KISS &
BREAK UP

D0104587

More in the Young, Loaded,
and Fabulous series:

PRETTY ON THE OUTSIDE

EVERYTHING BUT THE TRUTH

KISS &
BREAK UP

Young, Loaded, and Fabulous

KATE KINGSLEY

Simon Pulse
New York   London   Toronto   Sydney

SIMON PULSE
An imprint of Simon & Schuster Children's Publishing Division
1230 Avenue of the Americas, New York, NY 10020
First Simon Pulse paperback edition February 2011
Copyright © 2010 by Brubaker & Ford Ltd.
Originally published in Great Britain in 2010 by Headline Publishing Group
All rights reserved, including the right of reproduction
in whole or in part in any form.
SIMON PULSE and colophon are registered trademarks of Simon & Schuster, Inc.
For information about special discounts for bulk purchases,
please contact Simon & Schuster Special Sales at 1-866-506-1949
or business@simonandschuster.com.
The Simon & Schuster Speakers Bureau can bring authors to your live event.
For more information or to book an event contact the Simon & Schuster Speakers
Bureau at 1-866-248-3049 or visit our website at www.simonspeakers.com.
Designed by Mike Rosamilia
The text of this book was set in New Baskerville.
Manufactured in the United States of America
2 4 6 8 10 9 7 5 3 1
Library of Congress Control Number 2010929354
ISBN 978-1-4169-9401-5
ISBN 978-1-4424-1957-5 (eBook)

A big thank-you to everyone whose jokes
and anecdotes have inspired this series so far.
But especially, I'd like to thank Robbie Butler,
without whose wit, wisdom, talent, and trust
I might have gone insane. Honestly, Robbie,
I can't thank you enough.

CHAPTER ONE

"URGENT MEETING, 4 P.M.!" Alice Rochester read off the sign outside the junior class common room. She beckoned furiously to Sonia Khan. "Hurry up! We can't be late."

It was the first day back at St. Cecilia's after fall break, and the boarding school grounds were packed. Smartly dressed parents waved at each other from the windows of Porsches and Rolls-Royces. Girls squealed and gossiped about their Caribbean holidays. Chauffeurs grimaced as they hauled trunks and suitcases up to dorm rooms. And over all the chaos, the sun hung low in the October sky.

Sweeping through the common-room door, Alice dropped onto her favorite maroon couch and unfolded the official-looking letter that she'd nicked from Daddy's desk that morning. Sonia trotted behind.

"Ali," she pleaded, "just tell me what it says."

"Tell you what *what* says?" Alice asked innocently, dangling the letter just out of Sonia's reach. She loved having more information than her friends. Especially more than Sonia, who was ridiculously easy to wind up.

"That letter!" Sonia practically screeched. She lunged for it across the couch—but Alice dodged out of the way and Sonia crashed facedown into the cushions. "My nose!" she yelped, checking for damage. "Is it swollen? It feels swollen. If it's broken again then it's your fault, Alice."

Ping!

Smirking at Sonia's distress, Alice slid her iPhone from her pocket and skimmed her new text.

`Miss u already Sexy. See u at the social 2moro nite. Can't w8 for the costume. T x`

"OMG," gasped Sonia, who was reading the message over Alice's shoulder. "Tristan is *so* adorable. He obviously has, like, sex on the brain."

"Excuse me, Nosey," Alice snapped, cupping her hand over the screen. "Ever hear of privacy?"

But she was pink with pleasure. It was true. Tristan Murray-Middleton, her oldest childhood friend, was proving that he could be more than an amazing friend—he could be a model boyfriend, too. At least, the second time round. T and Alice had first got together in September at the beginning of junior year, but after a few dates, Tristan had freaked out and got scared off. Then last week, while he and Alice had been partying in Rome over fall break, they'd decided to give their relationship another go.

Things hadn't gone very far yet, not physically, but Alice was planning to change that in the very near future. Being a virgin at the age of almost seventeen was getting embarrassing (even though it was a fact only her three closest friends knew). Anyway, T was gorgeous and sensitive and popular, and he'd made it extremely clear that he wanted to *do* it. Alice was planning to oblige—as soon as they were alone.

UR gonna LOVE my costume, she typed, biting back a grin. Not telling u any more. U just gotta w8 & guess what I am . . . xox

With a shiver of anticipation, Alice hit send and slipped her phone back into the pocket of her gray wool school skirt. She'd planned tomorrow night's outfit down to the very last detail, and it was everything a Halloween costume should be: short, tight, and busty. Well, maybe "busty" was pushing it. Alice folded her arms over her chest. Somehow, before tomorrow night, she was going to have to grow boobs. Either that, or get over the fact that she was flat as a pancake. Because, at the Halloween party, T was going to see her naked for the first time.

"Move!" called a breezy voice. "Coming through."

A delicate jasmine scent wafted through the room, followed by the clatter of heels. A second later the whole sofa jittered as Natalya Abbott flopped down.

"Do I hear congratulations?" Tally beamed, her sea-gray eyes sparkling.

"What for?" Alice glanced enviously at her best friend's tousled white-blond hair and perfect figure.

"I'm on time for once!"

"Not," Alice protested. "You're the last one here." She gestured round the Tudor House common room, which, during the past few minutes, had filled to bursting point with the rest of the junior class. Girls were perched on radiators, tabletops, window ledges, and armchairs, comparing suntans and vacation escapades. In one corner, Gabrielle Bunter was actually bouncing up and down as she forced blond, cherubic Flossy Norstrup-Fitzwilliam to listen to some boring story. Gabby's flab was wobbling so much that she looked like a giant jelly bowl. Ugh. This was the problem with coming back to school after ten days' break: how quickly you started to feel like you'd never been away.

Alice heaved a long-suffering sigh and turned back to the letter in her hand. "Hoare?" she sneered.

"Now, now," Tally snickered, "I told you not to call Sonia that anymore."

"Oi," Sonia grumbled.

Alice giggled. "Shut up, Sone. No, really, can you believe this—our new housemistress's name is Mrs. *Hoare*!"

"Come on," Tally snorted with laughter. "Of course it's not."

"It is! Look, it says so in this letter Daddy got."

"Oh. My. God." Tally grabbed the paper. "How the hell are we meant to call her that without cracking up? We'll obviously have to ignore the woman for the rest of the year."

Alice shook her head. "It's just so weird that Miss Sharkreve's gone. Daddy says he's simply shocked that she left. He says he hopes our new housemistress is up to par, otherwise it might jeopardize our academic careers."

Tally rolled her eyes. Of course Alice's father would say something like that. Richard Rochester owned one of London's most eminent trading firms, was notoriously strict, and put a ton of pressure on Alice and her two brothers to do well. Everyone knew that the reason Alice worked so hard was because her father insisted she get into Oxford next year. He was counting on her to carry on the family tradition— especially since Alice's older brother, Dominic, had been too busy getting stoned at school to even think about Oxford. The fact that Dom was currently one of the coolest undergrads at Edinburgh didn't appease Richard Rochester in the slightest.

"Girlies, oh no," Sonia burst out. She was twisting a strand of her shiny, black hair round her manicured fingers. "I've just thought of something bad. Miss Sharkreve was our house-mistress for an entire half semester and she never once caught us breaking rules. Like, we never got punished for smoking, or for drinking in our rooms, or for sneaking out to town. What if this Mrs. Hoare woman is the opposite?"

"She'd better not be," Alice frowned, "or we're fucked for the Hasted House Halloween social tomorrow night. How are we gonna survive a school party if we can't sneak in extra booze? The whole point of being a junior is that you're supposed to be able to get away with shit."

"Guys, chill," Tally yawned, sinking back into the couch. "We'll find a way to have fun, whatever she's like. Anyway,

Mimah can just shove a couple of bottles down her top tomorrow. Smuggle the booze between her boobs." Tally giggled. "You can do that, right, Mimah? Give yourself a *booze* job?" Grinning, she stuck out her foot and nudged Jemimah Calthorpe de Vyle-Hanswicke, who was sitting scrunched up on the floor. Mimah had always been the bustiest member of their clique. "Mimah? Hello? Earth to Mime. . . ."

"*Stop* that. What the fuck do you want?"

Tally recoiled at Mimah's harsh tone. Biting her lip, she scrutinized her friend. Mimah's face was pinched and pale. This couldn't be good. Mimah had had a million family problems over the past few months—surely no more had surfaced over fall break?

"Shhh!" a whisper rustled through the room. Footsteps echoed in the marble foyer and the junior class rose to their feet. Two women swept through the door. One of them was St. Cecilia's headmistress, Mrs. Traphorn. Sonia craned her neck, but only Alice was tall enough to see the other woman over the crowd.

"What does she look like, Al? Ali!"

"Stop poking me!"

Mrs. Traphorn strode to the front of the room and positioned herself near the large flat-screen TV. Her companion hung back in a shadowy corner, obscured by a large floor lamp.

"Good afternoon, girrrls," Mrs. Traphorn droned poshly, rolling her *r*'s. "You may sit down."

As usual, the Trap had pinned her gray hair into a bun. She

was sporting a sleeveless cardigan, a plaid skirt, and clumpy shoes. Tally shook her head. Teacher fashion overload.

"Welcome back to school," the Trap went on. "I hope you've all had a verrry prrroductive fall break. I have an important person to intrrroduce to you today." She paused and patted her bun.

"For fuck's sake," Tally hissed in Alice's ear, "can't the old bat get on with it?"

"As you all know," the Trap droned on, "Miss Sharkreve left St. Cecilia's at the end of last fall break, to teach at a school in Scotland. We were extrrremely sorry to lose her."

Sonia snorted.

"But with me here today is Miss Sharkreve's replacement as junior class housemistress, Mrs. Edwina Hoare." The Trap clasped her hands. "Mrs. Hoare joins St. Cecilia's from Pembroke Ladies' School, where she was a beloved house-mistress for seventeen years."

"Seventeen years?" Tally sputtered. "If I had to stay at school that long, I'd kill myself."

"Shhh," Alice hissed. She was squinting at the house-mistress's obscured figure, but still couldn't make out her face. This was excruciating. If they ended up with a bitch or a weirdo, their whole junior year could go wrong. Fast.

"I'm sure I don't have to remind you," the Trap continued, "just before your vacation, St. Cecilia's saw the sudden depar-ture of its A-level English teacher, Mr. Logan."

Alice felt a set of nails dig into her arm. At the words

"Mr. Logan," Tally had tensed up and turned very, very pale.

"The good news is, in addition to her housemistress duties, Mrs. Hoare will be taking over Mr. Logan's vacant post."

Alice gave her friend a sympathetic look. Tally had been trying for the past couple of weeks to get over her infatuation with the hot young English teacher who'd broken her heart. Since the second he'd arrived at St. Cecilia's in September, Mr. Logan had flirted outrageously with Tally, tricking her (and everyone else) into thinking they were in love. The two of them had even shared a secret, passionate kiss on a school trip to Dublin. Then it had turned out that Mr. Logan was secretly dating Miss Sharkreve, and the two teachers had quit their jobs and left the school. Tally felt sick at the memory.

"That's all I'm going to say, girls," Mrs. Traphorn intoned from the front of the room, snapping her back to reality. "I'm sure you're very keen to get to know Mrs. Hoare on your own, so I'll leave you to it."

"Finally," Alice breathed. She leaned forward as the new junior housemistress emerged into the light. The next instant, her face contorted in alarm.

CHAPTER TWO

"Help," Sonia whispered, clutching Alice's wrist.

"Hello, girls," Mrs. Hoare said. She had a reedy voice. She was short and bony, with frizzy hair hacked into a triangle-shaped wedge. Her eyes were small and vulturelike. Her thin lips were coated in lipstick, which had caked and rubbed on to her teeth.

"Where did St. C's find this woman?" Tally mouthed. "It looks like they held an ugly contest and she won first prize."

Mrs. Hoare smiled sourly and raised her left hand, dangling several small sheets of paper in the air. "These are sticky tags," she announced. "'Why sticky tags?' you may ask."

"Oooh yeah," Tally muttered, "please tell us. Oh, please. I'm dying to know."

"Here's why," Mrs. Hoare snapped. "I want you all to take one, print your name on it, and stick it to your chest. You will wear these until I've memorized each and every one of your names. I've found that name tags are the best way to keep track of my students."

"Name tags?" Flossy Norstrup-Fitzwilliam sputtered under her breath. "What are we? Dogs?"

"Chop chop," Mrs. Hoare called, jiggling the sheets. "What's everyone waiting for? They won't bite, girls. They only *stick*." She cackled, clearly under the impression that this was a clever joke, and watched as the girls shuffled to the front of the room.

"Oi." Sonia poked Alice from behind.

"Ouch. What?"

"Look at Dylan." Sonia nodded toward a busty blond girl who was sticking a name tag to her yellow school blouse. "See how chirpy she's acting? What's her problem?"

"Who cares?" Alice peeled off a label. "She always looks chirpy. She's *American*."

"I know, but today she's, like, freaking me out. She was actually humming to herself in our dorm earlier on. It was a complete—"

"You!" Mrs. Hoare snapped.

"—nightmare. I wanted to punch her in the—"

"*You!* With the diamond watch!"

Sonia jumped. She'd never suspected that anyone, let alone an upstart new housemistress, might be addressing her so rudely. "M-me?"

"Yes. Did I say people could chitchat amongst themselves?"

Sonia gave her a blank look.

"Take a wild guess," Mrs. Hoare shot sarcastically.

"Uh, no you didn't?"

"Bravo! Class, we've got a genius on our hands. Now, do us all a favor, blabbermouth, and Shut. Your. Gob!"

Several people tittered. Sonia's eyes nearly popped out of her head.

"Can you believe this?" she hissed in Alice's ear as soon as Mrs. Hoare's back was turned. "As *if* our parents are paying this much money for us to be verbally abused by our house-mistress. I'm totally phoning Daddy after this and then that bitch will see who—"

"Shut up. Do you want to get *me* in trouble for whispering too?" Alice rolled her eyes and marched back toward the couch, shooting a glance at Dylan Taylor on her way. Sonia was right—the girl was glowing. And it was weird: What could possibly have happened over fall break to make her look so bloody happy? Ever since Dylan had arrived at St. Cecilia's from New York in September, her life had been hellish—and that was mostly Alice's doing. Because not only had Dylan dated Tristan over the summer (which was reason enough for Alice to hate her), but she was also cute, curvy, sparky, and blond. And the last thing Alice needed was someone like that hanging around, trying to hog all the boys' attention.

"Class!" Mrs. Hoare ordered, clapping her hands. "Settle down. You should all have made your name tags by now; it's not rocket science. I have several important rules to go over."

Tally snorted. "Why does that not surprise me?"

"First, the most important: No sneaking out of school."

"Oh, *really*?" Sonia muttered sarcastically. "Usually every teacher lets us sneak out whenever we want."

"I hear the St. Cecilia's girls have a habit of disobedience," Mrs. Hoare went on, glaring round the room. "Listen closely: That's about to change. None of you will leave the grounds during the week unless I give specific permission. If I find any of you have sneaked off into the woods for a cigarette, or made an unauthorized appearance in town, I will not be lenient. Finally, I understand that, because you're in your junior year, you're allowed to leave school on Saturdays and Sundays. But you may *only* do so if you sign out on my list first. I need to know where you are at all times or, I warn you, there'll be consequences."

Alice put up her hand.

"Yes?"

"I just thought I should remind you, Mrs. Hoare—this Thursday is Guy Fawkes Night."

Mrs. Hoare raised her eyebrows. "Excuse me?"

"You know, Guy Fawkes?" Alice prompted helpfully. She always liked to get on teachers' good sides. "'Remember, remember the fifth of November. Gunpowder, treason and—'"

"I know the rhyme, thank you very much. I'm a teacher, not a moron." Mrs. Hoare's eyes narrowed as she took in Alice's tall, model-like frame, her flawless olive skin, and her shiny brown hair. "And you think I should care about Guy Fawkes Night because . . . ?"

"Oh, sorry," Alice chortled apologetically, "let me explain. You see, there's a big fair that evening on Hasted Common, in town. They have a bonfire, fireworks, games. The junior class gets to go every year. It's a school privilege."

"Oh, a privilege, is it?"

"That's right."

"Well, I've got news for you, Alice, er"—Mrs. Hoare squinted at Alice's chest—"Roachmaster."

"Rochester," Alice corrected, attempting an airy voice.

"You will kindly not interrupt! Privileges must be earned. And from what I hear, the junior class hasn't earned anything at all this term. It's only October and you've already caused a scandal at a parents' charity show and lost your housemistress to another school. Which reminds me: I want everyone on their best behavior tomorrow night at the Hasted House Halloween social. The fact that Hasted is a boys' school is not an excuse to make a show of yourselves. Remember, you're young ladies, not to mention ambassadors of St. Cecilia's, and I expect you to behave that way."

Alice narrowed her eyes to slits. Judging from this bitch's attitude, it probably wouldn't help to explain that they'd known the Hasted House boys for years, that they had zero intention of being on their best behavior tomorrow night, and that they couldn't make a show of themselves any more than they already had at countless parties.

"This meeting is dismissed," Mrs. Hoare said. "I wouldn't want to keep you from your work, I'm sure you all have plenty to prepare for tomorrow's lessons. And girls!" she barked above the sound of people scrambling to escape. "I'm expecting you to wear your name tags at all time. No exceptions!"

"*No exceptions,*" Mimah mimicked, reaching the stairs before the others and stomping all the way to the first floor. *"No boys. No Guy Fawkes. No interrupting. Kiss my ass."* She scuffed her Converse on the corridor's regulation gray carpet. "I've never met such a bitch in my life. And the ho only just got here."

"The Ho!" Tally cackled, pushing open the door to the room she shared with Alice. "Oh my god—genius! That's got to be Mrs. Hoare's official name."

"Yeah," Sonia grumbled. "Suits her, rude cow." She flopped down onto Alice's purple and white quilt. "It looks gorgeous in here, girlies. I wish I could live with you two instead of with Dylan. Ugh."

Sonia surveyed the coveted corner room, which was famous throughout school for being one of the best in Tudor House. Golden late-afternoon sun poured through its three windows and flooded the alcove opposite the beds, which Alice and Tally had turned into their "entertaining nook." They'd furnished it with two school armchairs piled with cushions, a trunk doubling as a coffee table, strings of fairy lights, and a fluffy white sheepskin rug, onto which Tally flung herself facedown.

"Would someone like to tell me what the hell the Ho is trying to pull about Guy Fawkes Night?" she demanded, kicking off her gray suede ankle boots. "Does she actually think she can ban us from going?"

"I don't care what she thinks," Alice declared, glaring at Tally's boots, which had landed miles apart from each other on the carpet. She knew very well who'd have to pick them up later—and it wouldn't be Tally. "I promised Tristan I'd go, so I'm going. By the way," she sighed, her face going dreamy as she said Tristan's name, "T was telling me the other night how brilliantly the band's doing. They've got loads of gigs coming up. I wouldn't be surprised if they got a record deal soon."

"Oh, *please*," a voice sneered. Alice whipped round. Mimah was standing by an open window, practically spitting across the room. "Why do you always have to exaggerate? Of course T's band isn't about to get a record deal. They only bloody well got started a few weeks ago." She sucked in her cheeks, doing an impression of Alice's angular face. "*Oooh, my boyfriend's such a talented musician. He's such an amazing guitarist. He's gonna be world famous.* Get real."

"Oh. My. God," Alice grimaced, her eyes flashing. "*Someone*'s inner bitch escaped from its cage. Stupid me, thinking Jemimah Calthorpe de Vyle-Hanswicke was normal again. What is wrong with you?"

Mimah shoved her blunt black bangs out of her eyes and turned her back without a word. She glared out into the evening, over the pretty garden that surrounded Tudor House and beyond its low brick wall to the Great Lawn, the vast carpet of grass that lay at the heart of the school. Girls wearing the yellow and gray St. Cecilia's uniform flitted in and out of its shadows, between lampposts and buildings and fiery autumn trees.

"Mime," Tally said quietly. She'd crept off the rug and now slipped her slim arm round her friend's athletic shoulders. She'd suspected something was wrong before and now she was certain. "What's up? You've been acting funny all day."

Mimah rubbed her temples. "Nothing."

"Come on. That's a lie."

"I'm fine," Mimah insisted, sinking down onto Alice's bed. "I'm really sorry, Al. I didn't mean to lash out like that. Just PMS, I guess."

Alice nodded imperiously, but Tally looked at Mimah thoughtfully. She knew an excuse when she heard one.

CHAPTER THREE

*W*ell done, boys. Splendid practice today!" barked Brigadier Jones out on the Hasted House rugby field. The Brigadier, an ex-army officer who now devoted his life and soul to coaching sports at Hasted House, puffed out his chest and smacked a powerful fist into his palm. "Those puny bastards on the Glendale's team won't have a clue what's hit 'em."

"Rah, rah, rah! Go Hasted Hawks!" roared George Demetrios, high-fiving his two good mates, Tristan Murray-Middleton and Jasper von Holstadt, as they jogged off the field in their muddy white rugby shorts. "We're gonna destroy them."

"Glendale's are fierce, though," Jasper panted, his haughty, aristocratic face shining with sweat. "Brigadier, do you really think we can beat them next month?"

"Damn right I do, if we keep up at this rate," the Brigadier blustered. "Besides, we've absolutely *got* to win this time. Those gimps have beaten us the past six years running. Lucky we've got this star for a captain." The coach locked his arm round Tristan Murray-Middleton's neck. "Isn't that right, T? We're all counting on you, lad."

"Go, Big T!" George added, punching Tristan's arm.

"Ouch." Tristan rubbed his unruly hair, which was sticking out in all directions, and forced a smile, trying not to look doubtful. Sometimes it was great being team captain, but not at moments like this—not when everyone piled on the pressure and expected him to deal with it. The entire populations of St. Cecilia's and Hasted House would be there for the massive match against Glendale's, and if Hasted lost—one guess who they'd blame.

"T, follow me," Jasper said, squinting at the low, steely sky. "It's about to pour. Let's make hot chocolate—*and smoke a few joints*," he whispered. "I've got some great shit in my room."

"Can't, mate." T shook his head. "Love to, but we've got band practice. I said I'd play Seb and Rando my new song."

"Oh. Right. New song." Jasper whacked a clump of mud off his boot and watched T call to a pale, skinny boy who was lounging in the stands.

"Oi, Seb! Ready?"

"Ready." Seb Ogilvy brushed back his blond, haystack hair and leapt down onto the field, almost dropping the massive book in his hands.

"Doing a little light reading, are we?" T smirked.

"Yeah, and it's wicked," Seb gushed. "I bought it over fall break—it's a book on that street artist, Fade. Look how cool his stuff is. He's having an exhibition at this gallery in London in a few weeks and I'm definitely going. Anyway, what's your new song about?"

"You'll see," T replied. "But listen, I've been thinking, we've got to grow our fan base. The Paper Bandits have only played one gig so far, which is pathetic considering all our contacts. Rando knows someone at the Young Leaders Society. Their huge gala is coming up in a few weeks and—"

"Yo, bitches!" a voice butted in. "Wait."

Tristan jumped. He'd thought Jasper had gone to get started on his joints-and-hot-chocolate plan—but apparently not.

"What's up?" T asked. "We're talking business."

"*Business.*" Jasper swatted at the word like a bug. "Whatever. Who needs business when you can talk about fun? Ready for the big Halloween social tomorrow night?" He nudged Seb. "I bet Sonia will be looking hot."

"So?" Seb asked, turning red.

"*So?* It's about time you got your ass in gear and shagged her!" Jasper insisted, waving his hands in the air. "Shag, snog, whatever. Come on, she's fancied you for ages. And she's totally cute now, after her nose job."

"You think? So why don't you bloody well shag her yourself?" Forcing a laugh, Seb thrust his hand into his jacket pocket and clenched the engraved silver whisky flask that he carried with him everywhere. A swig would be perfect right now, but Tristan had recently ranted at him for boozing too much and the last thing he wanted was to set T off again.

Raindrops hurled themselves at the paving stones as the trio entered an echoing courtyard and hurried round the edge of the grass. No one was allowed to walk on the green, of course—the gardeners slaved away all year to keep it lush. Seb squinted up at the courtyard's four gray stone towers, built in the seventeen hundreds in the style of an Oxford or Cambridge college. He sighed. Tristan's dad, Sir Cecil Murray-Middleton, was always going on about Oxford. He was adamant that T go to New College, just like him, and become a powerful politician in the House of Lords. T hated all the pressure, but at least his father gave a shit what he did. Seb's dad, Sir Preston Ogilvy, had "better" things to do. Like jetting round the world, buying expensive wines to add to his collection, and coaxing high-society divorcées into the sack.

"Here's where we leave you, Jas," Tristan said, halting at the door of the music block. Unlike most of the school, this building was new, built of glass and steel. It was hidden tastefully behind a cluster of pines. "See you at supper. What are you up to now?"

"Oh, I . . ." Jasper's expression flickered, then steadied into its usual arrogance. "I was coming with you guys."

"To practice?" T raised his eyebrows. "Why?"

"What do you mean, *why*? Rando's my cousin and you two are my friends. Since when do I need a reason?"

"Mate, chill." Tristan pulled up one of his blue-and-maroon-striped rugby socks. "I just meant you'll be bored. You know nothing about music."

"What the—? That's the biggest lie I've ever heard. You've seen me deejay. How do you think I got so good on my decks?"

Tristan smirked.

"What?"

"Oh, nothing." T chuckled, turning into a blue-carpeted hallway that was practically shaking with the sound of drums. He burst into a practice room. "Not bad, Rando!"

Tom Randall-Stubbs jumped. "Sorry?" he yelled, suspending his drumsticks midair. "Can't hear, it's loud! Oh hey, Jas!" he exclaimed. "What're you doing here?"

"All right, cuz," Jasper yawned. He plopped his tall, tanned body into a chair and stretched his legs luxuriantly. "T's right, you do seem to be improving. Just thought I'd look in and see what's happening with the band, maybe listen to the new song. The Paper Bandits need some fresh tunes—the ones you've got are fine, but they're getting old." He drummed his fingers against a nearby guitar.

"I'll take that, thanks," Tristan snapped. He perched on an amp to tune up, while Jasper tapped his foot impatiently.

"Right. Quiet please," T announced at last. "Here it is: 'In My Own Backyard.'" In a husky tenor, he began to sing:

> *"I traveled far to find you*
> *But you were waiting, near me.*

21

I was blind, I don't know why
It took me years to see.

I never saw you as a lover—
You were my best friend.
I hunted love across the ocean,
But came home in the end.

Now at last, my love, I've found you.
The search was long and hard—
The hardship and the heartbreak
Left me lost and scarred.
Yes, my love, I've found you,
Of course I found it hard—
The last place I thought of looking
Was in my own backyard . . .
The last place I thought of looking
Was in my own backyard."

The slow, wistful music died into silence. Seb and Rando leaned back, dreamy expressions on their faces. Then:

"I don't get it," blared Jasper's voice. "Is that meant to be about you and Alice, or something?"

Tristan turned pink. "Of course not. It's art. You shouldn't take things so literally."

"Yeah. Okay. Sure. Apart from the fact that it clearly *is* about Alice. I mean, come on, 'lover' who used to be your 'best friend'? Subtle. And that bit about hunting love across the ocean—I mean, you met Dylan while you were in New York. Could you be any more blatant? I think you should rename the song 'To Alice, My Dearest Love.'"

Tristan clenched his jaw. "Thanks for chiming in—*even though you're not in the band*," he added under his breath. "I happen to like the title."

"Fine. Just trying to help, mate." Jasper yawned. "By the way, I was thinking, don't you reckon you should take out the word 'hard'?"

Tristan stared blankly.

"As in, 'I found it hard'?" Jasper prompted. "Sounds a bit perverted, don't you think? Like, *what* exactly did you find hard?" He winked luridly. "Know what I mean?"

"No. I have no idea what you mean, you complete weirdo." Tristan looked to Seb for help, but Seb was shaking with laughter. He ground his teeth. "Look, Jas, maybe you should leave, okay? The Paper Bandits have a vibe going, we're used to practicing together and—"

"So? All the more reason why you could do with a fresh opinion once in a while! Ever thought of getting a manager? I think I'd make a good one. I wouldn't let you get stale."

Tristan's eyes narrowed.

"Er, Jas," Rando jumped in hurriedly. "So, um, have you thought of a plan for tomorrow night?"

Jasper flicked his eyes to his cousin. "Plan? What for?"

"You know, for the Halloween social. Dylan Taylor's gonna

be there. I thought you'd been scheming how to get her to go out with you."

At the mention of Dylan's name, Jasper dropped his whole music-critiquing act and grinned. His first and only date with Dylan, a few weeks ago, had been disastrous to put it mildly, and he'd been hoping for another chance ever since.

"Good point." Licking his lips, Jasper flipped up the collar of his rugby shirt. "Dylan Taylor better prepare herself for the full-on von Holstadt charm."

CHAPTER FOUR

“Oh my god, you two look fab-u-lous!” Sonia squealed the next evening as Alice and Tally flounced into the dorm she shared with Dylan. “Those costumes are the sexiest things I’ve ever seen.”

“Thooonk youuu,” Tally intoned in a dead-sounding voice, thrusting out her perky B-cup chest.

“We are haaaappy you liiike themmm,” Alice added, goggling straight ahead. She’d been feeling jumpy all day, thinking about how tonight was going to be *the night* with Tristan—but now she’d got her nerves under control. Hasted House would be crawling with teachers. It was ridiculous to think that she and T would get enough time alone. Right?

“OMG. Adorable!” Sonia squeaked, bouncing over to Alice for a closer inspection. Her idol was wearing a shiny black tube top (cropped above the belly button to expose her perfectly flat stomach), a skintight silver miniskirt and thigh-high black fishnets, held up by suspenders. Tally’s outfit was exactly the same, except in reverse: silver top, black skirt, silver fishnets. Both girls were wearing spike-heeled ankle boots. Their faces were painted white, with dark bags around the eyes, and gory red slits at the throat.

"Whoa," Dylan blurted out. "What are you two going as? Dead prostitutes?"

Sonia rolled her eyes. "No, *Dylan.* Are you stupid or something? They're slutty corpses."

"Um, slutty corpses? Is that even a thing?"

"Of course it's a thing. And for your information," Sonia added, glaring at Dylan's open blouse and short skirt, "slutty corpse is a lot better than just plain *slut.*"

"I'm a flight attendant, actually," Dylan snapped, flushing red. She pointed at the little winged badge she was wearing on her chest, right next to her name tag for Mrs. Hoare. "See?"

"Oh, of course, how could I have missed it, stuck to your boob? Always have to draw attention to those watermelons, don't you?"

"Puh-lease. At least I'm making an effort. You're just wearing a designer dress. What are you supposed to be? A wolf in sheep's clothing?"

A snicker came from Alice and Tally's direction.

Sonia sniffed. "No, idiot. Isn't it obvious? I'm an Oscar winner. This is a red-carpet gown. And this"—she jiggled the gold plastic statuette she was holding—"is my Oscar."

Dylan burst out laughing. "I hate to break it to you, but wishful thinking doesn't count as a costume."

"Whatever." Sonia snatched her corsage and stabbed the pin through her yellow floor-length dress. "You're just bitter because I plan to be a world-famous director and marry one of the hot young male stars that I discover. . . . Can I help it if some of us have bigger ambitions than others, *stewardess?*"

Dylan clenched her bright scarlet Illamasqua lipstick. Deep breath. It was definitely not worth blowing her top over a stupid Halloween costume. And anyway, if the plan she'd formulated over fall break worked (and it was going to work), she wouldn't have to put up with these Brit-pack bitches much longer.

Dylan turned back to her mirror. She'd only come to St. Cecilia's in the first place because her mom had run off to London with Victor Dalgleish—an English quiz-show host and the most sleazy man imaginable. Dylan was sure her mother would dump Victor as soon as she realized how inferior he was to Dylan's dad. So, over fall break, while Dylan and her fourteen-year-old sister, Lauren, had been visiting their father in New York, Dylan had managed to convince their dad to make a surprise trip to London, where he'd win their mother back with chocolates and flowers and elegant dinners. He was going to be here in just a few weeks. And that was her ticket out.

"Sone, how long does it take to put up your stupid hair?" Alice whined from across the room. She marched to the door and opened it. "Come on. We're leaving in five minutes and we still have to go check on Mimah—she'll probably need help stashing the booze."

"Wait for me!" Sonia cried, grabbing her coat as Alice and Tally swept into the corridor. Out here, girls were dashing back and forth, borrowing last-minute accessories and showing off their costumes.

"Woo-hoo!" Cherry Rupert-Greene stopped in her tracks as Alice and Tally paraded by. "You two look shit-hot."

"Oh my god, so do you," Alice said in her fakest nice voice. "Let me guess—Lady Gaga?"

"Yeah! How's this?" Cherry straightened her blond wig and belted a few bars of "Paparazzi" into her fake microphone. Her father was the famous music producer, Ian Rupert-Greene, and she never let people forget it.

"What is that howling?" exclaimed Zanna Balfour, emerging from the bathrooms with her hands over her ears. "You're giving me a bloody migraine." Her eyes drifted to Tally and Alice, who were heading down the stairs, and narrowed in envy. "Shit, brilliant costumes, guys. Wish I could get away with wearing that."

"Cheers, darling," Tally called, blowing kisses up the stairwell. "Mwah, Mwah."

"Stop. Right. There!"

Tally shrieked.

Below them, in the foyer, stood Mrs. Hoare, glaring up. "Alice Rochester. Natalya Abbott," she cawed, eyeing the girls' name tags. "What on earth do you think you're wearing?"

"Ummm . . . our costumes?" Alice stammered. She was half terrified, half trying not to crack up. Mrs. Hoare was sporting a giant black witch hat—clearly her attempt to be festive—that made her look even more evil than usual. If possible.

"Those getups are completely and utterly inappropriate." Mrs. Hoare's pupils had shrunk to the size of pinpricks. "What a disgrace. What did I say about being on your best behavior tonight? I've got a good mind not to let you come to the social at all!"

"Oh, no! Please Mrs. Hoare!" Tally begged.

"You have to let them go," Sonia cried.

"I don't have to do anything, Sonia, er, Khan." Mrs. Hoare's sunken cheeks were tinged with red. "This is wonderful, just wonderful. We've got to get going right now, you don't have time to change, and I certainly can't leave you here unsupervised." She folded her arms, and Alice actually thought she caught the glimmer of a smirk. "Right. I know how to sort this out. Alice Rochester, Natalya Abbott, wait here."

Tally grimaced wildly at Alice as their housemistress stomped off down the hallway. What kind of vindictive plan did the Ho have now?

CHAPTER FIVE

B ack of the line, back of the line," Alice grunted, clutching Tally's sleeve. "There's no way we're going in first, looking like this. We have to hide."

She held on till the rest of the junior class had trooped past them through the arched doorway, into one of the towers of Hasted House. Luckily, Mrs. Hoare wasn't there to force them to walk faster. She'd already waltzed inside with the boys' housemaster, Mr. Brand.

"Darling, you're being ridiculous," Sonia trilled. She pouffed her shiny black hair over her shoulders, which she'd dusted with sparkly bronze. Little clouds of it puffed out behind her when she walked. "You two still look nice. I mean, at least, you don't look . . . *hideous.*"

Alice narrowed her eyes, fighting the urge to whack Sonia with her stupid statuette. "Why don't you just shut up, okay?"

"Fine." Sonia strutted ahead in her four-inch gladiator

sandals, her yellow layered dress swooshing round her ankles. "I was only trying to be helpful. Ow!" she squealed, tripping over a flagstone.

"Idiot." Giggling, Mimah straightened her cat ears, which she was wearing with a black jumpsuit and a black faux-fur jacket. The button nose and whiskers that she'd painted on her face stood out against her pale skin.

Alice stomped inside after the rest of the group, down a chilly stone corridor lined with school notice boards. One notice caught her eye.

JUNIOR RUGBY
HASTED HOUSE VS GLENDALE'S
Last Saturday of November!
Be there or be a loser

Alice grinned with anticipation. The annual rugby match between Glendale's and Hasted House was one of her favorite events of the year. Not that she was a massive sports freak or anything, but she loved watching from the stands at the boys' school, layering up in scarves, shouting, and waving homemade banners. Cheering Tristan on. One year she'd painted him a banner so huge that it had taken her, Tally, Sonia, and Mimah to all hold it up together. T had told her he still kept it under his bed.

Tally shivered as she and Alice filed behind the others into a hall that was even draftier than the corridor. "Does this school not have any fucking central heating?" she muttered.

"Of course not," Alice retorted. "That'd ruin the whole dramatic medieval thing, wouldn't it?" Unlike most of her classmates, Alice knew Hasted House back to front. Her older brother, Dominic, had studied here and her younger one, Hugo, who was fourteen, still did. In fact, Alice had been in this room before, for a music recital Hugo had given last year. It had high ceilings; vaulted windows; dark, polished floorboards; and a mezzanine accessed by two narrow curving staircases.

For tonight's dinner party, the place had been totally decked out. Orange and black streamers dangled from the mezzanine, as did a whole army of plastic spiders and bats. Floor-length banners hung in each corner of the room, painted with skeletons and vampires and zombies. The bulbs in the chandelier overhead were dimmed. Tables were arranged in a horseshoe shape, laid with orange cloths and black napkins, flickering jack-o'-lanterns and gigantic bowls of sweets.

"Yummm." Sonia drooled. Maybe she could grab a few chocolates while no one was looking. Not that anyone cared about her perpetual rabbit-food diet except herself.

Next to Sonia, Clemmie Lockheed was clapping her hands, dancing up and down. "Look at the effort they've made! Isn't it cute?"

"I love it," chimed in Felicity Foxton.

"Um, yeah," cut in Farah Assadi. "Except for one thing: Where the hell *is* everyone?"

Apart from the decorations, the entire room was deserted.

"Hello?" echoed Mimah's husky voice. "Anybody there?"

"Woooooh," someone hooted eerily, and the girls giggled nervously, then went quiet.

"I don't like this," whispered Bathsheba Fortnum.

Silence. Then:

"BOO!" roared forty voices.

"Eeeeee!" the girls screamed.

Boys burst from behind each banner, running and waving their arms.

"Help!" Flossy wrung her hands and shook her blond Little-Bo-Peep ringlets. Arabella Scott threw herself to the floor with her arms over her head. Zanna Balfour and Farah Assadi shrieked and flapped around in circles.

Mimah cackled. "Oh my god, their costumes are ridiculous. Freddie Frye's wearing gold leggings."

Tally gripped her arm. "You can see his *penis*!"

"OMG! Let's go get a closer look."

"Thanks for abandoning me, guys," Alice muttered, trying to hide behind Sonia as Tally and Mimah shot off across the room. Annoyingly, Sonia was at least four inches shorter than her, even in heels.

Suddenly, Alice stiffened. Oh god—the moment she'd been dreading. Tristan. His clear brown eyes were scanning the crowd and it was obvious, even from this far away, that he looked superhot. He was dressed as a hippie, in flared jeans and a beaded headband. His usually tousled hair was combed straight down over his ears.

"Hey!" he called, catching sight of her.

Alice's stomach cramped up.

"What are you two doing huddled over there? Al, you look—" T halted about two feet away, blinking. "You look g-great. I mean . . ." He eyed her outfit as Sonia stepped aside. "Wow. Okay. I know you said I had to guess, but . . . what the hell *are* you?"

Alice almost sobbed with embarrassment. Why, why couldn't she just melt into thin air? She looked like crap. And T was doing a terrible job of hiding the fact that he agreed. Her face was still powdered white but, on top of her costume, Mrs. Hoare had forced her to wear a mangy old lab coat that she'd dug up in some storage cupboard. It sagged down to Alice's calves. It was pocked with holes and stained with brownish marks—obviously the residue of some sort of deadly chemical. Half the collar was torn away.

But none of this was the worst part. The worst part was the pair of cracked goggles stuck to Alice's head, squashing the slutty-corpse updo that she'd spent ages creating. Who knew what kind of no-hygiene loser had worn them before?

Alice thought of the condom she'd carefully tucked inside her waistband, and cringed. There was no way T would want to have sex with her now.

Tally had been lucky—she'd got away with only having to wear a giant sheet, and had come as a ghost.

"Hmmm . . ." Tristan stroked his chin. "Hang on, you're a mad scientist?"

34

"What?" Alice creased her eyebrows.

"Yeah, sorry, bad guess. A dead scientist?" T squinted. "An evil experimenter? A . . . No . . . Yes! I've got it!"

"Huh? Got what?"

"Brilliant!"

"What are you *on* about?"

"Dr. Jekyll and Miss Hyde. Yesss!" T pumped his fist. "Bet you didn't think I'd guess it so fast. Trying to throw me off the scent, weren't you? I love the mad Dr. Jekyll bit—perfect." He raised his eyebrows, glancing down at Alice's fishnets and ankle boots. "Go on then, show me the rest. Don't I get to see sexy Miss Hyde?"

Alice's mouth dropped open. Was this actually happening? Did T actually believe she was wearing this junk on purpose? What was he, stupid? But then again . . . his mistake could work to her advantage. She entwined her fingers with his, drawing him aside. "I'll show you later, babe," she purred, stroking her thumb over his palm.

If only she could carry this off, she might be able to save face. They'd have to be supersneaky of course—Mrs. Hoare had warned her not to shed the goddamn lab coat, let alone anything else, under any circumstances. But still . . .

A whistle at Alice's side snapped her back to earth. George Demetrios-as-Wolverine was leching in her direction. "Hot outfit."

"Why, thank you." Alice hitched up her lab coat to reveal more fishnet. This getup obviously wasn't so bad after all.

"Work it, baby," George winked. "Let me guess. Air hostess."

"Huh?" Alice spun round.

Shit. George wasn't even looking at her. He was looking behind her at Jasper and at the girl whose arm Jasper was gripping: Dylan Taylor. Alice almost stamped her foot. The whole world knew Jas wanted to shag Dylan, but did he really have to inflict her on everyone else?

Dylan appeared to be wondering the same thing. She was pink in the face, snapping "no" at Jas under her breath as he tugged her forward.

"Dill, babe," he insisted, "don't be lame! You guys, help me. Rando!" Jasper beckoned to his cousin. "Dill here needs some convincing. She says she won't come to Guy Fawkes with me on Thursday. I told her she's got to. She can join our group by the fire. Am I right or what?"

Tristan fidgeted. He was still weirded out that one of his best mates was trying to get it on with his ex, but he'd decided to ignore that for now. He shrugged. "Fine. Whatever. Come if you want, Dill. I mean, yeah, the more the merrier."

Dylan turned even pinker. "Thanks, but I don't want to intrude. Anyway, maybe I'm stupid, but I don't even know what Guy Fawkes is."

"What!" George Demetrios cried, amid a general uproar from the boys. "What a philistine!"

"That is sooo American," choked Rando, his vampire teeth almost falling out of his mouth.

"Nice one, Jas," George guffawed. "Asking a girl on a date to something she's never even heard of."

Jasper cleared his throat. "Guy Fawkes Night is one of Britain's richest traditions," he began. "Four hundred years ago, a traitor named Guy Fawkes hatched a plot to blow up the Houses of Parliament, the headquarters of the British government. Nowadays, every November fifth, the people of Britain make effigies of him and burn them on bonfires across the country."

"*Boring*!" George coughed. "I hope no one ever pays you to take them on a tour of London. They'd die of boredom before you even got to Big Ben." He turned to Dylan. "Look, Guy Fawkes is really fun, I promise. Everyone drinks mulled wine and watches fireworks."

"And toasts marshmallows!" Rando said.

"And there's a fair with games and shit."

"Toffee apples!"

Dylan widened her baby-blue eyes. "Sounds freaky."

"*Sounds freaky*," Alice sneered quietly. Dylan probably knew exactly what Guy Fawkes Night was. Attention seeker. She was just lapping it up.

"Go on, Dill, come with us," Jasper urged. "Please?"

"Well, I guess I could, for a little while . . ."

Great. Just great.

"Oh, but wait." Dylan shook her head. "I think our new housemistress said we couldn't. I'd better not."

"Give me a break," Jasper protested. "You're not going to

let some housemistress stop you, are you? Al, you guys are coming, right?"

Alice scratched her nose.

"See, Dill? Al's coming. She knows how to sneak out. You'll bring her, won't you, Ali? You'll make sure Dylan doesn't get caught?" Jasper's expression was like a puppy dog's.

Alice smiled sweetly, clenching her fists. There was no way she could refuse, not in front of the guys.

"Of course," she cooed, and scanned the room for Mimah. It was time to get drunk.

CHAPTER SIX

*T*ally yanked her ghost costume straight so she could see through the jagged eyeholes she'd cut, in a rush, with Alice's nail scissors back at St. Cecilia's. She wobbled on her high heels. Bad sign. Wearing a sheet over your head when you were wasted was lethal—especially when George Demetrios was around. Tally had now stumbled into George (dressed as Wolverine) at least four times on her way to and from the bathrooms, which was where Mimah had stashed their bottle of rum. He kept insisting it was a "coincidence," but only idiots who'd never met George would believe that. Every encounter George had with a girl was minutely and deviously engineered—how else would a lech like him get any action?

Determined to escape the Wolverine clutches once and for all, Tally pushed her way to the far corner of the dance floor where Jasper had set up his DJ table and was spinning out tunes. The social had definitely taken off. Dinner was over, people's costumes were looking sloppy and drunken dancing was in full swing.

No one had managed to get drunk on the two meager glasses of wine doled out by the school, of course. Tally and her crew had nearly finished Mimah's rum and were already making a dent in Seb's whisky. Not to mention Jasper's vodka. So what if Mr. Brand and the Ho were sitting on the mezzanine, keeping a watchful eye over the room? That was all part of the fun.

"Guess who!" Tally cried, sneaking up behind Rando and throwing her hands over his eyes.

Rando eased his fingers along her soft, delicate ones. She felt him grin.

"Mr. Brand! I'm so flattered, I didn't know you felt that way!"

Giggling, Tally released him—and felt an electric spark as Rando's eyes met hers. Whoa. She'd never really noticed before, but Rando was cute. Correction: supercute—even with his long, satin vampire cloak and the trickle of blood drooling from the corner of his mouth. He was tall with a shock of dark brown hair, flushed schoolboyish cheeks, and a dashing, dimpled smile. Tally blushed underneath her sheet. Maybe this was exactly the distraction she needed after her disastrous affair with Mr. Logan.

"Dance with me!" she cried, flinging her ghost costume back over her shoulder like a cape.

Rando didn't respond. He was too busy gazing into Tally's

eyes, which were bright silver, like rain clouds pierced by the sun. He blinked down to her pink, curving lips, and sighed as quietly as he could.

"Come on," Tally's lips urged him. She'd grabbed Alice and was swaying seductively, her top glinting with the same silver as her eyes.

Rando shifted his feet awkwardly. A few weeks ago, he would have jumped at the opportunity to slide his arm round Tally's waist, draw her to him, smell her hair. She was the most gorgeous girl he'd ever seen. The problem was, he just couldn't get over a certain story Alice had told him before fall break about how Tally had stolen a book from a little old lady's secondhand shop in town. He'd never been so shocked in his life—or so disappointed. Maybe it wasn't fair, but you didn't expect someone who looked like Natalya Abbott to have criminal tendencies. Rando felt cheated—like he'd found a butterfly, but the more he stared at it, the more he could only see the caterpillar underneath.

At that moment the music stalled. The speakers farted out a disjointed beat. At the decks, Jasper was fumbling ineptly with his records.

"Rubbish!" George Demetrios cried.

"For fuck's sake, DJ," Tom Huntleigh heckled. "Get it together."

"Get him off!"

Smirking, Alice strolled from the dance floor toward Seb, who was chilling against one of the pillars that supported the mezzanine. She inspected his skinny suit trousers, brown blazer, jaunty fedora, and the unlit cigarette dangling from his mouth.

"Sebbie dearest, who on earth are you meant to be?"

"What are you talking about?" Seb retorted in a muffled voice, skillfully balancing the cigarette between his lips.

"Your costume, darling. I don't get it. Are you a gangster?"

"*No.* Come on, Al. I'm Jean-Paul Belmondo from *À Bout de Souffle.*" Seb cocked his fedora. "The icon of French New Wave cinema? How could you not recognize me?"

"Oh. Yeah. Of course." Alice flashed a smile, even though she had no clue what Seb was going on about. Jean-Paul *who?* The only Jean-Paul she'd ever heard of was Gaultier, the fabulous French fashion designer, and Seb definitely wasn't dressed as him. Still, there was no way she was admitting her ignorance: She had a cultural reputation to uphold.

"Hey," someone whispered in her ear. Tristan's fingertips brushed the nape of her neck.

"Hey," Alice breathed, her pulse quickening.

"I've got something to show you."

"What?"

"Just come with me," T said, enveloping Alice's hand in his own. He glanced up at the mezzanine. Good—Mrs. Hoare was rabbiting on to Mr. Brand while Mr. Brand glugged his wine. Neither of them seemed to give a shit what was happening at the raging party below. "This way." He clasped Alice's waist and ushered her out of the hall, down the corridor.

"Where are you taking me?" Alice said, sipping from her plastic cup full of rum and Coke. "Oh my god, are we going to your room? Do I get to see it?"

"I wish!" T grinned. "But do you know how much shit we'd be in if we got caught up there? This is bad enough." He pushed open a door. Inside lay a dark, empty classroom, bathed in moonlight.

"Finally," T uttered, "I've got you alone." Kicking the door shut, he pulled Alice close and kissed her. "Mmm, I love your lips. I've been thinking about them for days." He kissed her again, deeply, like he could never get enough, and pressed himself against her.

Heat rushed through Alice's body. Her knees went weak as she felt Tristan, warm and strong and passionate, against her. She glanced again at the classroom door. Maybe, just maybe, they could risk it. . . .

"Hey," she whispered, taking a step back, pushing her rum and Coke out of the way across the teacher's desk. She stared into T's hazel eyes, fiery with desire, and played with the top button of her lab coat. One by one, she unsnapped them all and shrugged the coat to the floor.

"Wow," Tristan breathed. Alice shone in front of him like an unwrapped present. He drew his gaze up her long legs; along the suspenders disappearing into her minuscule skirt; over her taut stomach; over the outline of her breasts through her shiny black top. It was so tight he could see practically everything. "You're incredible."

"Thank you." Alice kissed him again. Yes. This felt right. She was ready—at least, more ready than she'd ever been.

T pressed her against the whiteboard. He was breathing hard. The moonlight gleamed on his arm muscles, delineating each sinew and curve, and Alice gasped with the beauty of it. This was her perfect moment. If only she could freeze it in time and store it away to live and relive over and over again.

She moaned as T ran his hand down her tube top.

"Can I take this off?" he whispered. His fingers were playing over her bare midriff, sneaking toward her breasts.

Yes, she was dying to say, *yes, do it.*

But suddenly—

Slam!

Alice and Tristan both jerked backward as the classroom door burst open. Alice cracked her head on the whiteboard.

"Owww," she groaned, cradling her face in her hands. "My brain. Hurts. Broken."

The next second, a light snapped on.

"Argh." Alice blinked in the neon brightness and squinted toward the doorway, prepared to kill whatever idiot had ruined the moment.

Then she froze. There was Mrs. Hoare, her hands on her bony hips, her witch hat at a furious angle. "What in the devil's name is going on here?" the Ho screeched. "Alice Rochester, where is your lab coat? How dare you take it off? Boys and girls are not, under any circumstances, allowed in the same room unsupervised during a school social." She sounded like she was vomiting lines from the rule book.

"Uh . . . uh . . ." Alice darted her eyes round desperately for Tristan, but he'd disappeared. Maybe she'd knocked herself out. Maybe she had a concussion and none of this was really happening. Someone should call an ambulance.

"Bleeeurgh!"

Alice jumped a foot in the air as a horrible gurgling echoed through the room. In the doorway, Mrs. Hoare's face crinkled in disgust.

"Bleeeeeuuuurgh," burst the noise again, this time even more horrific. *"Blaaaaargh! Bluuurgh. Eurgh."*

Next came a feeble, hacking cough. Alice peered round wildly, her head still aching. It sounded like someone was barfing up their guts. Either that, or the Hasted House boys had gone overboard with their Halloween sound effects. Something rustled on the floor.

"Oh my god," Alice gasped, looking down.

Tristan's ass (which looked extremely sexy, even under the circumstances) was emerging from under the teacher's desk, followed by the rest of his body. His face was pale. Drops of brownish liquid stained his shirt. More drops trickled from the corner of his mouth, which he was dabbing with a filthy-looking rag.

"Gross," Alice muttered. What had happened to her sexy prince from thirty seconds ago?

Then, as T hauled himself to his feet, he caught her eye— and, quick as lightning, he winked. Suddenly, Alice realized what was going on. She clapped her hand over her mouth, trying not to crack up.

"Oh, goodness gracious," Tristan croaked loudly, pretending to register the Ho's presence for the first time. "Hello. I'm Tristan Murray-Middleton. I'm so terribly sorry, I had no idea you were there, Miss, er . . ."

"*Mrs.* Hoare," the Ho snapped. "And what exactly is going on?"

"Well, you see—*Ooooh. Eurgh. Blerg*!" Tristan pitched forward, clutching his stomach. He belched, and the Ho inched backward. "Oh dear, I am *so* sorry, Mrs. Hoare. I suddenly got ill during the social. I should have known better than to eat that shrimp at dinner; my entire family has a crustacean sensitivity. It gets frightfully messy at seafood restaurants."

The Ho shuffled further backward.

"Anyhow, when I started feeling ill, Alice kindly offered to help me to the toilets." Tristan leaned against the desk and reached for Alice's hand. She shrank away, even though she knew the vomit was fake.

"Alice Rochester and I have known each other forever, you see. The Murray-Middleton family and the Rochester family go back hundreds of years. When Alice and I were babies, our nannies used to bathe us together. We're practically brother and sister!"

Alice knit her eyebrows together. T was taking things a bit far. As subtly as possible, she moved her index finger in circles. *Wrap it up . . . Wrap it up . . .*

Mrs. Hoare was glaring suspiciously. "This is all very inter-esting, Mr. Murray-Middleton," she said, folding her arms, "but I can't see what any of it has to do with you two being in here—seeing as it's *not* the bathroom."

"Ah, yes, Mrs. Hoare, well noticed," Tristan said. "Very well noticed. This is indeed *not* the bathroom."

Alice shot him a look.

"So, er, let me explain," Tristan hurried on. "I was practi-cally unconscious with nausea and poor old Alice had no idea where the boys' bathrooms were—why would she, since she's not a boy? So, in desperation, she dragged me in here. And, well, you can see what happened." Tristan hung his head penitently. "Alice even took off the magnificent lab coat she was wearing as a Halloween costume so I could wipe up the mess." He held out the crumpled-up rag. It was soaked with what Alice now saw looked suspiciously like her rum and Coke, which must have spilled off the desk. "Here. Have a look."

Mrs. Hoare shrank against the door frame, holding her nose. "I can see quite well from here, thank you. You may throw that thing in the bin."

"Here, let me do it," cried Alice, rushing forward and grab-bing the lab coat. She dropped it into the wastepaper basket under the desk. "Tristan, old friend, are you feeling okay? I was worried you might die. Remember last time you had a crustacean incident, how you had to go to hospital and be put on a drip?"

Next to her, T erupted into a suspicious-sounding coughing fit.

"That's enough," Mrs. Hoare interrupted. She seemed more relaxed now that the sick rag was out of sight. "We're finished here. Young man, if you're so ill then I suggest you take a warm bath and get to bed. As for you, Alice Rochester, tomorrow is a school day, the party's over, and our bus is about to leave.

"And by the way," she hissed, catching hold of Alice's arm as Tristan limped ahead of them out the door, "I know your type. Don't let me catch you doing anything remotely suspicious again. I've got my eye on you, and next time, I might not be so trusting."

CHAPTER SEVEN

*A*n icy mist curtained Locke House. Mimah unlatched the front gate and hurried through the dark, leaf-trampled garden, scrunching her fingers into the sleeves of her lacrosse sweater. Shit, it was cold. So cold that practice this afternoon would have been torture, except for one thing: running up and down a field for an hour and a half, wielding a big stick, had forced her to forget about her personal problems for more than five minutes put together.

Now that practice was over, however, it was a different story. Which was why she was here.

"Jemimah dear!" cooed Mrs. Gould, the freshman house-mistress, as Mimah burst into Locke's cozy foyer. "What a surprise! You're looking like a bright-eyed bunny. Chilly out there?"

"Freezing." Mimah squeezed out a smile. Mrs. Gould was one of those permanently cheerful teachers who it was best to play along with. You never knew what kind of psychotic tendencies she was trying to compensate for. "Do you mind if I . . ." Mimah nodded toward the stairs.

"Yes, of course, my sweet chicken. She should be up there."

"Thanks."

"Toodle-oo."

Mimah trailed her hand up Locke House's well-worn banister. She got a warm feeling whenever she came back here—probably because freshman year had been one of the coolest years of her life. It was the year she and the girls had started going to raucous balls and house parties every weekend, wearing tiny dresses and lying to their parents, saying that they'd be "chaperoned." *Yeah, right.* It was the year the boys had started to look snogable instead of laughable. Oh, and the year their crew had been majorly bollocked for that notorious game of strip poker, where they'd all ended up stark naked in George Demetrios's living room, Sonia pole dancing around a marble column, Seb and Tally passed out over an antique ottoman.

Despite the errand she was on, Mimah chuckled.

Her destination was at the top of Locke's three flights of stairs. On the landing she paused, took a deep breath, and headed down a sloping attic hallway to the third door on the right. Four names were posted outside: Isabelle de Montfort, Victoria Wentworth, Imogen Drake, and Charlotte Calthorpe de Vyle-Hanswicke—her sister.

"Give it here!" A giggly voice floated into the hallway.

The door was ajar. Mimah squinted through the crack and

spied a tall, skinny blonde whose hair looked like she'd just walked backward through a lawn mower. Over her school uniform, she was wearing a shapeless knit rag with holes in it. This was the notoriously wild Georgie Fortescue, her sister's new BFF. And, shaking with laughter on the bed, rummaging through one of her dresser drawers, was Charlie.

Mimah blinked. Hmmm. Maybe her sister was dealing with this whole business better than she'd thought. Well, that would be a weight off her mind.

"Hi, girls," she declared, walking straight in.

"Mimah!" Charlie jumped off her polka-dot duvet. "What are you doing here? You can't just turn up out of the blue."

"Well, sorr-ee. Next time I'll make an appointment." Mimah bent to kiss her sister on the cheek, then stopped as she got a closer view. Okay, take that back: Charlie obviously wasn't handling their mum's bombshell all that well. She looked bad: pasty, undernourished, thin-skinned. Worse than she had in months.

"So, uh, you kids doing prep together?" Mimah asked, fake cheerful.

Charlie didn't answer, but a snort came from across the room.

Mimah wheeled on Georgie Fortescue. "Yes? Can I help you with something? Oh, and by the way, what the hell is up with your outfit?"

"Mime!" Charlie squealed. "Why do you always have to be so rude?"

"Sorry, but someone needs to tell her to lose that rag."

"That rag," Georgie replied, sticking her hands on her bony hips, "happens to be a designer poncho. Haven't you ever heard of boho-chic?"

"Yeah. Too bad those designers forgot the chic." Mimah smirked. Georgie's outfit was so not up to scratch for a diamond heiress who was one of the wealthiest pupils at St. C's. Then again, the poor girl's parents probably hadn't passed on much in the way of dress sense. From the moment their daughter had been born, the Fortescues had decided to have pretty much nothing to do with her, first hiring an army of nannies to deal with dirty diapers, then packing Georgie off to boarding school the second she turned seven. They had better things to do than deal with the whole "bringing the girl up" hassle; let the teachers handle that.

The problem was, in Mimah's experience, teachers just weren't as good at parenting as, well, parents.

Charlie stood up. "Um, Germ-imah, no offense or anything, but we're kind of busy. Hint, hint."

Mimah raised her eyebrows. "*Germ-imah?* Oh, that's mature. I come all the way over here to check you're okay, and you kick me out."

"I don't hear anyone kicking you out," Charlie said, smirking at Georgie in her infuriating little-sister way. She bent to the floor and snatched up a pile of material, which turned out to be her new Opening Ceremony winter jacket. "I mean, *we're* leaving, but you're more than welcome to stay. Make yourself at home."

"Charl, wait."

"Later!"

"Where on earth are you going? It's almost seven o'clock, Mrs. Gould will be coming round to take attendance in a—"

Slam.

"—minute." Mimah plopped onto Charlie's bed. Great. Her sister had just started behaving normally, months after their father had been caught feeling up a prostitute in the back seat of his Porsche, and now she was losing it all over again.

Mimah sighed. She thought back to the final day of fall break last week, when their mother had called her and her sister into the study of their Kensington house. Fine, it was probably Mummy's idea of "sensitive" to wait till then to tell them the bad news, but judging from Charlie's reaction, she'd fucked up.

"We're getting divorced," Mummy had blurted out.

Mimah froze as the weight fell.

"Hmm?" Charlie asked. As if pretending she didn't understand could hold off the blow. "Who?"

"Your father and I," Mummy said, taking a sip from her mug, which Mimah could tell even from the other side of the fireplace was full of something that bore no resemblance to tea. "We signed the papers two days ago. He's shacked up with some cheap French whore in Monaco. Says he wants to marry her." Their mother took another gulp. It was whisky, her regular drink. Mimah could smell it now.

"How long have you fucking known about this?" Charlie

screeched, jerking Mimah out of her pointless observations. Charlie's voice was dripping with blame, even though this whole thing was Daddy's fault. After all, he was the one who'd been caught fooling round with a prostitute half his age. Not Mummy.

"Charls, don't swear," their mother pleaded, dabbing at her eyes.

"*How long?*"

"A while. I don't know. A few weeks."

"And you waited till now to tell us? I've been having a good time this whole holiday, and now I find out I've been living a complete lie? You're the worst mother in the world. Thanks a lot."

As Charlie's words echoed in Mimah's head, a gust of wind burst open the dorm window, and the sting of cold air and wood smoke filled the room. Mimah jumped to her feet, rubbing her temples, and stared into the black night. She and Charlie were stuck here at boarding school. Their mother was permanently focused on the bottom of her whisky bottle. Their father was holed up who knew where in Europe with some awful woman. Someone needed to watch out for her sister—and the only person who could do it was standing right here.

CHAPTER EIGHT

I'm a total idiot," Tally exclaimed, waving her big wooden spoon. She turned to Alice, Mimah, and Sonia, who were waiting hungrily at the kitchen table. "I almost forgot it was Guy Fawkes tomorrow night. What's our escape plan? Has anyone actually thought of one? We need to get organized!"

"Shhhhh!" Alice hissed. "What is *wrong* with you?"

"Nothing. Why?"

"Oh, no reason. Just, I reckon the janitors on the other side of school might not have heard you. Want to announce our illegal plans a little louder?"

It was dinnertime on Wednesday and the girls were in Tudor House's kitchen, watching Tally ladle food from a battered school saucepan. Chicken liver pie had been the main attraction on the dining hall menu today, so the girls had decided to take advantage of the junior year privilege of cooking for themselves.

Well, "cooking" might have been an overstatement.

"Yuck." Sonia ventured a look at her friend's limp stir-fry and mushy noodles, and wrinkled her pert nose. Why on earth had they entrusted their dinner to Tally, the only person in the world who could actually fuck up instant ramen? Even though Tally lived practically alone during the holidays, fending for herself while her father and stepmother partied every night with their cokehead, wanker-banker friends, she could still barely fry an egg. She survived by eating out, or ordering in huge quantities of sushi, or sloping round to Alice's house, where the chef was always serving up some sort of three-course roast.

Whatever. Sonia wouldn't touch noodles with a ten-foot pole, anyway. Carbs made you obese.

Alice took a sip of Tango and lowered her voice. "Okay, listen up—I'm going over the plan one more time, and one time only, so you'd better memorize it. After this, I'm not mentioning it again."

Stuffing a piece of charred yet somehow undercooked carrot into her mouth, Tally rolled her eyes. Ever since the Ho had walked in on Alice and T on Halloween, Alice had been even more obsessed than usual with not getting caught. It was so bloody boring.

"Right." Alice leaned in. "Half-past seven tomorrow. Straight after dinner. The four of us—"

"Hang on," Sonia butted in.

"What?"

"Are you sure we should still go ahead with this? I mean, at Hasted House the Ho specifically told you not to do anything out of line. You could get suspended."

Alice smirked. "Actually, the Ho said, 'Don't let me *catch* you doing anything out of line.' And she bloody well won't. Will she?"

Tally grinned.

"So. Half-past seven, the four of us meet in—"

"Ahem!" Sonia coughed loudly.

"What *now?*"

Sonia jerked her head. Dylan had appeared in the corner of the kitchen. She was standing in front of her storage shelf, trying to lift out a loaf of bread without knocking down her rows and rows of American junk food: Oreos, Fritos, Goldfish snacks. Alice felt herself drool a little. All that fatty goodness looked like heaven next to Tally's stir-fry.

"Hi, girls!" Dylan said, fluttering her fingers sarcastically on her way to the toaster oven. She smiled to herself. How dumb did that crew think she was? She'd heard them muttering and she knew what they'd been muttering about—but who cared? Just five minutes ago, she'd got an e-mail from her dad confirming that he was coming to London in a few weeks—he was about to book his ticket—and that meant she'd be out of here fucking soon.

"Whisper whisper whisper," she mocked. "Are you girlies discussing tomorrow night?"

"Since when is that any of your business?" Sonia snapped.

But Alice pursed her lips. She'd been hoping Dylan had forgotten about Jasper and his booty-hunting invitation to Guy Fawkes. Clearly, that was wishful thinking. If only she hadn't promised to bring Dylan along. If only Jas hadn't decided he wanted to shag Dylan in the first place. Shit. If only she'd just said no.

"Actually, yeah." Alice shrugged. "We were. You can follow Sonia if you still want to come."

"What the—?" Sonia yelped.

"Great. I'll be there. Whoa!" Dylan's baby-blue eyes widened. Mrs. Hoare had just swept from the foyer into the kitchen, almost barging right into her.

"Ah, girls, I was hoping to find people in here," the teacher announced, not bothering to apologize. She had a smug, self-satisfied expression on her face. "You can spread the word."

Tally swallowed the giant mouthful of mush she'd taken, then politely put down her fork. "Sorry, Mrs. Hoare, spread the word about what? I'm not quite sure what you mean."

"Of course you're not sure what I mean. That's because I haven't told you yet." Mrs. Hoare leaned her skinny hands on the table and bent over the group, engulfing them in a cloud of garlicky breath. "Surprise, girls. I'd like to announce my new policy for Tudor House."

Sonia glanced at Alice. This couldn't be good.

"I've noticed the juniors are used to having the run of the St. Cecilia's grounds," the Ho went on. "Splitting into cliques, making certain people feel excluded. Well, that wasn't the way it was under me at Pembroke Ladies' School, and that's not the way it's going to be here. From next week, Wednesday nights will be known as Bonding Nights. After seven o'clock, the entire junior class will remain in Tudor House and bond with each other all evening. We'll visit each other's rooms, play games, watch videos, make new friends. And perhaps *some* of us," she said, eyeing everyone's plates, "might even learn to cook."

Mrs. Hoare squeaked out a laugh like a rusty hinge and looked round the table, clearly expecting everyone to join in.

When no one did, she cleared her throat. "I'll be in my study if anyone has any questions. Enjoy your dinner, girls."

As Mrs. Hoare barged out the door, Tally's porcelain complexion turned fiery. "Who the fuck does that creep think she is?" she hissed. She shoveled a forkful of soggy zucchini into her mouth. "I don't need to learn to cook. This food is delicious."

Sonia snorted.

Alice banged her palm on the table. "Someone needs to tell that bitch we're sixteen, not six. It's too late to make new friends. If we haven't bonded by now, we're not going to."

"*Bonding Nights,*" Dylan sneered, plonking down in front of her grilled cheese. "Yeah, right. Bondage Nights, more like."

Alice stared at her in surprise.

Tally guffawed. "OMG, hilarious! The Ho forces us into Bondage Nights. How fitting."

All five girls snickered, but eventually Alice's face grew

pensive. Mrs. Hoare was clearly sticking to her word, shoving her nose into everyone's business, keeping her insect antennae alert. Alice took a deep breath. But tomorrow night should be okay. . . . After all, the Ho had already caught her once this week, and lightning never struck the same place twice.

She hoped.

CHAPTER NINE

*S*tupid. Bloody. Physics!" whispered Farah Assadi, hurling her pencil away so hard that it hit Mimah Calthorpe de Vyle-Hanswicke, who was sitting on the other side of the antique oak library table. "These equations are impossible. Stupid Isaac Newton. Who cares about the stupid laws of motion?"

"Hmm, let me think . . ." Emilia Charles rolled her eyes. "Oh, the A-level examining board? Not to mention Mr. Vicks. He'll go mental if we mess up the test tomorrow morning. We were meant to be studying the whole of fall break."

"Give me a break," Mimah snorted. "Who does that? The only thing I studied over fall break was the quickest way to the pub."

"See?" Farah nudged Emilia. "Mimah didn't study either."

"Yeah, and just watch her get an A-plus anyway." Emilia grabbed Mimah's practice exam paper, which was scrawled all over with complicated-looking equations, and shook it in

Farah's face. "Some people don't need to study. And *some* people"—she looked pointedly at her best friend—"should have hit the books instead of sneaking out to seduce a sleazy club promoter twice their age."

Farah giggled and widened her almond-shaped eyes, which, much to the disapproval of her strict Persian family, she liked to pencil in thick, smoky black. "That guy wasn't twice my age. He was only thirty."

"Yeah, and that's at least five times your *mental* age." Mimah gave her trademark throaty cackle.

"Good one!" Emilia guffawed, punching Mimah's toned shoulder.

Farah made a show of laughing too. She and Emilia weren't usually suck-ups, but you couldn't help feeling flattered when Jemimah Calthorpe de Vyle-Hanswicke, one of the coolest girls in school, deigned to study with you. Plus, Mimah was BFFs with Alice Rochester, and if they were lucky, she might just drop a few party invitations their way.

Riiing!

"Gotta go!" Mimah sprang up from her chair the second the end-of-lessons bell clanged. "Hate to break up the study group, girlies—it's been sooo thrilling. Oh well, see you round. Ciao."

Almost before she'd finished speaking, Mimah was halfway through the library, hurrying over its oriental rugs, past its padded window seats that overlooked the school's front drive. It wasn't that she had anything against Farah and Emilia—they were lifesavers compared to the other geeks in her physics set—but that didn't mean she wanted them to be her new lapdogs. Especially not this evening. They might attempt to tag along to Guy Fawkes and it would be a hassle trying to shake them off.

Down in the marble entrance hall, Mimah pushed through a set of thick oak doors into the school's main courtyard. Quad was full of beautiful, old, redbrick buildings, dripping with ivy, but Mimah ignored all that. Instead, she headed straight for the dining hall at the opposite end of the courtyard, determined to shove her way through the teatime crowd. With any luck, she'd find Charlie there. Mimah had been on a mission to catch her sister all day.

"Jemimah," came a male voice.

"Yeah?" Mimah whipped round. Boarding school was so bloody annoying—people were always interrupting when you were in a rush. "Oh, Mr. Vicks, hi," she exclaimed, coming face to face with the Head of Physics. She glued a fat, ass-kissing smile to her face. "I was just practicing for tomorrow's test."

"Splendid," Mr. Vicks boomed. The man's eyebrows tufted out at least an inch from his forehead. *Shame he couldn't lend some of that excess fuzz to his receding hairline,* Mimah thought. "Listen, do you have a minute? I'd like a word."

"Um, yeah, sure." Great. Mimah clenched her teeth. The phrase "I'd like a word" coming from a teacher never meant anything good. "How can I help?"

"Cambridge. Have you considered it?"

"Huh?" Mimah blinked.

"Cambridge. The university." Impatiently, Mr. Vicks shuffled on the cobblestones. "Have you thought of applying there next year? I don't know if you're aware, but they have the best natural sciences program in the country. I think you'd make a good candidate."

"Oh. Cool."

"Cool?" Mr. Vicks repeated incredulously.

Mimah eyed the nearest wall, wishing she could bang her head against it. Mr. Vicks was a total weirdo, but he'd been Head of Physics for years, and he was by far the best science teacher on the St. Cecilia's staff. Now he was telling her she had a shot at Cambridge, and the best response she could come up with was *cool?*

"Uh, thanks," she added.

Mr. Vicks thrust his nose into her face. "Jemimah Calthorpe de Vyle-Hanswicke, I don't know why you're acting so pathetic. You're one of the most gifted physicists I've ever taught at this school and I'm confident you could get into any college you want. Especially with extracurriculars like yours—lacrosse, netball, tennis. And I hear you've never been in any trouble to speak of." He glanced toward the dining hall and licked his lips. "I must dash now, but think about it. I'm expecting great things from you."

Mimah watched Mr. Vicks hobble off, her jaw hanging open. Gifted. Great things. Cambridge. *Gifted.* She floated through Quad and onto the sweeping brick steps that led to the Great Lawn. Uni, grades—ever since her family life had started to go tits up, she hadn't thought she cared about that stuff anymore. In fact, she'd basically forgotten about the idea of university altogether. But now a vista of possibilities seemed to open into the distance. . . .

"Oops!"

"Ow!" Mimah snapped as someone whacked into her. She glared down at a weedy freshman. "Why don't you look where you're going instead of at your BlackBerry?"

"Sorry. Oh!" Weedy exclaimed, staggering a little as she realized who she was talking to. Her eyes flicked back to the text message on her phone.

"Got a problem?" Mimah demanded.

"No. It's just . . . Ummm . . . Never mind. Bye." Flashing a fake smile, Weedy stuffed her phone in her pocket and clattered down the redbrick steps to the Great Lawn.

Weirdo. Mimah frowned as she watched the girl run. It was then that she noticed the cluster of freshmen. They were gathered in the shadow of a large tree about fifty yards away, nudging each other, gaping at something Mimah couldn't see.

A squeal rent the air. Suddenly, a bundle of yellow and gray rolled into view, writhing on the grass. Mimah squinted and the bundle separated into two distinct figures—girls, tearing at each other's clothes, yanking each other's hair.

She grinned. Yes! A freshman catfight. Hilarious.

One girl managed to fight her way on top and started using

her knees to pin down her opponent's arms. She grabbed a handful of dirt and rubbed it in her captive's face.

And then the aggressor's stringy hair whipped to one side and Mimah caught a glimpse of her profile. The smile vanished from her lips.

CHAPTER TEN

The Great Lawn became a green blur under Mimah's zebra-print ballet flats as she raced toward the ruckus. "Move!" she gasped. "Out of my way."

"Oh, shit, move," the spectators murmured, pushing one another aside. "It's Charlie's sister. Watch out."

Snippets of gossip buzzed around Mimah like bees.

"She's been acting psycho all week."

"What'd she do this time?"

"Jumped on Chloe McPherson for, like, no reason."

"Yeah, Chloe was sitting on that bench and Charlie ordered her to move and Chloe was, like, 'No way, find your own seat.' So Charlie attacked her."

"Are you serious?"

"Charlie is such a freak."

"I am *so* reporting her to Mrs. Traphorn."

"Are you mad? You know who Mimah's mates are—they'd

kill us if we got Charlie expelled. Maybe Mimah can sort her out."

"Charlie!" Mimah shouted. She yanked her sister up. "What the fuck do you think you're doing?"

"Get off!" Charlie tried to jerk her arm away, but Mimah tightened her grip and dragged her sister off the grass, round the side of the art block.

"Those girls were saying you've been acting funny all week," she snapped. "Is that true?"

"No."

"Okay. . . . Then would you like to tell me where you and Georgie were going last night?"

"No."

Mimah rolled her eyes. "Wonderful. Since you're being so conversational, why don't you tell me what you were fighting about just now?"

"No!"

"Charlie . . . ," Mimah warned.

"Whatever," Charlie slurred. "That loser was pissing me off."

Mimah frowned. "Are you drunk?"

"No."

"We'll see about that." She leaned in. There was no booze on Charlie's breath. But something wasn't right.

"Jemimah." Charlie twitched away. "Get out of my face."

"Not until you tell me what's wrong! Look, if it's Mummy and Daddy's divorce, we can talk about it. I'm angry too. I was trying to chat to you about it yesterday, but—"

"Oh, fuck off," Charlie snarled. "I don't give a shit about that, okay? Why do you always have to be such a fucking goody two-shoes, sticking your nose in everywhere? Leave me alone!" Ripping herself from Mimah's grip, Charlie tore away across the grass.

Closing her eyes, Mimah rested her head against the art block's rough brick wall. This was worse than she'd thought. It was time to switch to Plan B.

CHAPTER ELEVEN

Sonia's gold Gucci watch read seven twenty-eight on Thursday evening, which meant that she and Dylan had two minutes to get to Mimah's room, which meant they were going to be late. Dylan's fault, of course. Sonia had been so pissed off at the thought of chaperoning her loser dorm-mate that she'd smudged her eyeliner three times and had had to start from scratch. Finally, she was done. Glaring at Dylan, she pressed her finger to her lips and crept toward the door of their room.

Dylan stifled a giggle. Sonia looked like she was doing a bad imitation of a cat burglar. The girl was literally the biggest drama queen ever.

"Remember," Sonia mouthed, her hand on the doorknob, "if we bump into the Ho on the way—"

"I say I spilled something," Dylan droned, "and you say you're taking me to the cleaning cupboard because I'm new and I don't know where it is." Sonia had repeated this plan to her about eight times during the past hour.

"Right," Sonia sniffed. "You don't mention Mimah's room, or Alice, or Tally. Got it?"

"Got it. Oh wait, one second!" Dylan gasped. "What liquid should I say I spilled? Shit, we haven't even planned that!"

Sonia looked panic-stricken for a second. Then she noticed Dylan's mocking grin and narrowed her eyes. "This is serious, *Dylan*. Believe me, if we get caught, your life won't be worth my little toe."

"Oh, no. I'm scared." Dylan stuffed all her fingers into her mouth at the same time. But, despite her sarcasm, she couldn't snuff the glow she felt at being included. True, Alice's crew had only invited her tonight because they had to, but that didn't mean she couldn't make the most of it. Night after night over the past two months, Dylan had watched Sonia sneak out to meet the boys at the pub in Hasted, or to gossip in Alice and Tally's lair, while she was left in their empty room with only a wall full of Sonia's glamorous party pictures for company. And now, finally, she was going too.

"Shhh," Sonia ordered, even though Dylan hadn't moved a muscle. Wafting a flowery perfume, she edged through the door. Her long, shiny hair tumbled down her back and skimmed the top of her butt, and her aquamarine blouse, tucked into her high-waisted jeans, shimmered in the dim stairwell. Its delicate silk billowed and rippled as she moved.

Dylan tugged at her hot-pink cashmere halter-neck. It was

itchy and kept bunching round her annoyingly gigantic boobs. For god's sake—couldn't Sonia, just for one night, look less than pristine and not make her feel like a muppet?

Tudor House was silent, its hallways deserted. The rest of the junior class had obviously taken Mrs. Hoare's Guy Fawkes embargo to heart and were studying behind closed doors. Losers. Then again, maybe they were onto something. Dylan shivered as the black November night breathed against the windows of the stairwell, sending jets of freezing air rattling through the panes.

"Stop." Sonia stuck out her hand. They'd reached the ground floor, and the entrance to Mrs. Hoare's suite was straight ahead. "Me first." Flattening herself against the wall, Sonia tiptoed sideways, like a crab—and then, just before disappearing round the corner into Mimah's corridor, she kicked the Ho's door with her studded ankle boot.

Dylan froze. Cold sweat broke out on her forehead. What the hell was Sonia trying to pull? And more important, how the fuck was she meant to escape before the Ho burst through that door and threw her into detention?

Dylan took a deep breath. *Calm.* Sonia was a bitch. She'd always had it in for Dylan, and if Dylan let her win, she'd never be able to look herself in the mirror again.

One. Two . . . Dylan bolted on three. She raced down the hallway, round the corner toward Mimah's room, skidded to a stop, and knocked.

The door cracked open.

"Quick," Mimah beckoned. "Get inside."

"Oh, it's you." Sonia looked like someone had just forced sour milk down her throat.

"Yeah," Dylan grinned smugly, "it's me. What's the matter? You seem kind of surprised. Oh, um, hi," she said, giving Alice and Tally a timid wave that came out looking more like a salute.

Pushing past Sonia, Dylan glanced round Mimah's dorm, which was definitely one of Tudor's worst. It was small. It was poky. It was dark. And it was shared with Gabby Bunter, the weirdest, most socially-impaired girl in their year. Gabby was hunched over her desk in the room's darkest corner. She was staring at a book, but was clearly too petrified by the presence of Alice and her crew even to turn the page.

Dylan's stomach fluttered. Funny to think she used to drop into this dorm almost daily. The last time she'd visited, she and Mimah had been the best of friends (or so Dylan had thought), practicing their raunchy dance routine for the St. Cecilia's fashion show. Unfortunately, Mimah had only been pretending to like Dylan and had pulled a nastier stunt at the fashion show than Dylan could ever have dreamed. She and Mimah had been avoiding each other ever since. That was hardly even six weeks ago, but it felt like a century.

"Let's get going," Alice said. She grabbed a blue and green plaid cape from Mimah's chair and opened the window as she threw it on.

A shard of wintry air cut through the room. Dylan shivered.

"Don't tell me you're planning on coming out like that," Alice scoffed.

"Um, yeah." Dylan glanced toward the bed, where Sonia, Tally, and Mimah were each pulling on a coat. "I thought we weren't wearing jackets. In case we got caught in the hallway. It would have looked suspicious."

"Yeah, no shit." Alice rolled her eyes. "Why do you think we dropped ours off here earlier? Sonia, you should have told her."

"Oopsie. Forgot."

Dylan bit her lip as Sonia, Tally, and Alice eased themselves over the window ledge and dropped outside.

Mimah was next. "You know the deal, right, Gabs?" she murmured, one hand on the sill. Her voice was low and menacing.

"Uh-huh." Gabby was staring down at her textbook.

"And you're not thinking of snitching on us, are you?"

"Uh-uh." Gabby's chubby cheeks wobbled as she shook her head.

"Good. That's the right attitude: team playing. You don't make *my* life hell and I won't make yours hell." Mimah gave Gabby a long, hard look. Then she took a leap and landed in the shadowy bushes below.

It was Dylan's turn. Teeth chattering, she swung one leg into the frigid air. But before she could turn, Gabby glanced up from her textbook and caught her eye. Shrugging, she gave Dylan a sad smile—a gesture of solidarity, perhaps, from one victim to another.

"Dylan," Alice hissed. "For fuck's sake, are you trying to get us caught? Move it."

Dylan snapped back to the escape. Forgetting all about Gabby, she swung her other leg over the sill, pushed off from the wall, and didn't look back.

CHAPTER TWELVE

"Where are they?" Alice fretted, the firelight playing over her flawless skin. "They said they'd be here at eight. It's past eight now. They're never late for Guy Fawkes."

Tapping her fingertips against her black hobo bag, she scanned the scattered groups of revelers on Hasted Common. Some were toasting marshmallows. Some were swigging cider and waving sparklers and belting out songs. None of them was Tristan. Or Seb. Or Jasper. Or Rando. Alice huffed. She and the girls had already walked twice round the huge bonfire without finding a trace of their Hasted House crew and she, for one, had no intention of waiting any longer.

Not that there was much else they could do.

"Babe, chill." Tally flicked a strand of her white-blond hair, which had fallen out of her perfect, messy bun. Alice was so bloody uptight about people being on time. Except when it was herself, of course; Alice Rochester could keep people waiting for as long as she liked. "They're probably having trouble with the crowd. I say we get drinks."

Mimah nodded. "Yeah, look: beer stall. Over there."

"Beer? *Rrretch.*" Sonia stuck her fingers down her throat. "I'm getting mulled wine."

"Whatever." Alice stamped her foot. "The boys should be here to get it for us. Since when do ladies have to get their own drinks?"

She folded her arms. Hasted Common was loud, smoky, dirty, and heaving with Hasted locals, the girls sausaged into cheap jeans that did no favors for their cellulite; the guys sporting pimples, mullets, and earrings in each ear.

"Ugh." Alice crinkled her nose. "I refuse to spend the whole night sharing germs with a bunch of tacky townies."

"And I refuse to stand here like a loser. Come on." Tally jerked her head and dived into the fray, trailed by Sonia and Mimah. Finally, Alice let out an exasperated sigh and followed.

Behind them, Dylan scrambled to keep up. Shivering in her tiny top, she watched her breath puff out in icy clouds. Outside the ring of firelight, the field was dark, freezing, unfamiliar. The smell of trampled grass saturated the air. Shouts flew overhead as carnies hawked their games. Strings of ratty soft toys dangled from their stalls. Cheers burst out every few seconds.

"Whoa!" Dylan cried, skidding to the side as a sinewy man swung a pair of fire torches into her path. Gashes of orange flame sliced through the blackness.

"Coooool," Alice exclaimed, stopping to watch.

Dylan shot her a glance. She'd never heard Alice sound so genuine.

"He's good," Alice said. "My brother, Dom, learned to do that last year at the Full Moon parties in Thailand. He met all these hippie travelers, and they sort of adopted him and taught him stuff."

"Thailand? Wow." Dylan took a step closer. "How'd he end up there? It's pretty far away."

Alice stared at her as if she'd just realized who she was talking to. Then she curled her lip and put on a retarded voice. "Dur, he got there by airplane. They're these big metal birds that take you places really fast. For fuck's sake." She rolled her eyes. "There's no need to look so impressed just because Dom went traveling round the world on his gap year. Everybody does."

Dylan sighed. Whenever she thought she was coming to grips with the English and their weird habits, they suddenly managed to make her feel like an alien again. Maybe she'd never fit in. Thank god she wouldn't need to, soon.

"Where on earth is Tally?" Alice said. She was craning her neck over the crowd, clearly dying to get back to her real friends. "She was here a second ago."

"Don't know." Dylan stood on tiptoe and looked in all directions, but Tally's white-blond hair and baby-blue coat were nowhere to be seen. "The nearest mulled wine stand's over there. Maybe they're in line."

"Maybe." Alice started toward the dodgem cars, skirting the ring-tossing and rifle-shooting games, cutting round the back of the Kamikaze. The crowd was almost nonexistent here, thanks to the dim lighting, but a skinny guy wearing a Kappa tracksuit still managed to bump right into Dylan as he passed.

She staggered. "Ow! He did that on purpose."

Alice sniffed. "Of course he did. Stupid townies. They hate us."

"Why?"

"Because we're posh and we go to boarding school and we're clever. They should love us, though. Why else do they think Hasted has fancy restaurants and nice cafés? Obviously, so our parents have places to take us when they visit. Otherwise it'd be a total dump."

"Oi, love," a voice interrupted. A fat, red-faced man planted himself in front of Alice. "How about I win you a nice soft panda?"

"Um, how about you don't?" Alice tried to push past, nearly suffocating from the amount of alcohol on the man's breath.

"Ooh er, a feisty one," he tittered, nudging his mate. "Gaz, look who's all high and mighty."

Gaz draped his arm around his friend, forming a wall in front of Alice and Dylan. His eyes were bloodshot. "Aw, Darren, that's a crying shame, that is," he slurred. "These girls should be more grateful. Come on, love. Don't you want a nice soft toy to cuddle in bed? To rub against on all those lonely nights?"

Darren snickered. "This one don't need any soft toys. She's got two right there." He pointed at Dylan's boobs. "I'd like to have a rub against those."

Gaz grinned like a shark as Dylan folded her arms over her chest.

"Oi, what are you hiding them for?" he said grabbing Dylan's hand. "Come on, gizza look."

"Get away from her," Alice cried. She slapped him.

"What the fuck was that? You fucking posh bitch!"

"These two tigresses need taking down a peg or two, don't you reckon, Gaz?" Darren sneered. He and Gaz closed in on Alice and Dylan, backing them farther and farther into the darkness, away from the Kamikaze's lights.

Alice's heart thumped. She was shaking like a cornered rabbit. She didn't like this. She didn't like the glint in the men's eyes. Where was Tally? Where was Mimah? Mimah was strong; she could save them.

Suddenly, Dylan made to dart round Gaz, but he blocked her with a sidestep. "Oh, no you don't."

"Help!" Alice screamed. Her cry was drowned out by the music and yells from the ride. "Heeelp!"

"You'd better shut it, you dirty slap—"

"What's going on?" demanded a voice.

Alice spun round. "Rando! Thank god." She drank in Rando's scruffy dark hair, his rosy cheeks scattered with freckles, his concerned brown eyes. She'd never been so glad to see anyone in her life. "Help us! These men are—"

"Oooh help us, help us!" interrupted Gaz. He and Darren were in stitches. *"Our hero!"*

"You think this little runt"—Darren guffawed, gesturing at Rando—"is gonna do anything? Except fall over when I hit him?" Flexing his arms, he advanced his huge bulk toward Rando.

But Rando, instead of retreating, put up his fists and assumed a defensive stance. His jaw was set.

Gaz cracked up. "Check it out, mate. Looks like you've got a fight on your hands!"

"Mummy, help, I'm scared," tittered Darren, turning to grin at his friend.

That was Rando's chance. Quick as lightning, he drove his right fist into Darren's cheekbone and followed up with a left-hander to Darren's gut.

"Ooooow!" roared Darren, more in surprise than in pain. He reeled backward.

"Ow," echoed Rando, shaking out his hand. He'd only ever punched one person before, and that was a boy his own size—not a bully six inches taller and four times as fat.

"Whack him back!" Gaz heckled from the sidelines. "You're not gonna let the runt get away with that, are you? Make him pay!"

"Oh, I will," Darren growled. "Come 'ere, you little bastard." His face contorted with rage; he pounded a giant, beefy fist into Rando's left eye.

"Argh," Rando groaned, doubling over. His brain felt like it was being crushed by a boulder.

Darren smiled maliciously as his foe staggered upright. "Want some more, do you?" he sneered, swinging back his arm to thump Rando again.

Dylan let out a whimper, her arms still clamped over her breasts.

"Stop it, you bully!" Alice screamed.

But before she'd even finished the words, Rando had flung himself to one side. Darren's fist whooshed through empty air and he stumbled forward with the force of his own body weight.

"Take that!" Rando grunted, kicking out. He booted Darren's ass with all the force he could muster.

Darren tottered. His eyes went glassy. Then his knees buckled and he thudded to the ground like a sack of dirt. "Urgh," he gurgled drunkenly.

"Pathetic!" Gaz jeered. "Get up, mate; you've got to teach this posh dickhead a lesson. Oi, get up!" He stomped over and nudged Darren with his foot.

Just then Darren lolled his head sideways and hurled. A stream of vomit oozed over Gaz's feet.

"Oh, you fucker," Gaz groaned. "That is digusting. And those are my new Nikes."

As he tried to clean his sneakers on the grass, Alice tiptoed forward and grabbed Rando and Dylan.

"Run for it," she muttered. The three of them dashed for the well-lit part of the common. They darted through the crowds, weaving around carnival booths. Finally, Rando stopped and looked back.

"I think we've lost them," he panted. "You girls all right?"

"Y-yeah," Dylan squeaked. She was shivering and pale.

"Oh my god, Rando," Alice cried, running at her friend and flinging her arms around him, "you're amazing!" She wasn't normally a huggy person—she hated all that touchy-feely crap—but right now she was overcome. "I can't believe you did that. Challenging two monsters three times your size—I've never seen anyone so brave. Oh, you poor thing," she added, reaching up to brush Rando's swollen cheek. "You're going to have a nasty bruise there tomorrow morning."

Alice smiled, and then froze. For some reason, Rando was blushing. His soft brown eyes held hers. She stepped back, confused.

The next moment, the weirdness was gone. Rando burst out laughing, his dimples creasing and his small, pointy teeth gleaming. It gave him such a mischievous air that Alice couldn't help smiling too.

"Thanks for embarrassing me, Al," he grinned. "I managed to look all manly there for a minute and now you've got me in the middle of a weepy scene."

She giggled. "Poor darling, you're still manly. I'm going to brag to all the others about what a hero you are."

Rando's dimples deepened even further. "Excellent! Come on then, what are we waiting for? Let's go find them so you can get started."

CHAPTER THIRTEEN

*F*uck me, I'm sweating my big hairy ass off!"
George Demetrios leered round the group
as if he'd just made a brilliant statement, and
stretched his arms above his head. It was ten thirty on Hasted
Common. The carnival crowd had thinned out and the air
had chilled to a subarctic degree, but the bonfire was still
glowing and crackling in the middle of the field, drawing
partiers into its warmth.

"Phew," George panted. "Did I mention I was fucking hot?"
Nudging Sonia aside, he grabbed a corner of Seb's cashmere
picnic blanket, wiped his forehead, and slurped down half
the whisky bottle.

Sonia's mouth dropped open. "Oh. My. God. Troglodyte." She
edged away toward Seb, whose navy jacket smelled deliciously
of marijuana and wood smoke. Unlike George Demetrios, Seb
was the opposite of a repulsive beast. He had delicate hands and
a gentle voice and fluffy down on his face instead of stubble.

"Sebbie, save me," Sonia bleated. She rubbed her cheek against his shoulder and gazed like a puppy into his eyes. "George is such a Neanderthal. I can't believe the zoo let him escape."

Seb coughed and sat up straight.

"Ow!" Sonia yelped as her head slid off his shoulder.

Tally smirked. "Um, I hate to break it to you, Sone, but Neanderthals don't live in zoos. They're not animals—they're prehistoric humans?"

"Whatever," Sonia hiccuped, cuddling against Seb again. "If they're anything like him, they *should* live in zoos." She narrowed her eyes at George Demetrios. "Ape."

"Babe," George slurred, "don't be like that. Here, have some booze. Peace offering."

"I don't *think* so. Not after your sweaty lips have slobbered all over it."

"Interesting . . ." George shot his eyebrows up and down like a lecherous old man. "I didn't notice you having an aversion to my sweaty lips at Bella Scott's Christmas party last year."

"Oooooh . . . ," heckled Mimah and Alice.

"Someone's asking for it," Tally jeered.

"Not," Sonia retorted. "I am not even going to dignify that with a response." She clamped her mouth shut, then immediately reopened it. "And for your information, *George*, I was drunk and stoned and half passed out at that party. It's not my fault if you took advantage of me."

"Yeah. *I* took advantage of *you*." George winked. "Suuure."

Around the circle Seb, Alice, Tristan, Mimah, Rando, and

Jasper cracked up. Dylan took a shy gulp from her beer can and ventured a grin. After three hours of drinking, she'd just about recovered from the whole breast-groping incident and was finally starting to chill. Plus, Alice was acting sort of . . . pleasant. She'd actually defended Dylan out there, against the murderous townies. And she'd been giving Dylan conspiratorial looks ever since they'd joined the others by the fire. Maybe danger was a good way to bond. Maybe the St. Cecilia's bitch crew was finally retracting its claws.

Or maybe not. As Dylan glanced up, she caught Sonia glaring at her across the circle. *Don't you dare think* you *can laugh at me*, the look implied. Sonia's lip curled. "Hey, everyone," she said, her eyes boring straight into Dylan, "I am *so* excited about next weekend. Who's coming?"

"Me!" George Demetrios cheered.

"You mean to YLB?" Tally bounced up and down. "Totally! I can't wait!"

"Me neither!" Alice squeezed Tristan's shoulders, careful not to disturb the joint he was rolling. "Tickets were, like, impossible to get this year. Unless you're us, of course."

"Apparently this one's gonna be even more debauched than the last one," George chuckled, rubbing his hands together. "Every hot girl in London's coming."

Jasper chucked a chip at him. "Including your mum?"

As the boys roared with laughter, Dylan's smile faded. What the hell was YLB? She glanced at Sonia, who adjusted her lipstick-pink pashmina and shot back a superior look. Dylan sighed as Rando leaned across her toward Tristan.

"Oi, mate," Rando muttered. He moved the cold beer bottle that he'd been holding against his swollen eye. "I've been meaning to tell you all night: Our surprise for YLB is on."

"Fantastic!" Tristan puffed out a cloud of smoke from the joint he'd just lit. "That's the best news I've heard all week! Wicked."

"Surprise?" Alice darted her eyes between the two boys. "What surprise?"

"The one you have to wait till next weekend to find out about." T grinned.

Alice swatted his knee and giggled. T was too cute to be annoyed at—even though she hated being kept in the dark. "Pass me the joint, will you?"

"Here." Stroking Alice's hair, T placed the roach between her lips. "Hopefully it'll help you forget about those beastly townies. I'm bloody glad you girls are safe. Another toast"—he raised his glass—"to Rando!"

"Rando!" everyone roared.

"Shut up!" Rando cried, burying his face behind his fingers. Alice noticed he was still wearing only his thin cotton T-shirt, green with faded letters across the front. He'd offered his coat to Dylan on the way back to the fire and hadn't asked for it back.

"Rando! Rando!" Tally and Mimah chanted, rocking back and forth.

"Stop it," Rando insisted. "You're embarrassing me."

"Why?" Tally cried, brandishing the joint Alice had just passed her. "You shouldn't be embarrassed. You're a hero!"

"I am so not a hero. I'm like, a . . . a *zero*."

"Whoa." Tristan sputtered out his mouthful of whisky. "Dude: hero, zero—that rhymes! Genius." He scanned the picnic blanket and grabbed a Tupperware box, which he overturned, scattering brownie crumbs everywhere. His cigarette hanging from his lips, he drummed out a tribal beat on the plastic.

> *"I've got a friend named Rando*
> *We play in the same indie band. Oh—*
> *He says he's a zero.*
> *But he's a hero.*
> *Give him a cheer. Go,*
> *Rando!"*

"Rando!" everyone echoed.

"Woo!" Tally cheered. She jumped up and pulled Alice to her feet. They stamped out the rhythm on the grass.

"Fine. If you're gonna be that way. . . ." Rando grabbed a beer bottle and his Zippo and started bashing along to T's beat.

> *"I've got a friend named Tristan.*
> *Tonight he got really pissed and*
> *Made up a dumb rap.*

It was really crap.
By the way, he's a twat. Yeah—
Tristan!
Tristan!"

"Dickhead!" T grinned, lunging at Rando's instruments.

Alice threw back her head and laughed. These were her boys. They were amazing. She raised her arms, swaying her hips to the beat.

Tristan stared at her as he drummed—at the firelight licking her olive skin, flickering in her eyes, glowing through her dark, flowing hair. She looked like a spirit sprung from the flames. He glanced at Rando, drumming by his side. Rando's focus was on Tally, of course. He'd always had the hots for Tals.

"Incredible," T murmured, "aren't they?"

"They are," Rando agreed.

He watched as T crept up behind Alice and slid his arm round her waist. Alice melted against him, like molten lava, as T whispered something in her ear. She smiled and together they slipped out of the ring of firelight, into the dark field.

Rando's Zippo missed a beat.

"Weird, isn't it?" said a voice at his shoulder. Tally wasn't dancing anymore. She was hovering in front of him, wisps of white-blond hair drifting around her face like sparks.

"Weird? What?"

"Seeing them as a couple. Alice and T. When we've all

89

been mates for so long." Tally swallowed. She was happy for her best friend—of course she was—but smiling for Alice sometimes got tough. It wasn't easy to watch Al slink away with her gorgeous boyfriend, leaving her out here in singlesville. Plus, Tally knew how jealous Alice would be if the tables were turned and Alice was the one who was out in the cold.

Laying her head on Rando's shoulder, she hooked her arm through his. "You and I will just have to keep each other company, I suppose," she said.

"Mmm," Rando mused. His black eye throbbed as he watched the bonfire die down.

CHAPTER FOURTEEN

There. Look," Tristan exclaimed as he and Alice skirted the last of the carnival games, leaving the Guy Fawkes crowd behind. He pointed to a row of skeleton market stalls whose metal poles stood jagged against the sky. Some were still hung with canvas dividers that partially curtained them from view. "I spotted vendors selling T-shirts and jewelry and stuff here earlier. We can hide out in the last one. No one will catch us, I swear."

Alice raised her right eyebrow as they ducked into a dim, cubicle-like space closed in on three sides. A neon bulb flickered in the next stall, illuminating the trampled brown grass. "What, you mean people won't be rushing to get in here?" she snorted. "It's just like a five-star hotel."

T laughed. "Okay, princess, I know it's not ideal. But at least it's out of the way and it's not at school where some teacher's gonna walk in on us. And at least we'll be together. We can go back to the others, though, I don't mind." He shook a wave of chestnut hair from his eyes.

Alice caught her breath. "Well . . . I do mind," she whispered, stepping towards him. Fine, maybe this wasn't the most romantic place to lose her virginity, but T was here and he was hot, and besides, an irresistible heat was spreading from her hips, downward, upward, through her whole body. T was wearing her favorite blue hoodie, the one that always smelled of him—a mixture of fresh air and sunshine and weed and soap. A few days' sexy stubble covered his chin. Standing on tiptoe, Alice brushed his slightly parted lips with her own. Tristan pulled her into a deep kiss. His tongue was in her mouth, his hands were under her jacket, running down the small of her back. She breathed shallowly. She felt his fingers slip under her strappy top and up, up toward the polka-dot push-up bra she'd worn especially for him.

She tugged him down toward the grass.

"Wait. Here." Tristan slipped out of his coat and spread it on the earth. "I don't want you to be cold."

"I won't be." Alice kissed his neck. "I've got you to keep me warm."

Tristan rolled on top of her, and Alice kicked off her shoes. This was it. This was definitely it. How would it feel? Would it hurt? She hardly had time to worry as T eased her pants down and traced his hands back up her legs. She caught her breath as his fingers caressed the insides of her thighs, then higher, higher. Gasping, she pulled him closer. She slipped her hands under his sweatshirt and felt his strong, smooth chest pressing against her.

"Alice," he breathed. "Please. I want you so much. I want to—"

"Stop."

"Huh?" Tristan froze.

"I didn't say anything." Alice shook her head. "Keep going. Please?"

He kissed her tenderly, fumbling with the button of her skirt.

"Don't push your luck!"

This time they both froze. Alice gripped T's wrist. "Who was that?"

"Chill," came a boy's voice, "I'm not gonna do anything. Why are you so jumpy?"

"Hmmm, let me think . . ." The girl's tone was sarcastic. "Oh, yeah, I don't trust you! Remember what happened last time you took me out? We're staying right here in the light, where I can keep an eye on you. Stay over there."

Alice's eyes widened. That American accent . . . "Oh my god. Is it—"

T pressed a finger to his lips. The two of them flattened themselves against the ground and peeked under the canvas divider. In the next stall, under the bulb, was Dylan. And next to her, Jasper.

"Shit," T whispered and chuckled, "he's a sneaky one. How did he coax her all the way out here?"

Alice shrugged. Dylan was still wearing Rando's coat, which was far too big on her. It made her look like a sack of rubbish. Shame, since she'd looked pretty hot earlier in her halterneck top. The girl had nice shoulders. And obviously there were the boobs. Alice sniffed. She didn't usually pay Dylan compliments, even in her head, but she could afford to be generous now that she'd won T fair and square.

Jasper was closing the gap between Dylan and himself. "Hey, listen," he began, "I know things between us haven't run smoothly—"

"*That's* an understatement," Dylan snorted.

"Okay, fine, they've been awful. But . . . Please, Dill, do you think you could give me another chance?"

"And why should I do that?"

"Good question," Alice hissed in T's ear. "He was a huge bastard to her on their date."

"Shhh."

"Because I like you," Jasper said. "And I thought, maybe, you liked me?"

"Egoist," Alice snorted.

Dylan sighed. "I don't know. Maybe I do. But . . ."

"What?"

"I don't belong in your group. All your friends hate me."

"Who? Who hates you?"

"Sonia. Mimah. Alice Rochester."

Alice rolled her eyes.

"That's rubbish," Jasper said. "I'm sure they think you're

fantastic. Anyway, who cares? You'd be dating me, not them."

"Yeah, well, that's the other thing. I don't know how long I'd be around to date you for, even if I wanted to."

"Huh?" T and Alice whispered together.

"That sounds a bit morbid," Jasper said. "Are you dying or something?"

"No! It's my dad. He's coming to London in a few weeks—I'm not sure exactly when yet—to make things right with my mom. He's going to take me and my whole family back to New York. I mean, that's the plan." Dylan's voice rose a little higher. "And I know it's going to work."

"Oh. Right." Jasper sounded deflated. "Well, I guess . . . maybe we could get to know each other better in the meantime? You'll probably think it's dumb, but I got you a present."

"What did he get her?" Alice pinched T's arm.

"How am I supposed to know?"

"It's a ticket to YLB." Jasper took an envelope from his pocket. "For next weekend. I managed to get an extra—I was hoping you'd be my date."

"No way!" Alice ripped up the handful of grass she'd been clutching. "I can't believe he's inviting her to YLB! That's, like, the most exclusive autumn invitation. Does he not realize?"

"Shhhhhhh!"

"Oh." Dylan flipped the envelope over. "Thanks, I guess. But . . . what exactly is YLB?"

Alice banged her head against the ground and rolled onto

her back, covering her eyes. "Oh my god. I can't watch this anymore. She doesn't even know what it is."

"What's YLB?" Jasper sounded shocked too. "It's the Young Leaders Ball. You mean you haven't even heard of it?"

"Does it sound like I've heard of it?"

Jasper laughed. "I guess not. Well, there's this charity in London called the Young Leaders Society, and every year they throw a gala to raise money for the promising young leaders of poor countries. They only invite England's most influential under-eighteens."

"I take it that means you?"

"Obviously. We're the nation's young leaders. *And* the only people who can afford tickets." Jasper laughed, even though he wasn't joking. "This year we're raising money for the Democratic Republic of Congo, so the theme's *Heart of Darkness*."

"What on earth is *Heart of Darkness*?"

Jasper grinned. "Who the hell knows? Apparently it's some famous book that takes place in the Congo during colonial times. Seb's read it. Anyway, everyone has to come in costume."

"Costume?" Dylan sputtered. "It was just Halloween. Can't you Brits stop dressing up for like, one second?"

"Why should we? It's our national pastime. Oh, you'll love this." Jasper chortled. "Last year the theme was Indian Summer. Guess what I wore."

"I give up."

"A bikini with the Indian flag on it. Ha! It went down

brilliantly. Go on, Dill, come with me. It would mean a lot, especially since you're leaving soon. I'm sorry for the way things went before—let me make it up to you."

Dylan sighed. "I don't know . . ."

"Please?"

There was a silence. Alice strained her ears. "Wait, what's going on?" she whispered. "Wait a sec, are they *snogging*?"

"Yeah!" Tristan grinned. "I've got to hand it to Jas, the guy's good."

Scrambling back onto her tummy, Alice peeped through the gap. Jasper's handsome face actually looked blissful. He wasn't doing his usual womanizing snog, the one where he subtly tried to make the girl feel loved while feeling her up and coaxing her clothes off all at the same time. He was kissing Dylan gently, eyes closed.

Alice turned away. She felt kind of pervy, watching.

"Hey," T whispered, drawing her close, "I reckon they've got the right idea. How about we get back to where we were before?" He brushed Alice's hair off her cheek and kissed her lips. She pressed her chest against him, inhaling his delicious scent.

A moan and a giggle burst from the next stall.

"Oh god." Alice flopped down. "I can't. I feel like we're in some sort of sex hotel, with our mates in the next room. This sucks."

"Yeah." Tristan shook his head. His face was flushed as he sat up, and his trousers looked a bit tight round the crotch.

Alice blushed. "I just want our first time to be special," she whispered, burying her face in T's warm, delicious neck.

"It will be, babe. It's you and me. How could it not?"

He stroked her hair and Alice sighed. Typical. Just when she'd decided to take the plunge, something had to get in the way.

CHAPTER FIFTEEN

ice hair," Mimah snickered the next morning. She poked Alice's greasy pony-tail with her highlighter. "I can see you've put loads of thought into that style. Experimenting with the classic 'morning after' look, are we?"

"Shut up." Alice swatted Mimah's hand away, then sat up poker straight as Mrs. Hoare barged in for double English, lugging a pile of printouts. As soon as the Ho had turned her back, she ripped a piece of paper from her notebook, scribbled something and shoved it in Mimah's face: UP YOURS.

"Ooh," Mimah chuckled, "someone's feeling crabby. Got a manover?"

"A *what*?"

"A manover. You know, like a hangover. But from too much sex."

"That is so not a word!" Alice giggled. "Anyway," she

dropped her voice even lower, "you know T and I didn't do it last night. I already told you what happened."

"Chill. It was just a figure of—"

"Quiet," the Ho barked. "Pencils out, class. Today we're going to be analyzing this poem"—she tapped her sheet—"by the great English genius Sir Alfred, Lord Tennyson and I want everyone's full attention. Full. Attention!"

"Owww," Alice groaned, clutching her head as the suck-ups at the front fought each other to hand out copies of the poem. The Ho's voice grated like nails on a chalkboard. She shoved back her chair, trying to escape from the noise, and immediately bumped into the back wall of the classroom. "Ugh."

Alice pretty much always sat at the front of lessons— if you wanted to get into Oxford, it was vital to be on teachers' good sides—but in Mrs. Hoare's case, she made an exception. They got enough of the bitch as it was in Tudor House.

"Seriously though," Mimah whispered, prodding her, "are you and T ever gonna seal the deal?"

"Oooh." Alice rubbed her temples. "Hangover headache. Hmm? What'd you say?"

Mimah folded her arms. "You heard me."

"Fine," Alice snapped. "Yes we are. Soon."

"Good, 'cause we're all rooting for you. In a few weeks I'm gonna start taking bets."

"Don't you dare!" Alice kicked her under the desk and

nudged Tally, on her other side. "Tals, help me. Mimah's being a bitch."

"That's nothing new," Tally smirked, flashing her annoyingly gorgeous grin. She turned back to her notebook, shielding it in the crook of her elbow.

"Hey, what are you hiding over there?" Mimah craned her neck. "Are you drawing something?"

"No." Tally fingered her gold, feather-shaped pendant (her new favorite in her collection) with a secretive smile on her face.

"You are so."

"Am not."

"Are so."

"Am *not.*"

"How old are you two? Six?" Alice interrupted.

"Mimah started it." Tally stuck out her tongue, then quickly pretended to make a note as the Ho's eyes grazed over them.

Mimah seized the opening. She reached behind Alice and snatched the notepad from under Tally's elbows.

"Oi!" Tally whispered. "Give it back."

But it was too late. Mimah clapped her hand over her mouth and rocked with laughter. "Oh my god."

"Let's see!" As she read Tally's doodle, Alice's jaw dropped:

Tom Randall-Stubbs
L3 O2 V0 E0 S2
Natalya Abbott

3–2–0–0–2
5–2–0–2
7–2–2
9–4
94% !!!!

"You worked out a love percentage?" Mimah gasped for breath. "You total loser. You really are six! I haven't done that since like, fifth grade."

"Piss off." Tally lunged for her paper but Mimah jerked it out of reach. "Okay, fine. So I think Rando's cute. So what?"

"You never did before," Alice remarked.

"Huh?"

"I said you never did before. All those times last month when I tried to get you to go for him, you wouldn't. And now, suddenly, you've changed your mind?"

Tally stared at her. "Yeah. Why do you have to sound so accusing?"

Alice blinked. "I'm . . . I'm not accusing. I'm just . . . I think it's weird behavior, that's all."

"What's so weird about liking a cute boy? Especially after last night." Tally closed her eyes. "He was so heroic, rescuing you guys and then giving Dylan his coat. And that cute little smile. And that song he made up? It was so funny! Not that it was better than Tristan's, Al. And anyway, ninety-four percent? Come on, it's fate!"

She and Mimah tittered.

"Girls!" Mrs. Hoare snapped. "I'm sure nothing you're saying can be as interesting as what I'm saying. Which of you is going to answer my question? I'm waiting."

All three of them tucked their heads and pretended to study the poem.

"Well? Does not one of you have anything intelligent to say?" Mrs. Hoare advanced down the classroom. "That's funny, I thought St. Cecilia's was supposed to be a good school. What do you think your parents are spending all this money on? To pay for you to learn how to apply lip gloss?"

"Yeah, that's an important skill," Mimah said under her breath. "Maybe you should learn it sometime."

Alice glared at her. The last thing they could afford was to set the Ho off on a rant.

"Did you say something, Jemimah Calthorpe de Vyle-Hanswicke?" Mrs. Hoare snapped.

"Nope."

"Glad to hear it." She swept back to the front of the room.

"Psst." Tally slid Alice a note: LET'S GO SHOPPING 4 YLB COSTUMES THIS WEEKEND??

Alice nodded.

Tally beamed. WICKED, she scribbled. YOU + TRISTAN. ME + RANDO. SONIA + SEB. MIMAH + ??

YLB IS GONNA BE *INSANE*!!!

Alice glanced at Tally's stunning profile and frowned. Yeah, YLB was going to be insane. So why was she in such a bad mood all of a sudden? She had Tristan, he adored her, they were going to see each other next weekend, and if everything went according to plan, they were going to have sex.

Still, something was bothering her. And she couldn't work out what.

CHAPTER SIXTEEN

Tristan was fresh from the shower, dressed in a clean blue polo shirt, when he strode into the room he shared with Seb late on Saturday afternoon. He flicked a few droplets from his towel-dried hair, his chestnut eyes gleaming.

"Seb, dude—we just played such an awesome match against St. Jude's. Tom Huntleigh did an incredible tackle on their prop and then Rupert scored a try in the last thirty seconds. We are so going to beat Glendale's this year, the afterparty is gonna be mental."

Seb, sitting on his bed with his head turned to the wall, didn't move.

"Seb? Oi, Seb. Sebastian!" Tristan chucked a towel at him.

"Whatthehell!" Seb jumped. He pulled out his earphones. "Dude, I didn't know you were back. Why'd you come sneaking in like that?"

Tristan snorted. "Don't tell me." He nodded at Seb's laptop screen. "You're engrossed in one of your Italian 'arthouse classics' again."

"Nope." Seb flipped into a sitting position on his blue-and-green-checked duvet. "French. It's called *The 400 Blows*, it's directed by François Truffaut and it's, like, the most important New Wave film. You've got to see it. I'll lend it to you before I return it. I found it in the Modern Languages section of the library."

"Whatever, nerdo." T grinned. He loved giving Seb a hard time, even though he counted on the boy to keep him in the loop about sixties and seventies culture. Seb was the world expert on all that stuff—his favorite artists were Andy Warhol and David Hockney. His favorite bands were Pink Floyd and The Velvet Underground. Sometimes T thought his best mate had been born about four decades too late.

"So how was the rugby?" Seb asked.

Tristan rolled his eyes. "Just carry on with your film, I wouldn't want to deprive you. I'm perfectly capable of amusing myself till it's over."

"No, that's cool." Seb tossed his Bose headphones aside. "I've been waiting for you to get back so we could work on your new song. We've got a shitload of practice to do before . . . you know."

"Good point. We do not want to fuck that up."

T stooped and peered under his bed as he retrieved his guitar from its corner by the window. Yep, it was still there, neatly rolled up—the six-foot banner Alice had painted last year for the Glendale's rugby match, proclaiming GO TRISTAN! GO HASTED HOUSE!!! in honor of his first stint as team captain. T smiled. He couldn't wait for Alice to come and see the team win in a few weeks—this time as his girlfriend, not just his friend.

Settling himself on the edge of his mattress, T struck a minor chord. "It's called 'Verge.'"

Seb nodded, his bass poised, just in case inspiration struck.

"We thought we'd left them all behind
When we sneaked away the other night—
Away from the crowd, away from the light,
Just us two.

We lay in the grass and I kissed your lips
And I thought to myself, this is it—
It's the night when I finally get to
Make love to you.

Oooh,
Will we ever be alone?
Will you ever be my own?
Will we ever hear our two hearts
Beat as one?

But before I could slip you out of your dress,
Before I could lift your hair, or caress,

We heard footsteps nearby and I thought,
This can't be true.

I've waited for weeks, I've waited for years,
To hold you in my arms like this.
Why can't I have just one moment of bliss
With you?

Oooh,
Will we ever be alone?
Will you ever be my own?
Will we ever hear our two hearts
Beat as one?"

By the end of the song, T's eyes were closed. He'd obviously got carried away by his own ridiculously frustrated music. He was probably having detailed sexual daydreams about Alice right this second. Seb cleared his throat.

"Oh. Sorry." T's eyes popped open. "So, er, what'd you think?"

"I like it. It's catchy, melodic, romantic. The only thing is . . ."

"Yeah?"

"Well, I wonder if it's a bit close to the bone?" Seb squinted. T wasn't exactly good at dealing with criticism. "I mean, aren't you basically broadcasting what happened with you and Alice the other night? You've got to be careful with that stuff."

"I guess." T looked pensive. "But what am I supposed to

do? I can't not make my music personal. Good art comes from the heart."

"Totally. But can't you write something from the heart that's not completely autobiographical? Isn't that what song-writers—and novelists and directors and shit—aspire to all the time?" Seb's expression was rapt. "I've been thinking, I reckon great art is, like, a distillation of the artist's experi-ence. You know: you feel something and then you try to communicate the essence of your emotion, using whatever your medium happens to be. Paint. Music. Words. Film."

Tristan blinked. Sometimes Seb went *waaay* over his head. He grinned. "Uh, okay, Professor Ogilvy. If that's your only objec-tion, I think we're good." He leaned forward over his guitar. "Oh, and speaking of getting personal—you and Sonia. What's up?"

Seb glanced toward his computer, where *The 400 Blows* was on pause. "Nothing. Why? Should it be?"

"Only if you want to honor that promise you made a few weeks ago. The one where you swore you'd ask her out? After fall break? Remember?"

Slowly, Seb let out a breath.

"Oh yes, mate." T clapped a hand on his friend's shoulder. "The time has come." He smiled. "Honestly, you don't need to be nervous. Look at me and Al. I managed to get together with her and we'd been best friends for ages. Times change. People change."

"Yeah." Seb stared, without seeing, at the David Hockney lithograph above his bed. It was a blue and green picture of a swimming pool in LA and had been the first big investment he'd made with his trust fund. "I guess."

"Well, I *know*." Tristan reached behind a row of books on his shelf and fished out the little red tin where he kept his weed. "Ask her this weekend, at YLB—you're not going to get a better opportunity." He flattened a Rizla between his fingers. "And if you don't, I'll just have to do it for you."

CHAPTER SEVENTEEN

*T*ally grabbed a fistful of popcorn from the bowl in Alice's lap and snuggled deeper into the common-room sofa. "I had no idea this BBC *Pride & Prejudice* series was so romantic!" she whispered.

"Shhh," Alice hissed, her eyes glued to the flat-screen TV.

It was Wednesday evening and Tudor House's first Bonding Night was in full swing. All round the darkened room, girls were folded into comfy chairs and spread out on duvets and cushions on the floor. Chocolate wrappers and cake crumbs and empty cocoa mugs littered the carpet.

"It's educational," Mrs. Hoare had announced a few hours ago when she'd walked in wielding the ancient-looking *Pride & Prejudice* box set, plopping her bony butt into the cushiest armchair. "Not to mention sexy."

Farah Assadi snorted under her breath as the opening credits rolled on. "Sexy? That old trout wouldn't know sexy if it slapped her in the face."

Mimah stuffed a piece of brownie in her mouth. "OMG, this program's, like, older than my mum. Is the Ho trying to send us back to the Stone Age?"

Several episodes later, the entire junior class was hooked. The story was reaching its climax. Smoldering, lovelorn Mr. Darcy had just dived headfirst into a pond to cool his raging hormones, and it looked like he was about to bump into the beautiful Elizabeth Bennett at his gorgeous country manor. Tally held her breath. What would happen when they met again?

"Bedtime!"

The scene froze. Brandishing the remote control, the Ho propelled herself out of her chair and planted herself in front of the TV. Even though she was short and skinny, she still managed to block the crucial part of the screen. "Chop chop, girls, off to your rooms. I shouldn't have let you stay up this late—it's eleven o'clock."

No! Alice thought silently, at the exact same time as Dylan popped up from the pillow she'd been lying on.

"Please," Dylan cried, "this is the best part. Can't we watch a little more?"

"Ooh, someone's getting ballsy," Sonia hissed in Alice's ear.

Alice smirked and peeped at the Ho, who was tapping her foot on the carpet. "Hmmm. You're Dylan Taylor, aren't you? The American import."

Dylan nodded. "Yeah."

"I think you mean 'yes,'" Mrs. Hoare snapped. "And I don't know what manners they teach you back in the colonies, but in England, girls listen to their housemistresses. And that means no answering back. I expect this room to be tidied and empty of people by the time I come back to check. You have fifteen minutes."

As the Ho swept out, most of her minions scrambled to their feet in a rubbish-gathering, blanket-folding frenzy.

"Ass kissers," Farah Assadi muttered, rolling her eyes. "Dill, I can't believe the bitch spoke to you like that."

"And *I* can't believe she'd do this to us," moaned Cherry Rupert-Greene. "I was enjoying that episode. Doesn't she *want* us to enjoy her stupid Bondage Nights?"

"Maybe she thinks we'll bond more if we all hate her together," Emilia Charles smirked.

"Now we'll never get to see the rest," Alice grumbled.

"Hmmm," Tally winked, "that's not necessarily true." Disentangling herself from the couch, she strolled over to the television and reached behind the screen. "Look who's left the box set here."

"Ooh!" Alice rubbed her hands together. "Let's take it and watch the rest in our room."

"My thoughts exactly. We can connect your big desktop to the speakers and have a viewing party in the entertaining nook."

"Wicked! And we've got loads of booze. Mime, Sone, come on."

"Wait!" squealed Cherry Rupert-Greene. "This is *so* not fair. Can we come too?"

"Oh, go on," Arabella Scott chimed in. "It can be a pajama party."

Sonia flapped her hands. "Keep it down! The Ho has super-sensitive ears. She might hear."

"Pleeease?" Cherry whispered.

Alice glanced at Tally. Come to think of it, they hadn't hosted a party in their dorm all term—which was a travesty since, thanks to their decorating efforts, the room was looking fucking amazing.

She twisted her hair into a long, shiny coil and shrugged. "Fine. Who wants to come? We can only have four extra people or you'll mess up our stuff."

"Me!" Cherry and Bella shot up their hands.

"And me," Farah added, linking her arm through Emilia's.

Dylan lowered her eyes. Of course. Bella, Cherry, Farah, Emilia. There was no room for her. There never was. Even if she *had* kissed Jasper von Holstadt. Unobtrusively, she stood and gathered her duvet and pillows, and padded toward the door.

"What do you mean you can't come?" came Farah's low, grainy voice as Dylan reached the threshold.

"Babe, don't tempt me." It was Emilia speaking now. "I've got a Latin quiz first thing tomorrow and you know I haven't studied. It's such a shag."

"Right, then there's space for one more. Dylan!" Alice's

tone was imperious. "You can come if you like. Even though you're the one who pissed off the Ho in the first place."

As she turned back, Dylan bit her lip to stop her smile. She knew this was the most enthusiastic invitation from Alice Rochester she was going to get.

CHAPTER EIGHTEEN

All seven of the other girls had already claimed their spots when Dylan rocked up to Alice and Tally's dorm ten minutes later, her face washed and her blond hair haloing round her shoulders. Sonia was sprawled across an armchair, painting her toenails silver. Bella, Cherry, and Farah were lounging on squashy pillows and silk cushions, plaiting each other's hair. Mimah was stuffing something under a duvet, and Tally and Alice were flitting about, slipping bottles of booze from their hiding places.

Dylan hugged herself with contentment. It was so secretive and festive in here. Strings of fairy lights glowed down into what she could only assume was the "entertaining nook," a large alcove in one wall decorated with photo collages and a fluffy white sheepskin rug. Scented candles flickered, perfuming the air. Everyone was talking in low, animated tones.

"Mind if I sit here?" She pointed to a cashmere knit cushion next to Bella Scott.

"Nope." Bella shifted over. "Nice slippers."

"Thanks." Dylan wiggled her toes inside the soft white angora poking out from under her pajama bottoms. "My dad gave them to me in my Christmas stocking last year."

"In New York?"

"Yeah."

"Cool." Bella had always thought Dylan Taylor seemed all right, and now that Alice Rochester appeared to be endorsing her, it was probably safe to be friendly. "*My* family's spent Christmas in loads of weird places, but never New York. Last year we were in Copenhagen 'cause Daddy was shooting a film there. It was pretty cool. Well, actually it was bloody freezing, but whatever."

Dylan laughed. Bella seemed almost normal for someone whose father, Sir Lucian Scott, was a world-famous movie director. Bella was regularly whisked round the Oscars and the BAFTAs and to Cannes, and was on first-name terms with everyone from Lindsay Lohan to Johnny Depp.

"Vodka-cranberry?" Alice asked. She was standing above Dylan, wearing skimpy tartan shorts and a floaty white top. Dylan peeked enviously at her taut, tanned stomach, just visible under its hem. Alice was so graceful and carefree. Dylan knew *she* could never pull off that look, not with her balloon-sized boobs. The best she could do was the boring cotton tank she was wearing, and even then she had to strap herself in with an industrial-sized bra.

"Bottoms up," Alice said, pouring two lethal-looking

combos. "And if you're planning to spill anything, spill it on one of Tally's cushions, not mine."

Cherry giggled as Alice stepped over Bella's feet toward her. "Oh, gosh, just a little for me." She twirled her overly highlighted blond hair. "I'm kind of a lightweight."

"Yeah. I've seen you at parties." Alice rolled her eyes. "If you puke on my rug, you're dead."

"Better be careful," Mimah grinned, punching Cherry's shoulder. "Here's an idea—why don't you line your stomach with these?" Reaching under her duvet, she pulled out a gigantic box of chocolates. CHARBONNEL ET WALKER, read the gold lettering on the lid.

"Oh my god!" Alice gaped. "Where did you get those? They're my favorite *ever*."

"From Daddy." Mimah selected a big piece and popped it in her mouth. "He's trying to get back in my good graces."

"Nice." Alice grabbed a marzipan-filled nugget and shut her eyes in ecstasy as she chewed. "Mmmm. Make him send you a few more of these first."

"Cheers, everyone!" Bella raised her glass and gave the sort of thousand-watt smile she'd probably cultivated for the paps at her father's events. "Girlies, booze, chocolates, and a costume drama: I've never had a more perfect Wednesday night."

"Hear, hear." Farah gave a throaty chuckle. "All we need is a game of I've Never and we're set."

"Oooh." Tally twisted round from the computer, where she'd been programming the DVD. "That's an idea!"

Dylan gulped her vodka-cranberry. Tally couldn't be serious.

"Is-is it?" Sonia's voice echoed her thoughts. "I don't know. I'm not sure I want to tell everyone my secrets."

"That's lucky." Mimah smirked. "Because I'm pretty sure no one wants to hear them."

"Shut up."

"Go on, guys." Tally had abandoned the computer and was casting her mischievous gray eyes around the group. "It'll be so juicy. We've got loads of vodka."

"But what about *Pride & Prejudice*?"

"We can watch that anytime."

"But what if the things we say get spread around?" Dylan balled her clammy hands into fists. She'd had more than enough experience with the St. Cecilia's gossip vine.

"Hmm. Good point." Farah scratched her cheek. Dylan examined the other faces around the circle. It was hard to believe, but her own apprehension was reflected on every one of them. Apparently there was no one here without a secret they wanted to keep.

"I've got it!" Alice announced at last, snapping her fingers. "We make rules. A code of conduct."

"Like what?" Tally asked.

"Like this: Number one—whatever is said in this room stays in this room. No exceptions. No excuses."

"Number two:"—Mimah joined in—"Traitors will be found out and punished."

"Punished?" Sonia muttered fearfully. "How?"

"I guess you'll have to wait and find out," Alice breathed. The candles guttered, dimming the alcove even further. There was a silence.

Then Tally nodded. "I'm in."

"I'm in too," Mimah said.

The others nodded their assent. Farah threw back half her cocktail. "I'll go first."

"Wait," Dylan interrupted. Her heart was pounding. Maybe she shouldn't have come. Maybe this was the worst idea ever. "Let me . . . let me just check that you Brits play the same way as we do. I'm always messing things up."

"You can say that again," Sonia grumbled. "Look, the game's idiot-proof, okay? Someone makes a statement like, 'I've never pissed my pants,' and if you *have* done it, you drink. Got it?" She sipped from her glass.

Mimah cackled. "Busted! You just drank. Does that mean you *have* pissed your pants?"

"Bed wetter!"

Everyone cracked up.

"Quiet, contestants," Farah ordered. "We're starting." She cleared her throat, and declared in a loud voice, "I've never snogged more than one person in one night."

"Oh, come on," Tally scoffed, gulping from her glass. "Everyone's done that. Unless they've never been to a ball or something."

"I know. I'm starting easy," Farah chuckled. "Gotta get the group lubricated before the real dirt comes out."

"Someone's played this game a lot," Alice smirked, stretching her long legs in front of her. "Your turn, Tals. Go."

"I've never . . ." Tally tapped the arm of her chair. "Hmmm . . . I've never lied to get a boy to like me."

"Excuse me?" Sonia screeched, as everyone else drank. "No way! Why would I need to lie? I'm comfortable just being myself."

Mimah guffawed, almost spewing out her mouthful. "Yeah, sure. That's why you totally *didn't* get a nose job!"

"And you totally get *all* the boys you fancy," Alice snorted. "Not."

"*Seb Ogilvy,*" Tally coughed.

"Wait," Bella giggled. "Wait, wait. Sonia fancies *Seb Ogilvy?* No way!"

"Oooh, he's dishy," Farah smirked. "So skinny and pale, just like a sexy piece of chalk. Anything happen yet?"

"No," Sonia snapped. Farah was so bloody smug. "But it will. Soon. And remember," she grunted, "nothing we say leaves this room."

"Don't worry," Farah winked. "Your secret's safe with me."

"Me too," Cherry hiccuped. "Can I have another drink?"

"And me." Dylan shook her empty glass.

"Fill 'em up!" Tally cried, sloshing vodka their way. "We can't play this sober."

"Anyway," Sonia sniffed, "my turn." She narrowed her eyes at Dylan. "I've never fancied someone else's boyfriend."

"Hell, yeah!" Cherry drank. "Alice, I totally fancy your boyfriend."

"Me too." Bella raised her glass. "You lucky sod, Ali. Tristan Murray-Middleton is hot."

"Is he a good kisser?" Cherry squealed, then covered her mouth. Half the room toppled over giggling.

"Hang on, hang on," Farah cackled, her eyes glinting with mischief. "Dylan and Alice have *both* kissed Tristan. Why are we only asking one of them?"

"Oh my god, that's right!" Cherry clapped her hands. "Tell us, both of you: Is he good?"

Blanching, Dylan glanced at Alice, whose face was clenched as she glared into her drink. Great. She'd fallen right in the middle of Alice Rochester's least favorite pastime: being reminded that her boyfriend was Dylan's sloppy seconds.

"Come on!" Cherry pounded the carpet. "Tell us; you have to."

"Excuse me," Dylan said archly, "but we don't have to do anything. In case you hadn't noticed, we're playing I've Never, not Twenty Questions. This isn't a free-for-all."

"Exactly."

Dylan jumped. Alice Rochester was looking at her from across the circle. She actually had a grateful expression on her face. "Sorry to disappoint," Alice continued, "but if you want to know whether T's a good kisser, I guess you'll have to snog him yourselves." She grinned. "Oops, you can't. He's going out with me."

"You tease!" Cherry hit her with a chocolate wrapper.

"Fine," Farah said. "In that case—Dylan, why don't you tell us if *Jasper von Holstadt* is a good kisser?"

"What?" Bella cried. "How would she know?"

"Didn't you hear? I thought everyone knew those two snogged the other night."

"No. No way!"

"All right, all right, break it up," Mimah interrupted. "What is this, an exposé on Dylan Taylor's love life? Because who really cares?" She refilled her glass with vodka, totally ignoring the cranberry juice. "My turn. Ready? I've never given a blowjob."

"Whoo!" Tally cheered, drinking. "Now we're getting to it."

Farah, Mimah, Bella, and Dylan giggled as they drank.

"Wait," Alice blurted without thinking, "every single one of you has given a guy a blowjob?"

"Um, yeah." Bella's eyes were wide. "Haven't you?"

"I thought you'd done everything," Cherry added.

"Well, think again." Alice folded her arms. "In my world, giving a guy a blowjob is way more intimate than having sex."

Farah laughed lewdly. "Not in mine."

"Hang on." Cherry was still staring. "You mean you've had *actual* sex but not *oral* sex?"

"Is that an official question?" Alice tried to keep her drink steady.

"Fine." Cherry's eyes met hers. "My turn: *I've never had sex.*"

"Hell, yeah," Mimah whooped. "Wait, I'm drinking five times—to signify each guy!"

"Wait, wait," Farah hiccuped. "You're on five too? Yeah!" She drained her glass and high-fived Mimah across the circle.

Alice hesitated. Cherry was still watching her. She could feel Farah, Bella, and Dylan starting to stare. Her cheeks were on fire. She was sure they were burning like beacons of shame. She gripped her glass.

Then, without meeting any of their eyes, Alice drank.

Tally, Sonia, and Mimah exchanged looks. They knew she was lying. But she couldn't admit to being a virgin. Her street-cred would go up in smoke.

Then Alice realized something else: Dylan hadn't drunk. Her glass was still sitting in her lap. So, Alice thought, her fists unclenching, Dylan and Tristan really hadn't had sex. She and T really would be each other's first. Well, sort of. Alice knew T had shagged a St. Swithin's girl last year while he was totally wasted at some party, but he claimed he couldn't remember a thing.

Suddenly, the room seemed to melt away before her. Who cared if she'd lied in a stupid game? She knew the truth. Her best friends knew the truth. And anyway, this weekend the truth was going to change.

CHAPTER NINETEEN

I can't, I'm late!" Mimah cried over the banister in exasperation. "I've got to go meet the girls." She stuffed a slinky red evening dress into her oversize Mulberry tote, on top of the five others that she'd already culled from her wardrobe.

"Sweetie darling, I insist," her mother's voice carried back. "I only need two minutes; it's important."

"Let me guess," Mimah muttered to herself, "you want me to dash to the liquor store and pick you up a resupply of Jameson. Typical. *Fine*," she called. "But it's already three o'clock. I have to get to the salon."

Rushing back into her bedroom, Mimah swept up a selection of shoes: her toweringly high Christian Louboutins, a pair of purple Jimmy Choos, and the mean-looking Nicholas Kirkwood ankle boots she'd bought on a fall break spree at Dover Street Market—and which Sonia (along with an entourage of sales assistants) had convinced her that she couldn't live without. Having wedged these into her bag, Mimah topped off the pile with a sheaf of sequinned masks and a tangle of necklaces, earrings, and diamante tiaras, plus, of course, her makeup. Then she stomped down the polished ebony stairs.

The Calthorpe de Vyle-Hanswickes' house was dark. It had always been dark, but since Mimah's father had left last spring, it had grown even darker. The heavy curtains had been shut tight for months—which did no favors for the gloomy Victorian wallpaper or for the austere oil paintings that lined the halls. Drafts skittered down the passageways. Behind the thick doors, the gas fireplaces lay cold and empty.

Well, except for one, whose light was pulsing feebly into the ground-floor corridor.

"Mimah?" her mother croaked from the study. "Is that you?"

"Yes." Mimah banged the study door open just to make some sort of noise, cradling her tote in front of her like a shield.

"Please, darling, my head," Mummy drawled aristocratically. She was lounging in her robe by the fire, her slippered feet resting on a footstool. "Got your costume for the Young Leaders Ball? How wonderful. Whose house are you getting dressed at?"

"Tally's." Mimah's eyes traveled to the table beside her mother. There was the requisite bottle of whisky, almost full. Okay, so Mummy didn't need a new one. At least, not yet. "Tally's is near the Kensington Roof Gardens," she added.

"That's where the gala is." *And it's the only house not full of prying parents,* she added to herself. Which meant they'd have plenty of freedom to get pissed before the ball.

"Lovely. Lovely." Mummy wasn't even listening. She was staring straight ahead, reaching for a packet of pills—one of at least four scattered within a two-foot radius. *Diazepam. Xanax. Prozac.* The labels read like a psychiatrist's dream.

"Mums . . ." Mimah chewed her thumbnail. "Why do you . . . Do you really think it's a good idea to take so many of those?"

"Oh, Mimey, don't criticize me. Please." Teary eyed, her mother pushed a tablet between her lips. "I can't bear it. I just can't. You have no idea what it's like."

Mimah ground her jaw. Oh really? She had no idea what it was like? Last she checked, it was her *father* who'd taken off and turned into a total sleaze. If her mother weren't so permanently out of it, only ever thinking of herself, Mimah might tell her a few things. Earlier on, she'd even been considering telling her what Mr. Vicks had said about Cambridge. But she hadn't.

"I need to ask you a favor," Mummy gasped, rubbing her forehead.

Mimah gritted her teeth. *It's about my whisky supply,* she recited to herself.

"It's about Charlie."

"Charlie?"

"I got a phone call from the school. Apparently she's been cutting lessons. Snapping at teachers, neglecting homework, acting up in class. Do you know anything about this?"

Mimah paused, letting her tote sink to the floor. "No," she lied. What good would it do to tell her mother *yes*? It would only stress her out. As if she weren't stressed out enough already.

"Obviously they didn't want to take any disciplinary action— we have such a long legacy with St. Cecilia's. But what am I going to do?" Mummy's voice strained like a rubber band about to break. "I'm going to have to come to the school, of course. I'll come with you tomorrow afternoon. We'll drive down. Yes, that's what we'll do. I'll drive." She stared round vaguely, as if wondering where her car keys had gone. As if wondering where her clothes had gone. She probably hadn't got dressed in days.

"No!" Mimah said suddenly.

"What are you—?"

"Mums, don't worry, please. I'm sure they're overreacting. Look, I'll have a chat with Charlie and sort her out. Next week. Tomorrow," she amended, seeing that her mother was about to protest.

There was no way Mimah could let Mummy turn up at school. Not only was she clearly in no state to negotiate with someone like Mrs. Traphorn, but no one could be allowed to see her like this. None of Mimah's crew knew about this latest family drama—she hadn't told them and she didn't want them to find out. They were bored of hearing about her problems. Sure, you were allowed to be a downer sometimes, like maybe once a year for an hour or so, but there was only so much people would put up with. If you lived in the fast lane, you had to move on fast. She knew from experience that she'd definitely reached her sympathy limit.

"Oh, Mimey," her mother sighed. She unscrewed the top from a new bottle of pills and slumped back in her chair. "Thank goodness. I knew I could rely on you."

CHAPTER TWENTY

*A*lice relaxed into her comfy leather chair at Richard Ward, Chelsea's most exclusive salon, and shook her empty champagne flute in the hand that her manicurist wasn't massaging.

"I'd just adore another glass." She flashed a smile at her hairstylist's assistant. "If you wouldn't mind."

The assistant, who'd been hovering in the background watching the stylist sculpt Alice's mane into glamorous waves, leapt to attention. This was one of the swankiest salons in London and you had to stay on your toes if you wanted to keep your job. It wasn't like there was a shortage of trainee hairdressers who'd kill to work here. After all, what could be more of a privilege than waxing, buffing, and polishing members of the elite Sloaney set?

"Opinions please, darlings!" Sonia trilled from a few seats down. "Ali, Mime, how do I look? Be honest please—I can't go to the gala looking second-rate."

"But, Sone, you always look second-rate," Alice snorted, twisting round.

"Miss Rochester, please keep still." Alice's manicurist steadied her pot of deep red nail polish. "We don't want this to smudge."

"Hmm? Oh, sorry." Alice craned her long, swanlike neck. "Ooh, I like it."

Sonia's hair had been swept into a chic pile on top of her head, adding at least three inches to her height. The do was fixed with crystal pins and arranged so that little curls and wisps floated down over her forehead and eyes.

"Not bad," Mimah agreed. She sipped from her Kir Royale. "It'll look even better when you do your makeup. I'd go for a smoky, seductive style."

"Yes, yes, seductive!" Sonia clapped her hands. "But do you think it's sexy enough? Do you think Seb will like it?"

Alice and Mimah exchanged eye rolls.

"Duh," Alice said. "He's a boy, isn't he? Just pretend to ignore him for a while when we arrive and you'll have him eating out of your hand. That's how guys' minds work."

"Speaking of how guys' minds work . . ." Mimah twirled the stem of her champagne flute. "Do you reckon Jas is gonna get any from Dylan tonight?"

Sonia snorted. "Well, if he doesn't, it won't be because he didn't try. That boy's on such a mission. He's always like this with girls—and then, as soon as they shag, he'll dump her like that." She snapped her fingers.

"I don't know," Alice mused. "I have to say, he looked genuinely into her when T and I saw them snogging the other night. I was wondering if we should have invited her this afternoon."

The other two stared at her.

"To the *salon?*" Sonia gasped.

"Did you actually just say that?" Mimah said. "You hate Dylan Taylor."

"I know," Alice said defensively. "But she is Jasper's date. And our group has to stick together."

Sonia sniffed. "Well, I am not babysitting that loser all year just because she happens to be fooling around with Jas. It's bad enough sharing a room with her."

"That reminds me . . ." Alice raised her right eyebrow with a mysterious air. "Maybe you won't have to share a room with her much longer."

"Huh? Al, don't get my hopes up. What are you on about?"

"Oh, didn't I tell you? Dylan might—"

"Miss Rochester, please." The manicurist jumped back as Alice jerked her arm.

"Yeah. Sorry. Anyway, I can't believe you don't know."

"Don't know what?" Sonia almost screeched.

"That Dylan's leaving St. Cecilia's."

There was a silence. Then:

"No way!" Sonia said.

"Way. Her dad's coming over in a few weeks. He's getting back together with her mum and taking her whole family back to New York."

"Seriously?" Mimah gaped. "You mean Victor Dalgleish is history?"

"He will be, soon."

Mimah's eyes narrowed. "Hang on, how do you know any of this? Don't say Dylan told you. What are you two, BFFs now?"

Alice grimaced. But before she could answer, "Wow!" the stylist's assistant whistled.

"Ow," Alice snarled. One of the rollers had got snagged in her hair.

"Sorry, Miss Rochester. But your friend looks amazing."

Alice snapped her head round. Tally had appeared from the direction of the dressing rooms, wearing a black skintight catsuit with immense platform heels. Her eyes were charcoaled in black. Her hair was cascading sensually over her shoulders.

"Niiice," the manicurist said, dropping Alice's hand. "I didn't know your friend was a model."

"She isn't," Alice snapped.

"Well, she should be."

Tally spun a twirl. "What do you think, girlies? I had to put on the whole outfit—one of the beauty consultants here offered to make me over for free, as long as I let her take some pictures for her portfolio."

"I don't blame her," said the manicurist. "You look stunning."

"*Totally* Heart of Darkness," Sonia added.

"Seriously," Mimah chimed in. "You're definitely going to win the best-dressed prize."

"Oh, don't be ridiculous!" Tally beamed. "Al, what do you think?"

"Nice," Alice said dismissively.

"Really?"

"*Yes*. Do you think I'm lying? I'm sure Rando will fancy the pants off you." Alice pressed her lips together. "That reminds me," she said, glaring at her phone, "I haven't been able to get through to T all afternoon."

"Oooh, babe." Sonia frowned. "Not good. Do you think he's ignoring you?"

"For fuck's sake, don't listen to her," Tally jumped in. "I'm sure it's something to do with that surprise the boys said they'd planned for tonight."

Alice downed the last drops of her champagne. "I bloody well hope so. Whatever this surprise is, it better be good."

CHAPTER TWENTY-ONE

i, no hogging," Seb whispered. He pinched the butt-end of the joint that he and T had been smoking and took one last toke before the spark turned to ash. The remains he shoved into the pocket of his safari trousers. Hopefully, there were no security cameras in the private lift that was whisking the two of them up six floors to the Kensington Roof Gardens. Otherwise, they were fucked.

Tristan tapped his foot nervously. "Mate, tonight seriously better go well. YLB is a huge deal; there'll be at least two hundred people here. If we mess up—"

"Will you please chill about us messing up? The more you stress, the more—"

But before Seb could finish, the doors slid open. Pounding music and colored lights flooded the elevator, surging over him and T, washing them right out into the party. On all sides, London's most gorgeous under-eighteens were mingling, dancing, knocking back champagne, and air-kissing each other. Flossy Norstrup-Fitzwilliam and Freddie Frye were doing the cancan on a low-slung table, making its exotic orchid arrangements shake as at least ten people cheered them on. Over in a corner, blond, floppy-haired Tom Huntleigh was trying to snog Bella Scott. Melissa and Olivia Wyndham-Rhodes, the dumb, beautiful twins famous for their antics at Malbury Hall school, were parading round wearing identical stuffed parrots on their heads. They stuck up at least two feet in the air and kept whacking the palm fronds hanging from the ceiling. And, through the glass doors leading to the vast, leafy roof gardens, T caught sight of a vodka luge and a trio of fire jugglers.

"Boys!" shrieked someone in his ear. An incredibly hot redhead in a mask blasted between him and Seb like a whirlwind. "Welcome to the Young Leaders Ball! The Young Leaders Society is honored to—*hic!*—have you here tonight. Oh my, my, my, who are *you?*" The girl stumbled toward Seb, batting her eyelids.

"Huh?" said Seb.

Leaning in unsteadily, the girl chucked him under the chin and then kissed him, lingeringly, on the lips. "Mmmmm. *Hic!* You taste of lychee martini. I *adore* lychee martini. Night night, now."

"Whoa." Seb wiped his mouth and stared after the redhead as she tottered toward another group of arrivals. "What was that about? Who was she?"

"Who cares? We just got here and you've already scored." T snickered. "Now all you have to do is ask Sonia out."

Seb rolled his eyes. "Oh, great. Did it ever occur to you that I'm just not that into Sonia? Maybe that's why I haven't asked her out of my own accord."

"Yeah, sure, mate," chuckled Tristan, digging him in the ribs. "But you take stuff with girls too seriously; you need to lighten up and enjoy life a little. Give Sone a chance. You never know until you try, do you?"

Seb sighed and looked at the pink, floodlit bar, which was lined end to end with champagne flutes. "This way," he said. "I need a drink. Or ten."

"What can I get you, gorgeous?" asked the outdoor bartender, winking at Tally.

"Hmmm," Tally mused, flashing her flirtiest smile. "My third margarita, of course."

Tally had started on her margarita kick the second she'd noticed how adorable the cocktail mixer was, with his long, wavy hair and cocky self-confidence. Now he grinned at her slyly as he frosted the rim of her glass. "Salty with a hint of sweet—just how I like 'em," he leered. "My drinks, I mean."

"Um, right," Tally said, taking her cocktail. Talk about getting fresh. Maybe it was time to switch to white wine. And maybe it was time for Rando to show up. Where was he?

Aimlessly, she wandered the gardens, set high above Kensington High Street. Hundreds of feet below, London may have been noisy, foggy, and cold, but up here the ball was a subtropical paradise. Strings of lanterns twinkled overhead, illuminating fountains filled to the brim with flower blossoms. Giant leaves screened off private seating areas. And dozens of heat lamps made the air balmy—which explained why a trio of sluts over by the sushi bar had thrown off their pashminas and were swaying barefoot to Pixie Lott.

"Natalya! My darling rose," boomed a voice.

Tally stopped in her tracks. *Great.*

"Archibald!" she cried, forcing herself to smile at the double-chinned man who was poking his nose in her face. Sir Archibald Wellesley-Wesley was the chairman of the Young Leaders committee, as well as a friend of Tally's awful step-mother, and he'd always had a soft spot for her. Just like every other man on the planet.

"The ball looks fantastic this year," Tally said, backing away as subtly as she could. "I'm having such fun. Such great fun."

"Jolly good! And do call me Archie," said Sir Archibald, beaming red as a radish. "Or even Sir Archie, if you like. Heh, heh." He advanced on Tally. Just then something brushed against her legs. Something rustling and snakelike.

"Oh my god!" she shrieked. "What is that?"

"What's what?" Sir Archibald stuttered. "What, what?"

"That!" Tally pointed at the thing hanging from the chairman's waist. It was brown and droopy, and was swishing round his knobbly knees.

"Oh, you mean this?" Sir Archibald jiggled his hips. "That's just my African grass skirt. Frightfully fun, isn't it? Ha! I bartered it off an old Zulu chieftain in Zimbabwe. Not strictly Congo-themed, but whatever, frankly. Damned if I can tell the difference between all those African countries."

Tally coughed, choking on her margarita.

"Sir Archibald?" said an aide, touching the chairman's arm. She was wearing the same uniform mask as all the young socialites who volunteered for the Young Leaders Society in order to have a charitable extracurricular on their UCAS forms. "I've got two gossip columnists from the *Telegraph* clamoring at the door. Can we let them in?"

"The *Telegraph*, eh? Will you excuse me, dear?" Sir Archibald patted Tally's arm. "Got to placate the media, you know. Always after a free booze-up, that lot. Have a smashing time. And don't go breaking any boys' hearts. They're young. They can't handle it like I can." He chuckled and a fleck of spittle flew onto Tally's cheek.

Ew, ew, ew. Tally held her breath until Sir Archibald and his skirt had swished away. Then she wiped her face frantically with her sleeve. "Oh, god, gross. He always bloody does that. I'll probably catch herpes or something now. Help."

"Talking to yourself again?"

Tally wheeled around. "Rando!" she cried, her cheeks flushing pink. She stared into Rando's face, wincing as she saw the faded bruising around his left eye. Poor, heroic thing. He'd really risked his life to save Alice the other night. "I've been looking for you everywhere," she blurted.

"I mean, not *looking* looking but, like, you know, keeping an eye out, seeing if you'd arrived." Tally bit her tongue. Did she want to sound any more stalkerish?

"Oh, thanks," Rando said, checking his watch. "I guess I am kind of late. But it's not my fault." He gestured behind him, to where Dylan and Jasper were standing, gazing into each other's faces. As Tally watched, Jasper whispered something in Dylan's ear and grazed her neck with his lips.

"Whoa. How did you get stuck coming with those two?"

Rando shrugged. "Good old cousin Jas wanted some moral support."

Tally grinned. "I see. He needed you along to keep his nerve up."

"Exactly."

"I bet he pulled all your heart strings . . ."

"Yep."

"Pleaded and begged, said he couldn't do without you . . ."

"Uh-huh."

"And then, as soon as you met up with Dylan, he acted like you weren't even there."

"Aha!" Rando declared. "I can see you've played wing woman before."

"Very perceptive," Tally giggled. "I'm actually the wing-woman queen."

"We should team up, then. We could rent ourselves out: Wing People United." Rando winked, his cheeks dimpling.

Tally's heart fluttered.

"Well, well, well," Jasper leered, strolling up with Dylan. He was wearing a Congolese wooden mask on top of his artfully-tousled hair. "What are you two ladies gossiping about?"

"You," Tally retorted. "Hey, Dylan. You look pretty."

"Hey. Thanks. You too." Dylan tried to keep her voice casual, even though she literally couldn't believe Natalya Abbott was speaking to her. Never mind complimenting her. She wasn't sure Tally had ever addressed a single word to her up till now.

"Whatever. Listen, you guys," Jasper butted in, "guess what I just found out."

Rando shrugged. "You have genital warts?"

"Shut up. That Dylan"—Jasper brushed Dylan's hand—"didn't know I was a DJ."

"Ha!" Rando snorted. "By 'DJ,' do you mean 'pretentious fool who messes with his decks in his bedroom'?"

"Fuck you. Is that the kind of backup I'm supposed to expect from my cousin? I spin at parties. I'm very musical. I should be in a band."

"Oh, naturally," Rando said. "Who cares if you can't play an instrument?"

Jasper flipped him the finger and turned to follow Dylan, who'd gone in pursuit of a tray of canapés. "Oh, Tals, darling, by the way," he threw over his shoulder, "do me a favor and take care of my poor dateless cousin tonight, will you? He's a bit deprived. Give him some loving."

Tally blushed. What was Jasper hinting at? Could he tell

she liked Rando? Could he tell she'd *happily* give him some loving? Shit. Hang on a second, why was she so nervous? Rando was the one who'd liked her in the first place, wasn't he? Tally lifted her margarita to her lips—but before she could take a sip, a wasted rugby-player type rammed her side. Tequila sloshed everywhere.

"Ow!" she cried.

"Are you okay?" Rando jumped toward her. His eyes traced the droplets of liquid on her porcelain shoulder. "You're soaked."

"Am I?" Tally murmured, locking his gaze. Rando's face was so close that she could make out the faint freckles dotting his nose. Their mouths were so near that she could feel his breath on her lips.

Suddenly, he shook himself and stepped backward. "Uh . . . Where's Alice?"

"Alice?"

"Yeah, you know—the others?"

"Oh." Tally cleared her throat. "Over there, by the pagoda."

"Cool." Rando shoved his hands in his pockets. "Guess I'd better go say hi. I don't have long—I've got to be somewhere important soon."

Seb's phone vibrated and he pulled it out of the pocket of his safari trousers.

Do it now u wimp, read T's text. Or else.

"Are you okay, Sebbie?" Sonia asked, tickling Seb's knee

with her fingernail. "You look nervous." She stared at him longingly. Seb was so pale and arty and delicate, she could just stick him in a little crystal charm and wear him round her neck.

"Yeah, yeah, I'm great," Seb said. He waved his phone. "Just, er, irritating spam."

He sighed. As if it weren't enough that he'd made the effort to start talking to Sonia. Now he had to jump in and ask her out before he was ready. His palms had gone clammy. Maybe he should smoke a cigarette. Sonia did look pretty tonight. Anyone else, any more experienced guy, would probably be snogging her by now. He had to ask her out—he'd never hear the end of it if he didn't. Maybe T was right—he didn't have to *marry* Sonia, for god's sake. There was nothing wrong with a bit of fun.

"Oi! Sebastian Ogilvy!"

Seb coughed on his cigarette.

"Just the man I wanted to see," called Marcus Hungerford, an old acquaintance of Seb's who went to Glendale's.

"All right, Marcus." Seb nodded. "Nice bow tie. Very old-school."

"Thanks, mate. So, tell me you're throwing another after-party tonight. That one last year was the debauchery of the century."

Seb shook his head. "Sorry, mate."

"What do you mean, sorry?"

"My house is a no-go. My dad just got back from Dubai

and he's keeping his vintage champagne under lock and key."

"Bugger!" exclaimed Marcus. "I've been looking forward to raiding your wine cellar all week."

"Yeah, me too. Just our luck. Such a shame. Well, see you later." Seb watched Marcus wander off. "*Good riddance.* I wasn't sure he'd buy that story."

Sonia's eyes widened. "Sebbie! You mean you were lying?"

"Of course I was lying. My dad isn't in town; he only bothers to show up in London about four times a year. And he can't lock up his booze—I know where the key is."

"But Sebbie, why did you fib?"

Seb shrugged. "How else was I supposed to get that sponge off my back? If he knew my house was free, he'd badger me till I agreed to throw an afterparty—and he's a fucking nightmare guest. Remember last year when he decided to dance on the glass coffee table? He fell right through it on to his ass."

"Poor thing."

"Poor coffee table, you mean. Marcus's ass didn't break."

"Oh, Sebbie!" Sonia squealed. "You are too naughty. You have such a way with words. But, if you're not having an afterparty, then what are you up to for the rest of the weekend?" She fluttered her eyelashes.

Seb took a deep breath. "Um, actually . . ." He scratched his head. "I thought maybe . . . I was wondering if you'd like to . . . meet up?"

Sonia gasped. She glowed. For a second Seb thought she might howl with glee.

"Really?" she squeaked. "Me?"

"Yeah. I mean, I'm sure you have to check your calendar and everything, so if you can't make it—"

"What time and where?" Sonia interrupted.

Seb snapped his mouth shut. Whoa, the girl really did like him. Okay. He could do this . . . even though he felt sort of sick. He massaged his temples. "Well, I was thinking, I've been reading all about this street artist called Fade. He's getting really big, and this famous dealer is organizing his first major exhibition at the Workhouse Gallery in Hoxton." Seb cleared his throat. "I was wondering if you wanted to go? Sometime tomorrow afternoon? We could have lunch at Shoreditch House."

"Oh. Lunch?" Sonia looked at her perfect nails. Lunch was ambiguous. Lunch meant no cozy bars; no snuggling on comfy couches with their lips just too close to resist; no drunken confessions of lust; maybe no alcohol to lubricate things at all. But still, Sebastian Winston Patrick Ogilvy actually wanted to meet up with her. Alone! Yes, this was definitely a date. A day date. A dayte! Hadn't she read somewhere that daytes were the new black?

"Sounds perfect," Sonia gasped. "I can't wait. I've never been to Shoreditch House."

"Hey, you two!" Over by the pagoda, Alice was standing next to Tristan and waving. "Get over here. *Tatler* wants our picture."

"Ooh, hurry," Sonia cried, grabbing Seb's hand while

145

fishing in her clutch bag for more lipstick. Appearing in *Tatler's* monthly society pages meant you'd be scrutinized by every Londoner who mattered. If only she could convince the photographer to take a close-up just of her and Seb—it could be their debut in society. Everyone would know they were an item.

"Group shot!" ordered the photographer, ushering her and Seb to opposite sides of the tableau. She was standing next to Jasper. Great. Seb was all the way over by Mimah.

Flash!

"And again," the photographer instructed. "Say 'Congo' everyone."

"Congo!"

Flash.

"Beautiful."

Alice smiled up at Tristan. "Shall we get another drink?" she said, sliding her hand into his. "Maybe find somewhere to snuggle up for a bit?"

"Oh." Tristan looked at her. He'd forgotten—she didn't know. "I want to. I'd love to, but I can't. I—"

An aide came running up. "Tristan Murray-Middleton?" he asked.

Tristan's face paled. "Yes?"

"It's time. Ten minutes."

"Time for what?" Alice demanded.

"The Paper Bandits set," the aide whispered. "Shhh, don't tell anyone. It's meant to be a surprise."

"OMG!" Tally jumped up and down. Then, clapping her hand over her mouth, she whispered, "the Paper Bandits are playing now?"

"How could we not have known about this?" Mimah whispered. "Are you serious?"

"They can't be," Jasper scoffed. He looked green with envy. "T, Seb, you guys are tiny, why should you play at YLB? No one's ever heard of you."

"Not for long," beamed the *Tatler* photographer. "Three of London's most eligible teens serenade the Young Leaders Ball? This is the scoop of the evening! Mate," he asked the aide, "where's the best place to shoot this from?"

Alice grabbed Tristan's arm. "T! Did you hear that? The Paper Bandits are going to be famous! Was this your surprise?"

Tristan nodded, his face one big grin. "I'm sorry I didn't tell you before. The Young Leaders Committee said we weren't allowed to. They—"

"Don't even begin to apologize," Alice said, shutting him up with a kiss.

T held her against him and kissed her again. And again. She felt warm and soft and delicious. He didn't want to stop, but he had to. Later, back at her house, in her big four-poster bed, they wouldn't be interrupted. . . .

"Come on," Rando nudged him. "We'd better go set up."

"Oh, hang on, guys," the aide called. "One more thing. Sir Archibald Wellesley-Wesley said to tell you—there's an agent in the audience tonight. Apparently he's looking for new talent. And he's heard about you."

Tristan trembled, his pulse pounding in his ears.

"Shit," Seb whispered, giving voice to T's very thoughts. "This is it, isn't it? The night that makes or breaks us."

hhhhhh," someone hissed. The crowd snickered. "Hellooo?" called a boy with a European accent. "Is anything happening up there?"

The restless audience of gala guests craned their necks at the dark stage, behind which Seb, Rando, and Tristan were crouching, waiting for their call. Rando peeked out.

"Shit, guys," he mouthed, "I don't know if I can do this. There are hundreds of them!"

Seb looked even chalkier than usual. Tristan breathed in through his nose, out through his mouth, in through his nose, out through his mouth. A heart attack was coming on, he knew it. He might keel over and die before he even got on stage.

The babble of voices crescendoed.

"Get on with it!" a girl shouted.

"I wonder who's playing. The Arctic Monkeys?"

"I'll bet it's Kasabian."

"Sugababes!" shouted a boy and a bunch of people cheered.

Seb shot the others a panicked look. "Oh no, oh no. They think we're someone famous. This is gonna be horrific."

"Ladies and gentlemen!" boomed a girl over the loud-speaker.

The voices in the crowd eased off.

"The Young Leaders Society is delighted to present . . . three talented lads from Hasted House: Tristan Murray-Middleton. Sebastian Ogilvy. And Tom Randall-Stubbs. Please welcome the Paper Bandits!"

The crowd applauded. Struggling for a view as the band ran on stage, Alice, Tally, Sonia, and Mimah screamed so hard it hurt their throats.

"Rando! Rando!" Tally yelled. "Oooh, he's so adorable. Look at his poor eye. I think he might like me."

"I can't believe they're playing," Mimah cried, wringing Alice's hands. "By the time you marry T, he's gonna be a pop star."

"Hasted House boys in a band!" giggled Olivia Wyndham-Rhodes. She was standing next to Tally, cradling her parrot head. "I'm dying to hear what they sound like."

"I've heard they're good, Livs," said her twin, Melissa. "Apparently they played a secret venue in Hackney last month. That new place—Formica, or something."

"I heard that too," chimed in Bathsheba Fortnum. "But it was, like, a top-secret gig. I wish I'd been there—Tristan Murray-Middleton is one of the hottest guys at Hasted!"

"Sheebs fancies Tristan, Sheebs fancies Tristan!"

"*Everyone* fancies Tristan."

Up on stage, T slung his guitar strap round his neck and blinked at the audience. The bright lights bruised his vision but, right at the front, he spotted Alice, her face radiant with pride. Suddenly, he had an idea. He tapped his microphone.

"I'd like to thank the Young Leaders Society for having us here tonight," he announced. "We're honored to support your fantastic work. And now," he added, his expression flashing with gallantry, "I'd like to dedicate this first song to my beautiful girlfriend, Alice."

A high-pitched squealing rose from the audience.

"Awww!"

"That's so romantic! I'm jealous."

"Alice? Does he mean Alice Rochester? Lucky ho."

"OMG!" Tally tugged Alice's arm. "Babe, I've never heard of anything so adorable. What's the song?"

Warmth flooded through Alice's core as if an ember had been lit in her heart. "I don't know," she said, her eyes shining.

The melody began. Everyone hushed to listen.

> "*I traveled far to find you*
> *But you were waiting, near me.*
> *I was blind, I don't know why*
> *It took me years to see . . .*"

"Oh, Al," Tally murmured. "That's beautiful. He's like your knight, questing for you all over the world."

"Yeah," Alice said. But her forehead was creased.

Tristan sang on. By the time he reached the last verse, several audience members were standing with their eyes closed, faint smiles on their lips.

"Yes, my love, I've found you,
Of course I found it hard—
The last place I thought of looking
Was in my own backyard . . .
The last place I thought of looking
Was in my own backyard."

"Wow," Tally sighed as the notes died away. There was no reply, so she looked at Alice. "What?"

Alice shrugged. "I don't know; it's just . . ."

"What?"

"The words. I mean, 'waiting'?"

Tally stared at her.

"He makes it sound like I was just there twiddling my thumbs until he decided he wanted me."

"Uhhh . . ."

"And how about 'backyard'? What am I? The boring bloody girl next door? I don't want to be Jennifer Aniston! I want to be Angelina Jolie."

Tally cracked up. "So get your lips Botoxed. Babe, pull it together," she prodded, seeing Alice fold her arms. "You are *so* overanalyzing. Boys' minds aren't that subtle. I'm sure T was just being poetic."

"Maybe."

"Not maybe—definitely. It's not like he's Shakespeare—he's probably just trying to make things rhyme."

"Yeah . . . I guess . . ." Alice felt her hair, checking that its bouncy waves were still intact. She looked a bit happier.

Up on stage, Tristan grinned at Seb as the Paper Bandits' third song came to a close and the whole party cheered. "Going well, isn't it?" he shouted above the noise. "They seem into us."

"Totally, mate—they're eating it up."

Rando played an elaborate drumroll and the cheering grew still louder.

"Hey, let's play the new one," T called.

"Wicked," Rando yelled back.

T leaned into the mic. "This one's called 'Verge,'" he said. "I'm sure it'll be a familiar feeling to all you boarding-school kids out there."

"Don't talk about school!" someone shouted.

Laughing, T held up his hand. "Sorry, mate. One, two—

> *"We thought we'd left them all behind*
> *When we sneaked away the other night*
> *Away from the crowd, away from the light,*
> *Just us two."*

Alice and Tally swayed together to the beat. "At least this one can't be about you," Tally said. "You and T don't go to the same school."

Alice put her finger to her lips. "Shhh. I want to hear."

> *"We lay in the grass and I kissed your lips*
> *And I thought to myself, this is it—*
> *It's the night when I finally get to*
> *Make love to you.*
>
> *"Oooh,*
> *Will we ever be alone?*
> *Will you ever be my own?*
> *Will we ever hear our two hearts*
> *Beat as one?*
> *But before I could slip you out of your dress,*
> *Before I could lift your hair, or caress—"*

"Alice!" Tally hissed. "Where are you going?"

But Alice didn't answer. She'd cut her way to the edge of the crowd, and stormed indoors. The bar area now held only a smattering of people. The rest of the two hundred guests had poured outside to the gig.

Pushing into the girls' bathrooms, Alice clenched her fists and paced back and forth in front of the sinks. It was quiet in here. Deserted. Until, a few seconds later, the door swung open again. Tally, Mimah, and Sonia burst in.

"Al, babe," Tally cried, "are you okay?"

"Oh. My. God." Alice stared, wide eyed, at her best friends. "I have never been so embarrassed in my life. Did you hear that song? It was exactly what happened to me and T the other night at Guy Fawkes. I thought that was a private moment! And now everyone knows I'm a"—she lowered her voice to a strained whisper, checking the bottoms of the stalls for feet—"virgin."

Mimah and Tally exchanged looks.

"Hon," Tally began, "no one knew he meant you. He didn't name names."

"He dedicated his first song to me, for fuck's sake! Everyone knows I'm his girlfriend."

"Okay, Al, calm down," Mimah said. "I can see why you're upset, but the song doesn't actually say you're a virgin. It just says you got, you know, interrupted. Like, maybe you'd done it before, but this time it didn't work out."

"And he called it 'making love'!" Sonia gushed, clasping her hands together. "Oh, Al, that's so swoonworthy! You're T's muse."

"Great. What if I don't like being his muse? I mean, what if I was Picasso's muse and he made me look as chubby and weird as those women in his paintings? If being a muse is like looking into a fun-house fat mirror, then I don't want it, thank you very much."

"Ali!" Sonia gasped. "You're not fat."

"Okay, that's it," Mimah jumped in. "Sonia, shut up. Al,

you're taking this way too far. Tally's the drama queen in this group, not you."

Despite herself, Alice felt her lips twitch.

"Look," Mimah went on, "we four are the only people in the world who know you haven't had sex yet. Tristan doesn't even know, does he?"

"No," Alice murmured.

"Not that it even matters whether you're a virgin or not," Mimah continued, "but I can see why you don't want anyone to know. The point is, people who don't know—which is everyone—would never work it out from that stupid song. And if anyone asks you—which they won't—you can totally lie. And, much as I hate to say it, Sonia's right: Tristan obviously likes you so much, he's writing odes about how much he can't wait to 'make love' to you."

By the time Mimah had finished her tirade, Alice was leaning back against the sinks, practically smiling. She smoothed a crease from her ball dress and nodded. "Thanks, Mime. I reckon you're right. Anyway," she added coyly, "I bet T's next love song will be about something totally different. He's spending the night at my house tonight."

"Oooh!" Sonia squealed. "Dishy! Why didn't you tell us before?"

Alice rolled her eyes. "Do I have to tell you everything? Come on, let's go back to the gig."

The bathroom emptied out and the girls' chatter faded. Everything was still, except for the low beat of music from the bar and the faint rush of water through the pipes.

Then, slowly, the door of the very last cubicle creaked open. A blond head peeked out. Two anxious blue eyes scanned the bathroom and, seeing no one, blinked in relief.

Dylan Taylor slipped out of the stall. Thank god she could finally stretch her legs—she'd been huddled on the toilet, hugging her knees to her chest, throughout the whole of the clique's gossip session. She'd been shaking, too, trying to breathe as little as possible. Because if they'd discovered her, that would have been the end.

Dylan drifted toward the sink, her strapless black dress flowing out behind her, and studied her own face in the mirror. Funny how calm she looked, when her thoughts were hurtling in her head like leaves in a gale.

Alice Rochester was a virgin, just like her. And Alice was so mortified about it that she was prepared to lie to pretty much anyone to save face. Well, now Dylan knew her secret. And knowledge was power—if she chose to use it that way.

CHAPTER TWENTY-THREE

*A*ce performance, you guys!" Jasper called, rocking up to where Tristan, Seb, and Rando were packing away their instruments behind the stage. The cheering had finally died down after the Paper Bandits gig and most of the guests were refueling on booze.

"Didn't think you had it in you," Jasper went on. He lit up a cigarette and blew a stream of smoke into the center of the group, where it hung like a challenge.

Tristan coughed ostentatiously and batted away the fumes. What the hell was Jasper's problem? It was like he wanted the Paper Bandits to fail. Like, if he couldn't be a part of the band, then he didn't want it to exist at all.

"Thanks, Jas," Rando said, oblivious as usual to his cousin's attitude problem. "Glad you enjoyed it. We were shitting a brick when we first went on."

"Yeah, that was pretty obvious," Jasper remarked, sucking

in his cheeks. "I thought I'd make a suggestion, actually. Just to help you guys on your style."

"Oh, wonderful," T muttered. "Why did I know this was coming?"

"Next time," Jasper went on, "I'd consider adding a bit of keyboard to your set. Mix up the sounds a little, you know? Seb plays keyboard, don't you—"

"Young men!" called Sir Archibald Wellesley-Wesley, bumping Jasper out of the way as he bustled around the side of the stage. Sir Archibald's red cheeks were wobbling and so was the grass skirt dangling from his potbelly. "Splendid performance, simply splendid. And this fine gentleman," he blustered, indicating the man at his side, "quite agrees."

"All right, boys," the man said. His accent was cockney and his face was savvy. "Let me introduce myself—Dick Crawley of Sound & Fury Musical Agents. Pleasure. Enjoyed the show."

"Thanks very much," Tristan said. Dick's handshake was firm and a bit intimidating. "Tristan Murray-Middleton. It was terribly nice of you to come."

"Nice nothing," said Dick, shaking hands with Seb and Rando. "I was here for myself, not for you—I'm always on the lookout for new talent. But I know this is a party and you'd much rather be chasing tail than talking business, so I'll be brief."

Tristan chuckled. "Oh, don't worry about that," he said, elbowing Seb. "I think a lot of babe-getting has already been accomplished."

"Fast movers, are we?" Dick remarked. "Good. That might work in your favor." He leaned forward authoritatively. "Look, boys, I'll tell it to you straight: I liked what I saw tonight. I think you lads could do well as a sort of teen heart-throb band. You've got catchy songs, a ready-made boarding school following, and looks that'll send the A-level girls round the bend. Girls will be the bulk of your fan base, naturally."

"Oh, er, naturally," T echoed. Talk about a surgical deconstruction of his art. "Uh, thanks."

"You're welcome," Dick said. "But here's the thing. If I took you on as an agent, I'd want to strengthen your look."

Rando blinked. "Our look?"

"You got it. Here's what I'm saying." Dick jerked his thumb at T. "You've got the charming, hot, charismatic bandleader. . . ." He pointed to Rando, "The boyishly cute drummer, and," he turned to Seb, "the arty, alternative bassist. But where's your mysterious, brooding type? Where's the band's darker, wilder side—for girls who like a bit of danger?"

Tristan cleared his throat. "Er, I see what you mean, and I don't mean to blow my own trumpet or anything, but . . . my songs *can* be rather dark and dangerous. I've been told they channel a, er"—he coughed modestly—"a sort of Jeff Buckley vibe."

"Who told you that? Your mum?" Dick guffawed.

Jasper snorted with laughter from the fringes of the circle.

The agent jumped. He turned to where Jasper was standing, smoking, and his face sharpened. "Who's this, then?"

"Hello," Jasper said, stepping forward. "I'm Jasper von Holstadt."

"Charmed, I'm sure. Are you involved in the band?"

"Well . . ." Jasper crushed his cigarette under his shoe. "Not strictly, but I do sort of advise them about—"

"No," Tristan interrupted. "He's not."

"He's a friend," Seb explained.

Dick was eyeing Jasper keenly. "A friend, eh? Well, he's got exactly the look I was talking about." He scanned Jasper's tanned skin, dark hair, dark eyes, and arrogant, handsome face—as if Jasper were a horse he might bet on. "Yes . . . He's the perfect foil to Tristan's clean good looks. Tell me, Jasper, what instrument do you play?"

"Instrument?" Seb blurted. "None."

"Yeah, good luck with him," T chortled. "He's about as musical as a stone."

"Oi," Jas retorted. "Shut up, okay? I've had it with you guys joking about my musical talents. As if you're all Beethoven or something. I could play an instrument if I wanted. I'm a DJ," he informed Dick. "I'm sure I could learn the drums or something pretty quick. I mean, how hard can it be to bang a bit of plastic with a stick?"

"Excuse me!" Rando protested.

"Yeah, not sure about that," Dick said. "The Paper Bandits already have a drummer. Hmmm, but that doesn't mean percussion's out. You could play the triangle. No—the cowbell! Perfect. It'd get you up on stage where the girls can see you."

Tristan's mouth was as thin as a piece of string. "No offense or anything," he grunted, trying his best to sound polite. "But exactly how is Jasper meant to look brooding, never mind mysterious, while he's shaking the bloody cowbell?"

Dick waved his hand. "Oh, don't trouble about trifles; there are ways. I know every trick in the trade, boys."

"I bet you do," Seb said under his breath.

"Guys, this is wicked," Jasper grinned. "Oh, go on, you guys, how fun would it be if I was part of the band too? We could all rehearse together. We could sneak weed and whisky into the music rooms. And, like Dick says, I might help your image." He stared, with wide eyes, from Seb to Rando to Tristan.

"If I might throw in my two cents as well, boys," Dick said. "I suggest you give it a try for a few weeks—with me as your agent and Jasper here as your fourth—and we'll see how things go."

Tristan studied his feet in silence. "Thanks very much again for your interest," he said finally. "Can we think it over and let you know?"

Dick half shrugged, half nodded. "But I'll need an answer by tomorrow. This is a one-time-only offer."

CHAPTER TWENTY-FOUR

Dylan lurched out of the lobby of the Kensington Roof Gardens onto Kensington High Street, singing a medley of Paper Bandits songs at the top of her lungs. It was four in the morning. One of her sandals was dragging off her foot and a damp wind whipped up, tangling her hair over her eyes.

"Come on, Jassie, dance with me!" Dylan hiccuped. She propelled herself toward Jasper, stumbled, and knocked them both backward into the side of the building, where Tom Huntleigh and Bella Scott were sucking each other's faces off.

"Afterparty!" shouted George Demetrios, charging out of the lobby with Bathsheba Fortnum, Tally, Rando, and Sonia in tow.

"Afterparty? Where?" Tally slurred.

"At Jamie Darlington's. His parents are in Switzerland. You wait here, I'll text you the address." George jumped into a waiting black cab with Bathsheba, who was clearly his project for the night, and winked luridly at his friends. "Later, babies."

"Wait!" Dylan called, trying to run after the taxi. "I wan go affapary too."

Jasper caught her hand. "No way are you going to the afterparty," he laughed. "You can hardly walk. Look, here's another cab. I'm taking you home."

"No fun," Dylan complained, lolling her head back and forth as Jasper helped her onto the seat. Then, stumbling round, she waved both hands at Tally, Sonia, and Rando out the window. "Bye-bye, guys!"

"Ugh." Sonia rolled her eyes.

"Wow," Tally said, turning to Rando. "Jasper likes Dylan for real, doesn't he? I've never heard of him making sure a date gets home. Especially a drunk date. He's usually trying to take advantage and get some."

Sonia snorted. "Oh, come on, Tals, don't be so naive. Of course he doesn't like Dylan. He's totally gonna jump her in the cab and then he'll ignore her for the rest of her life."

"Optimistic, aren't you?" Rando said. "Actually, I reckon Tally's right—Jasper seems well into Dylan. You should have seen him getting ready to meet her tonight; it was like being backstage at a bloody fashion show. I reckon he genuinely wants to go out with her."

"Yeah, right," Sonia sniffed. "You mean he genuinely wants to go out with her tits. Anyway, he can't go out with her, 'cause she's leaving. He clearly knows that and is taking advantage of a quick shag. Shit!" She gaped at her watch. "I didn't realize how late it was! How am I supposed to look hot for my date with Sebbie tomorrow if I don't get my beauty sleep? What if I get a wrinkle and he doesn't fancy me? Help, Tally! Why didn't I think of that earlier? Oh my god, oh my *god*!"

Ignoring her, Tally plucked Rando's sleeve. "Coming?" she asked coyly as a taxi pulled up. "You and I can drop Sonia off and then head to Jamie's afterparty."

"Oh . . . I don't—"

"Go on!" Tally wheedled. "It'll be so fun."

"But . . ." Rando shifted his feet. "How about Alice? Shouldn't we wait for her?"

"Oh my god, good point," Sonia exclaimed, thrusting her head out the window. "Where is Al, anyway? I haven't seen her since the tequila shots. Or was it the vodka shots? Or was it the—"

"Shut up!" Tally hissed, dragging Rando onto the seat. "She's over there. Don't bother them. Let's go."

The taxi door slammed, and down the street Tristan lifted his head, parting his lips from Alice's but keeping his hands in her long, soft hair.

"Has everyone gone?" she whispered.

As if in answer, a breeze rustled the leaves of the tree above them and T smiled as their dim shadows swayed over Alice's face. "Yes," he said, touching her cheek. It was soft—as soft as he imagined her skin would be under her dress, under her bra, when he felt the whole length of her body against him in bed. . . .

Alice slid her hand from his back pocket and drew her coat around her shoulders. "Let's go home."

"Yeah."

T's limbs felt warm and loose as he and Alice strolled, fingers entwined, along Kensington's dark, empty streets. *Whoa.* Suddenly, the pavement tilted. T blinked. His bloodstream was buzzing with all the celebratory drinks he'd knocked back after the Paper Bandits gig. *Subtle,* he ordered himself, *be subtle.* Alice wouldn't exactly be pleased if she knew he was wasted.

They passed a closed-up pub shrouded in beer-smelling air, then a row of expensive boutiques. A dark gray cloud bank drifted across the moon, blotting out its silvery light.

"I love this time of morning," Alice said softly. "I love that behind all those dark windows, people are sleeping, their heads buried in their pillows. None of them knows we're out here. None of them has the slightest idea how their street looks and sounds right now."

T squeezed her hand. "It's like London's ours. Everyone's wasting the night except for us."

Alice barely felt the pinching of her leopard-print stilettos as they turned into the Rochesters' road. Nor did she feel the cold—not even when, as they reached her gate, an icy predawn rain began to scatter down.

The Rochesters' house was tall, wide, white, blocked from the street by a high, ivy-covered wall. At the front rose a lofty bay window, through which loomed shelves lined with books, flower arrangements in urns, imposing paintings, a grand piano.

Alice hurried up the front steps, the rain soaking her through.

"Shhhhhh!" she whispered, fiddling with her key, locking the front door behind her. She slipped off her soaking shoes, finally shivering a little. Now that she was here with T, like this, the foyer looked unfamiliar—bigger, more shadowy— even though it was the same as it had always been. She let her feet relax for a second on the antique oriental rug, then led T toward the stairs.

Crash!

"Shit," he gasped as he banged into a side table. The mirror above it jittered like crazy. He flattened himself against the opposite wall. Alice cowered with her hands over her head. Then she caught Tristan's eye and giggled.

Shaking with silent laughter, they collapsed onto the staircase's bottom step. T slicked back Alice's wet hair. He held her face in his hands.

"It's ruined," Alice murmured. "The style. I just had it done."

"I like it like this," T whispered, kissing her. "Natural."

Drops of moisture glistened on his face. Alice brushed them with her lips. He kissed her more deeply, more passionately, pressing against her until the edge of the next step seared a line into her back.

"We should go upstairs," she whispered.

Hand in hand, they crept up the two landings to her room. She shut the door and turned to T, her heart pattering against her chest as fast as the rain against the windows. He reached behind her, unzipping her dress, peeling the wet fabric from her skin. His eyes devoured her honey-colored shoulders, her lacy black bra, her taut stomach. He knelt and kissed her belly button, and Alice gripped the back of his head as he lifted her onto the bed. She was breathing hard. It was weird being here, on the mattress where they'd fallen asleep side by side so many times. But nice weird. Exciting weird. She tugged Tristan's shirt over his head. He kicked free of his trousers and boxer shorts and pulled her to him, their mouths and tongues together, their legs intertwined.

We're naked. Alice's heart raced. *We're naked. We could do anything.* Her body yearned for Tristan's. Nothing could tear them apart.

"Should I get a condom?" she asked. It felt like she was talking to the darkness.

"Uh, yeah . . ." T's voice was shaky. "Wait, I don't know . . . I'm not sure I can . . ."

"What?"

Tristan closed his eyes. "I'm not sure I can do it tonight."

Something caved in Alice's chest. All of a sudden, she thought she might cry. "Oh. You—you don't fancy me enough?"

"What?" Tristan lifted her head. "Are you mental? I fancy you like crazy. I'm a bit drunk, that's all, and it's not . . ." He moved Alice's hand—down—and Alice caught her breath. "It's just a mechanical thing; it sometimes happens when I drink too much. God, this is so embarrassing," he murmured, burying his face in Alice's neck. "I really, really want to. But . . . it's not gonna work."

"Don't worry," Alice whispered. She closed her eyes. Maybe she should tell him. She wanted to. She bit her lip.

"Oh no. You're disappointed," T groaned. "Oh god, I'm such an idiot."

"No, no." Alice ran her hand over his shoulder. "You're not, it's not that. Actually . . . I'm kind of relieved." She took a deep breath. Was it completely insane to be admitting this? "I don't want to have sex while we're drunk, either," she whispered. "I'm . . . I'm a virgin."

T's eyes shot open. "What? You—you are?"

Shit. He thought she was a loser. Alice nodded, her cheek nestled in the pillow. She willed herself to look at T, even though all she wanted to do was bury her head under the covers.

"Hang on." T looked confused. "I thought you did it with Boy Stanley-Soames. In Rome."

"Uh-uh." Alice shook her head. "You're my first. I mean, you will be. But please," she cried, feeling a jolt of panic, "don't tell anyone. Everyone will think I'm a freak if they know. Promise!"

Tristan ran his hand over Alice's cheek, his mouth curving into a smile. "I promise," he whispered. "And I'm glad. We can make it special. Tomorrow we won't be drunk. And we have all day."

He kissed her, slowly, and Alice kissed him back. After a while, he pulled her to his chest and they drifted to sleep, naked in each other's arms.

CHAPTER TWENTY-FIVE

By Sunday afternoon, the alleyways off Brick Lane had turned into black rivers of rainwater, made deeper every second by the downpour. Sonia leapt on her toes over the crooked pavements. The East London sludge had better not contaminate her pink kitten heels. Maybe wearing them had been a bad idea. Maybe carrying her matching pink umbrella had been a bad idea too. Sonia had only wanted to look pretty for Seb, but now she realized she was channeling totally the wrong vibe. She stuck out like a sore thumb among the Shoreditch crowd in their uniform of jeggings, hoodies, and vintage leather boots.

Seb, on the other hand, fitted right in. There he was, huddled outside the Workhouse Gallery, smoking a cigarette, wearing skinny jeans, pointy shoes, a blazer, and a gray fedora pulled over his eyes. He was the epitome of coolness.

Except, Sonia noticed suddenly, the hand holding his

cigarette was trembling. She stared. Seb was nervous! He was actually nervous about a date with her. She'd never seen anything quite so adorable.

"Sebbie!" she waved. "Yoo-hoo!"

"Oh, hey." Seb chucked his cigarette butt into the gutter, where it hissed and sank into the dirty stream. His cheek looked like it was twitching with nerves. Sonia had to restrain herself from jumping forward and planting a kiss on it.

"So," Seb said, "I've been reading a lot about Fade."

Sonia flicked her hair. She'd put it up in a special quiffy ponytail that she'd copied out of *Now*. "Who?"

"Fade." Seb stared at her, holding open the door. "The artist we're here to check out?"

"Oh." Sonia rolled her eyes. "Yeah. Stupid name."

"Not really. I mean, it's just a pseudonym."

"Why would an artist need a pseudonym?" Sonia snorted. "Are his paintings that crap? Like, he doesn't want his friends to know it's him?" She shrieked with laughter.

Seb winced. The gallery's main room was built entirely of concrete and Sonia's voice echoed everywhere. Some of the other viewers shot them glares before turning pointedly back to the murals, which were spray painted and chalked directly onto the walls. Stamped into the floor, just inside the door, were stern block letters spelling WORKHOUSE. The gallery was completely silent except for the shuffling of shoes and the *drip, drip, drip* of rain.

"Fade grew up in Birmingham," Seb muttered, so softly

that it was like they were at school, whispering in lessons. "He spent his childhood graffitiing his name on all the ugly buildings—you know, as a way of reclaiming the city for himself. Then he decided that painting murals made more of a statement in the modern world."

"Oh. Cool." Sonia had no idea what Seb was going on about. She stared at a row of photographs showing murals that Fade had spray painted onto buildings. Most of the murals were of people with political and philosophical slogans scrawled over their heads. "How come he doesn't get arrested?" she demanded.

"That's the genius of it!" Seb tugged excitedly at his fedora. "No one knows what he looks like. Whenever he's photographed, he covers his face."

"Oh," Sonia said knowingly. "Like a terrorist."

"Huh? No, not like a terrorist. He's not violent. He doesn't consider himself a criminal."

"But he is a criminal!" Sonia protested loudly. "He defaces other people's property. That's a crime!"

Seb darted his eyes around. "Uh, well, that depends—maybe he just has a different way of defining 'property.' Maybe he wants to challenge people."

"I'll challenge him!" Sonia cried. "If he came and spray painted on *my* building, I'd set the police after him. I'd have him thrown in jail for the night—then he'd see what private property meant. Ha!"

Now other people were really starting to stare. A girl

with dreadlocks, wearing a cropped, faux-fur jacket, rolled her eyes.

"Uh, let's go and look at the next room," Seb whispered.

"Okay," Sonia whispered back. She inched closer to Seb and linked her arm through his. It was so intimate, talking in murmurs. Having their own private intellectual debate. She crossed the floor at his side, enjoying the loud clip-clop of her kitten heels. Hopefully, Seb liked her new perfume—she was debuting it today.

"Oh, wow," Seb said, pausing in front of a big, complicated mural. "I haven't seen this one before. It isn't in my book."

"Hmm, really?" Sonia edged so close to Seb that she could smell the fabric softener on his clothes.

Seb broke into a sweat. "Oh, look, it, uh, it says here that this is a new piece. It was created especially for the Workhouse."

"What?" Sonia scoffed. "That is the stupidest thing I've ever heard."

"Shhh," Seb pleaded. Sonia was practically shouting. They'd probably get kicked out in a second for being rude about the art. "What do you mean? Why is it stupid?"

"Sebbie, it's so obvious," Sonia said. "The whole point of this Fade character's art is that he's some kind of urban warrior—reclaiming public space, blah blah blah. And now, at the first available opportunity, he sells out—starts selling things in galleries so that pretentious trendies like these people"—Sonia waved her hand at the browsers—"can congratulate

themselves on their cutting-edge taste! Ha!" She smiled trium-
phantly, her voice echoing off the walls.

Seb looked at the floor, his cheeks burning red under his
blond haystack hair. "Yeah . . . ," he mumbled. "Maybe we
should go to lunch. Are you hungry? I booked us a table at
Shoreditch House."

"Oooh, yes!" Sonia cried, seizing Seb's arm as they walked
toward the door. "And afterward, we can catch the train
together back to Hasted. Won't it be fun?"

Seb's eyes widened. "Oh, but, I can't get the train back
straight from lunch. I have to go home first, pick up my stuff,
organize some—"

"Don't worry, silly," Sonia trilled. "I'll come with you; I don't
mind." She snapped open her pink umbrella and pressed
herself against Seb so that it covered him, too. "I'm sure we
can amuse ourselves at your place. I can think of plenty of
fun things to do."

CHAPTER TWENTY-SIX

*M*orning, sleepyhead," Alice smiled, as Tristan stirred on the next pillow.

It was kind of pathetic, but she'd been gazing at him while he slept—at his eyelashes fluttering against his cheekbones, at his soft, kissable lips, at the stubble around his jaw. *He's mine*, she'd said to herself, and the thought had sent quivers through her body.

It felt strange, waking up with T for the first time. Of course, he and Alice had woken up *next* to each other countless times when they were just friends and had fallen asleep on one or other of their beds—but it was strange waking up with him like *this*. For a start, Alice had no idea what to do. Usually, in the past, she'd have ruffled T's hair, or squashed him with her pillow, or whipped the duvet off him just to wind him up, but doing those things now might feel like she was trying to go back to the way things were. And she wasn't. Definitely not.

"Morning, gorgeous," Tristan said, reaching for her, drawing her into a kiss.

Okay, clearly she was the only one feeling at a loss.

"How are you feeling?" he asked, sliding his hand under the covers, over her shoulders. "Hey, what's this?"

"Oh." Alice smiled sheepishly, plucking at the strap of her lacy top. Earlier on, while T had been sleeping, she'd sneaked over to her chest of drawers and slipped on some pajamas. It had been one thing being naked in the dark, drunk and in the heat of the moment. It had been quite another waking up starkers in the gray morning light. "I guess . . . I was cold."

Tristan grinned. "We can't have that, can we? Let me warm you up."

He eased Alice's top up over her belly button. She sucked in her tummy. With the light filtering through her curtains, T would be able to see how small her boobs were. He'd be able to see every freckle and lump and hair on her body. But he didn't seem to mind—he didn't seem self-conscious about being naked at all. *Relax*, Alice told herself.

It was weird: For some reason she felt detached—like she was watching herself act out a sex scene in a movie. Maybe once you got round to having sex yourself, you'd read and watched films about it so many times that it was hard to tell what you were doing naturally and what you were mimicking.

Alice shook her head. *Stop thinking so much.* The rain was drumming on the windows, enclosing her and T in their own private lair. It was like they were the only people in the world: She couldn't see out through the glass and no one could see in.

T's mouth was exploring her breasts. Alice closed her eyes and trailed her hand down his chest, past his belly button. "Can . . . can I touch you here?" she whispered.

"That feels good," T gasped, his eyes closing. He cupped the curve of Alice's hip. He ran his fingers between her legs.

"Don't stop," she breathed, pressing into him.

"Alice . . . I want to make love to you. Please."

Alice bit her lip. *Yes.* She was ready. She'd been ready for weeks. Her heart racing, she propped herself on her elbow, reached into her bedside table and passed T one of the condoms that she'd been stowing there for ages, for exactly this moment.

Suddenly, his face went serious as he rolled it on. His entire body looked tense, all his muscles taut.

Alice trembled. "I-I'm a bit nervous."

"Me too," T whispered, kissing her.

"But—why? I thought you'd done this before."

"Not with someone I care about," he murmured, gazing into her eyes. "Not with someone I love. I love you, Alice." His breath was hot on her skin.

I love you, too. Alice opened her mouth to say it. But then—

Ring ring! Ring ring!

"Fuck!" Tristan jumped a foot in the air. "What the hell is that?"

Alice giggled. "Chill. It's your phone."

"Oh. Yeah." T chuckled, tangling his fingers in her hair. "Let it ring. They can leave a message. Sorry," he whispered, as the noise cut off, "did that totally kill the moment?"

"A little. But I'm sure you can get me in the mood again," Alice said, smiling coyly and kissing Tristan, savoring his taste.

He thrust his hips against her. They were about to do it—

Ring ring! Ring ring!

"Stupid fucking phone!" Tristan pounded the pillow. "Hang on—I'll throw this at it."

Alice grinned and gave him a shove. "Maybe you should just get it. I bet you've got a stalker—they might slit their wrists if you don't pick up."

"There's only one stalker I want and she's right here," T said, nuzzling her neck. "But you're right, I'll get rid of them. Be back in a sec."

He rolled out of bed. Alice closed her eyes, still feeling his kisses and his hands all over her body. But she couldn't help sighing with relief. What was wrong with her? Were most girls this awful at losing their virginity? Were most girls this terrified? Tally and Mimah hadn't been—they'd both done it and got it over with, and now they could have sex all the time with whoever they wanted. Well, that's how they talked about it, anyway. Maybe Alice was incapable of having sex. Maybe she'd die a virgin granny and everyone who was anyone would know about it and laugh behind her back.

"No way!" burst T's voice from across the room.

Alice sat up in alarm. Then she saw T's face. Whoever he

179

was talking to had obviously given him good news. Great news.

"I can't believe it," he went on. "This is all happening so fast! Thanks, I'll tell the others right away. Cool. Bye."

T hung up and vaulted onto Alice's bed, making its springs creak. "Babe, guess what? That was Dick Crawley, the agent from last night? He says there's gonna be a picture of us in *OK!* next week—in the society pages."

"Cool!"

"And guess what else? He's arranged for us to do a photo shoot in London next weekend—as long as Jasper comes too. Apparently we need a professional portfolio now that we've got an 'image.'" T smiled and rolled his eyes. "It might be worth having Jas, if stuff like this starts to happen. Anyway, I've got to call the others. You don't mind, do you?"

"Of course not." Alice swallowed. "I'm so pleased for you." And she was. Really, she was.

"Thanks, babe," Tristan said, planting kisses all over her face. He looked like a little boy who'd just been given a puppy. "I'll take you out for an amazing dinner next Saturday, after the shoot. We'll go somewhere special; it'll be so romantic."

"That sounds lovely," Alice murmured. She snuggled against T's chest as he dialed Seb, and felt the happy vibrations of his voice against her head. Gently, she stroked his stomach, the sexy part just below his navel, where a trail of hair led down, down, down . . . Alice let out a long, silent sigh. If she and T didn't have sex soon, she might actually burst.

CHAPTER TWENTY-SEVEN

*H*ello?" choked Seb, lunging for his phone. His hands were shaking. Thank fuck someone had rung. For the past ten minutes, Sonia had been edging closer and closer to him on the couch in the Ogilvys' TV room while he piled up DVDs to bring back to school. He got the feeling she was moving in for the kill, which was ridiculous, since he'd purposely picked mid-afternoon on a Sunday for their date—the least sexy time of the week. Or so he'd hoped. As he stood up, his phone pressed to his ear, Seb suddenly caught a glimpse of himself in the mirror above the couch. Shit—he looked terrified out of his mind. This was pathetic. Sonia was just a *girl*, after all.

Her eyes followed Seb to the other side of the room. "Where are you going? Who is it?" she whispered. Poor Sebbie Webbie—he really was nervous, Sonia could tell. He'd sat frozen in his seat like a frightened bunny the entire time she'd been closing the gap between them. Not that she blamed him;

as far as anyone knew, the boy had practically zero experience with women. The fact that he'd refused the advances of some of the hottest chicks in London (including Mimah Calthorpe de Vyle-Hanswicke) only made him more attractive. Sonia fluffed her hair. She selected a walnut from the antique wooden bowl in front of her and cracked it open with massive silver tongs. If only she could get Seb to forget his fear. If only she could get her hands on some alcohol and stuff it down his throat. . . .

"That was Tristan," Seb said. He ventured back toward the couch. "The agent from last night wants us to do a photo shoot next weekend. I thought he was a bit of a sleaze, but he seems to know his stuff."

"Of course he knows his stuff," Sonia proclaimed, popping the walnut in her mouth. "He's a professional. And agents are known for being sleazy—I've researched it because, when I'm a famous director, I'm going to have to work with them all the time. Speaking of directing, Sebbie, we should watch some films together sometime." She dangled a DVD box with an incomprehensible Italian name on it. "Like this one. Looks arty. I just love arty things."

"Oh, right," Seb said, adding it to his pile. "Me too."

"I know," Sonia said, staring into his eyes. "I've always liked that about you, Sebbie. You're so original. You know what you think is cool and you don't care what anyone else thinks. I admire that." She touched his sleeve. "I really do."

Seb stared back at her, biting his lower lip. His heartbeat stalled.

"Thanks, Sone," he said softly. "Umm, right . . ." He pulled away. "I've got to get some wine."

"Oh." Sonia gave a little sigh.

"Yeah, it's Rando's birthday soon and we're throwing him a drinks party at school." Seb stuck his thumbs in the pockets of his skinny jeans. "So, er, it's in the cellar. Why don't you wait here and I'll be back in a minute."

Sonia jumped to her feet. "No, I'll come too. I'm not missing my chance to see the famous Ogilvy wine cellar. No way." Straightening her baby-blue high-waisted skirt, she clopped out of the TV room after Seb. This was just the opportunity she'd been waiting for. They passed the billiards room, its deep red walls casting a pinkish reflection in the corridor, and entered the drawing room, with its lofty ceilings and tall, narrow windows. Watery light filtered through the panes and illuminated swirling dust motes. The dark, polished floorboards creaked under their feet. Sonia pictured Seb here all alone during his father's many absences, reading in front of a crackling fire or projecting huge, shadowy films onto the walls. Maybe this was why Seb loved movies so much: In this big, empty mansion, those larger-than-life characters were his only company.

The stairway down to the cellar was lit by dim sconces built into the mahogany walls. This part of the house was spanking clean and in perfect repair, thanks to the fact that it was home to Sir Preston Ogilvy's pride and joy. Sometimes Seb joked that his father would have been happier if his mother had given birth to a bottle of 1787 Château Lafite, the world's most precious wine, instead of a son.

"Whoa," Sonia breathed as they entered a vast chamber filled, floor to ceiling, with bottles upon bottles upon bottles climbing the walls in wooden racks. "This is enormous."

"This is nothing," Seb replied. "It's only the first room. Come on, let's go to the tasting room. That's where my dad keeps the bottles I'm allowed to touch."

He led Sonia through a long corridor, past cabinets showcasing rare and historic bottles, into a space that looked like a private bar. Wine bottles lined the walls. In the middle of the room was a wooden counter, stacked with sparkling glasses in every imaginable size.

Seb pointed to a seating area furnished with a leather couch and matching leather chairs. "My father likes to sit there and taste different wines for hours on end," he said. "Sometimes he entertains his girlfriends down here. That's what those are for." Seb nodded to a set of speakers built into the walls and blinked. "I spied on him once, when I was seven or eight," he said. "It was after my mum had left. Dad had invited this woman back here and got her drunk on his best Bordeaux. He started playing old-fashioned love songs and they danced. Then they shagged, right there in that chair. A foolproof method." Seb smiled ruefully at Sonia. "When they started going at it, I ran away."

Sonia blinked at him. This was the longest speech she'd ever heard from Seb and somehow it had made her sad. He looked like such a romantic figure, such a lost and lonely soul, with his bright blond hair and pale, expectant face. She longed to take him in her arms and comfort him, to let him know that someone in the world wanted him, right here. Right now.

"Why don't we have a drink?" she said. "It'd be a shame to come all the way down here and not toast the lovely day we've had."

He looked at her. Sonia was beautiful with her exotic black hair, bright eyes, and caramel-colored skin. Maybe she was a little frivolous and a bit bitchy, but she was loyal as hell to her friends and she'd never said a nasty word to him. He should just do it—he should just kiss her for fuck's sake.

"Okay." Seb nodded. "Here." He ducked over to a rack of red wines and selected a bottle of Merlot. "Shall we . . . shall we drink it on the couch?"

"Oooh, yes," Sonia beamed, practically squirming with delight.

She sat, watching Seb's long, delicate hands as he poured them both large glasses. She patted the seat next to her. The sofa was small and soft. It had probably been picked out especially by Seb's dad as a seduction spot, which was totally gross, but at least it suited her purposes.

"Cheers," Seb said, his hand trembling. His wine kept jumping up the side of his glass, leaving thick trails as it trickled back down.

"Cheers."

He and Sonia both took giant gulps. They looked at each other. The seconds ticked by. Seb knocked back the rest of his glass. He poured another and drank that, too.

"Seb," Sonia murmured. She put her hand on his sleeve. "I've had a wonderful day, I really have. I just wanted to say thank you."

Slowly, she leaned in and kissed him on the cheek, breathing deeply, inhaling his smoky, rumpled scent.

Seb's heart raced. Now. It had to be now. He closed his fingers around Sonia's slim arm, and as her lips brushed away from his cheek, he kissed her.

It felt strange at first—nothing like how Seb had imagined. The feel of her mouth was soft and slippery—more slippery than he'd expected. And her taste was so real, so different.

"Mmm," Sonia sighed, moving in for more.

Seb panicked. Sonia sounded so involved, so . . . *into* it. The opposite of how he felt. He didn't feel a trace of the longing he knew he was supposed to feel. The longing he felt when he looked at—

When he thought of—

"Oh," Seb groaned, pulling away. "I'm sorry. I can't do this. I—"

"What? What's wrong?" Sonia's face was wrenched with worry.

"I just . . . I need to be alone. I need the bathroom."

Sonia gasped. "Oh no! Have you got the runs? I told you that lamb at lunch looked weird."

"No," Seb said, backing away. "I just need to be alone."

Sonia's expression changed. Her mouth fell and the light in her eyes went dim. "Oh. I get it," she whispered miserably. "It's me, isn't it? I've put you off; it's my fault. I'm a bad kisser. I'm fat."

"No!" Seb said. "You're great. It's nothing to do with you. Promise."

On legs that felt like jelly, he escaped the room and stumbled down several corridors to the basement bathroom. Once the door was safely locked, he looked at himself in the mirror for the second time that afternoon. Was it really true? Seb examined his ashen face, his frightened but comprehending eyes. As soon as his lips had joined with Sonia's, it had felt wrong. As he'd known, deep down, it would. That shadowy thing which had been gathering in his mind for months, maybe years—he finally saw its shape.

Seb breathed a deep breath and looked in the mirror again, straight into his own eyes.

I don't fancy girls. The words echoed around his head. *I don't fancy girls.*

"I'm gay," he whispered and his reflection whispered it back.

Seb swallowed. He stood there for a long time looking into his own eyes. Gradually, they cleared.

It was okay. He didn't have to tell Tristan. He didn't have to tell Sonia or Rando or Jasper or George Demetrios, or anyone. The only person he had to tell was himself. *I can lie to as many people as I want,* he thought, *as long as I don't lie to myself.*

As soon as those words popped into his head, Seb felt his mood rise like the sun among clouds of fear. It was like Tristan had said last night: You never knew how something would be until you tried it. Now he knew what he was going to try next.

CHAPTER TWENTY-EIGHT

*A*lice snuggled into her usual couch in the Tudor House common room and tucked her slippered feet under her butt. Cradling her mug of hot cocoa, she leaned forward and selected a biscuit from the plate Sonia had laid out. Sunday evening debriefing sessions were the best way to purge your hangover before the week began.

"Right," Alice yawned, "first topic on the agenda: Tals, gossip from Jamie Darlington's afterparty."

Tally winked. "Ooh, I've got something good. Wait for it. Tom Huntleigh and"—she glanced round the room and dropped into a loud whisper—"Tom Huntleigh and Bella Scott got it on. Big time."

"Boring," Mimah snapped. "Tell us something we care about. Those two were practically humping all night at the ball."

Hearing the strain in her own voice, Mimah pursed her lips

and glanced toward the windows. As soon as she'd arrived back at school this afternoon, all her worries had come flocking back. She knew she should go and find Charlie. She knew she should have that talk with her like she'd promised Mummy yesterday, before leaving for the Young Leaders Ball. But she couldn't face it right now. It was freezing outside and dark, and judging from her recent chats with her sister, this one was going to be hell.

Tally was staring at her. "Mime, are you okay?"

"Of course."

"Then chill, will you? I haven't got to the juicy bit yet." Tally grinned. "So, as soon as we get to Jamie's house, Tom and Bella lock themselves in the upstairs bathroom and don't come out for hours. No one knows what the hell they're doing. Finally, when Jamie manages to get in, there are empty champagne bottles everywhere, the entire bathtub is sticky, and Bella and Tom are passed out on the floor. They totally had a champagne bath!"

"Ewww!" Sonia doubled over with laughter.

"And they drank the champagne after sitting in it!" Tally cackled. "What idiots."

"Um, excuse me," Alice interrupted. "This story is fucking fascinating, really—but what happened with you and *Rando*, Tally? Duh, that's what I was asking."

"I know," Tally giggled, sipping her hot chocolate. She'd loaded it up with four spoonfuls of sugar, just how she liked it. "Well, it's kind of embarrassing, but . . . nothing."

"Nothing?" Sonia burst out. "Like, *nothing* nothing?"

"Well, we flirted all night. It was like we were at the party, you know, *together*. He kept getting me drinks and we talked all about everything and smoked joints together in one of the bedrooms." Tally's eyes were dreamy. "But he never made a move."

"Um, point of information:"—Sonia butted in—"Why the hell didn't you jump on him?"

"Because I wanted him to jump on me. It's so much more romantic that way. Plus I'm not a psycho predator, unlike some people." Tally smirked at Sonia. "Explain to me again what happened with Seb? You kissed him and then he bolted? What an achievement. Did you eat raw garlic for lunch?"

"No," Sonia glared. "I ate *lettuce*. And, anyway, *he* kissed *me*."

"Yeah, right."

"He did! You just don't want to believe it because it means my weekend was more successful than yours. Well, bite me."

Tally scoffed. "You wish."

"Girls," Alice interrupted, "give it a rest. Sone, seriously, what's up with the running away? What did you do to him?"

Sonia arched her eyebrows. "Well, I have a theory. Before Seb kissed me, he was telling me all about this special tasting room in the wine cellar that his dad uses to seduce the girl-friends he brings home." She paused for a dainty sip of tea. "I probably shouldn't be telling you any of this, because Sebbie told me in a very intimate moment and he wouldn't want anyone else to know. But anyway. One time, Sebbie sneaked into the tasting room and saw his dad. Shagging someone."

"No!" Alice gasped.

"Yes." Sonia picked an invisible piece of fluff off of her sweater. "Oh, yes. It was bad. He saw them going at it for ages. He saw everything. And guess where this was, this scene of horrible sex?" She paused for dramatic effect. "It was on the same couch, in the same room, on the same cushion, that Seb kissed me."

"Whoa," Tally breathed. "No wonder he ran off."

Sonia nodded. "I should probably be a psychologist. I'm very sensitive to this sort of thing."

"I wonder if Tristan knows," Alice mused.

"Don't tell him," Sonia said quickly. "Or Seb might think I've been gossiping. The poor boy needs someone he can trust."

"And that's you, is it?" Mimah snorted.

Sonia glared at her. "Yes, as a matter of fact. You're just jealous, Jemimah. Everyone knows you used to fancy Seb. Well, I'm the one he kissed. Me. *Moi.*"

Mimah narrowed her eyes, but before she could retort, Mrs. Hoare sauntered into the room. Standing near the doorway, the Ho pointed her finger at Sonia and squinted.

"What's she doing?" Alice grunted.

"Help. Nervous," Sonia muttered, darting her eyes around.

"Sonia Khan," Mrs. Hoare announced.

"Uh . . . yes?"

Striding across the carpet, the Ho swung her finger round the group. "Alice Rochester. Natalya Abbott. Jemimah Calthorpe de Vyle-Hanswicke. Oh, bravo to me! Aren't you girls impressed by how good I'm getting with all your names?" Chortling, she settled herself into the chair next to Sonia's.

Sonia shifted sideways and widened her eyes at Alice.

"The last few weeks have been so hectic," the Ho went on, "I feel I haven't had a chance to get to know many of you." She smiled, revealing a smudge of lipstick on one of her snaggleteeth. "How was everybody's weekend? I hear there was a very jolly charity party in London. Did you all go?"

Sonia stared into her slimming oolong tea. Alice cleared her throat awkwardly. Just then a head peeked round the common-room door.

"Excuse me, I'm sorry to interrupt, but is—"

"Charlie!" Mimah exclaimed.

"Oh, hey, Mime," Charlie said, going pink. "I just came by to, er, see you." She gripped her bag, fiddling with its tasseled zipper.

"Hi, Charl." Alice waved. Charlie was the same age as Alice's fourteen-year-old brother, Hugo, and she'd known her for years.

"Come have some biscuits and hot chocolate," Tally cried. "Tell us all the freshman gossip. Who's been making trouble lately? Who's in and who's out?"

Abruptly, Mimah jumped out of her seat. "Never mind that," she snapped. "Come on, Charlie, let's go talk somewhere. You know, catch up."

She tugged her sister out of the room, feeling Mrs. Hoare's eyes burn into her back.

CHAPTER TWENTY-NINE

*W*hat are we doing in here? Why the hell can't we talk in your room?" Charlie asked, pushing aside a pair of Hunter boots and a jumble of scarves so she could squeeze onto the bench in the Tudor House cloakroom.

Mimah shut the door. "Because Gabby fucking Bunter is in my room, as always, gobbling After Eights and watching repeats of *Star Trek* on her computer."

"Ew, Gabby Bunter!" Charlie howled with laughter. "I saw her in Quad the other day. If she gets any fatter she'll fall through her mattress in the middle of the night and get stuck in the bed frame!" She puffed out her cheeks and flailed her arms, doing an impression of Gabby on the floor.

Mimah giggled too. Then, as the laughter died from Charlie's face, the light faded from her own, as well. Charlie looked even paler now than before the weekend. Her eyes were rimmed with dark circles and her hair was gnarled around her shoulders.

Mimah rubbed her eyes. "Charl, I—"

"Is Mummy coming to school?" Charlie interrupted stiffly. She looked down at her hands, which were knotted together in her lap.

"No, she's not."

"Oh." Charlie's fingers began to uncurl and Mimah noticed a glimmer of calculation in her eye.

"But only because I begged her not to," Mimah went on, her voice hardening. "I told her I'd talk to you. Sort you out. You know the school called her, don't you?"

Charlie met her eye for a split second.

"I'll take that as a yes. What the hell were you thinking, skipping lessons? You didn't think teachers would notice how blatantly you were breaking the rules?"

"Rules are made to be broken," Charlie scoffed. "Since when did you become such a goody-goody? You used to be fun."

Mimah's face burned. "Oh, shut up. Don't be so superior. You know I'm always up for fun—but you've got to be subtle about it, that's all I'm saying. Otherwise you'll get suspended. And how 'fun' do you think that'll be, sitting at home with Mummy for weeks on end?"

Charlie stared straight ahead.

"Not very," Mimah informed her. She rubbed her temple.

It was horrible having to be all teacher-ish like this. Charlie was right—she was used to being the one *breaking* the rules, not sticking up for them. Suddenly, she felt a surge of resentment toward her mother for putting her in this position in the first place—for being a weak, stupid, pathetic pill popper.

"How is Mummy?" Charlie asked. Her voice was meeker now.

Mimah shook her head. "The same. Maybe worse. She—"

Beep! Beep!

"Oh, hang on." Charlie grabbed her phone from her pocket and cupped it so that Mimah couldn't see the screen. Mimah studied Charlie's profile, instead. As her sister read, a shutter in her face seemed to open. Warmth gleamed out from the inside—but only for a second. The next instant the shutter closed and Charlie looked up, shoving her phone toward her pocket.

"You were saying?" She waved her hand. "About Mummy or whatever?"

Mimah gritted her teeth. *Mummy or whatever?* Why was *she* doing all the bloody work, when Charlie was the one who'd fucked up?

"I was saying that Mummy's worse," she snapped. "She's still popping pills, she never goes out, she never sees anyone. When I arrived on Saturday afternoon, she was lying in bed drinking whisky with the curtains drawn. Not that you seem to care," Mimah spat. "All you care about is your bloody social life—and what clever tricks you can get away with. You don't give a shit about anyone else. About me having to look after Mummy and do everything for her."

The dark circles around Charlie's eyes seemed to grow darker. "Hey," she croaked, "that's not fair. I've come to see you, haven't I? Why do you think I did that? I thought it would be n-nice—I thought it would be nice to talk." Charlie's eyes were brimming with tears. She jerked to her feet and brushed her hand over her face. "I need the toilet. I'll be back."

As the door clicked shut behind her sister, Mimah stared down at the sneakers, the umbrellas, the boots, and the gardening gloves on the cloakroom floor. She'd been way too harsh. She was supposed to be helping Charlie, not hurting her. But it was impossible. How was she supposed to help when she couldn't even find out what was wrong?

Just then Mimah noticed the glint of metal at her feet, and as she reached down, her heart leapt into her throat. It was Charlie's phone. Maybe it could give her some clue. Urgently, she opened the inbox and found the text Charlie had just read.

`Me 2. So bad. B careful. Can't w8. Xx awesome`

Mimah screwed up her face. What the hell did that mean? Who was this weirdo who signed their messages "awesome"? What couldn't they wait for? And why did Charlie have to be careful? Mimah squinted at the sender's name. A lot of help that was—it was just a set of initials—FHB. Who on earth was that? Certainly not Georgie Fortescue. Scanning Charlie's inbox, Mimah noticed that the initials came up again and again and again. Maybe if she read more she could find out who it was. Maybe she'd understand. She scrolled through the messages—and suddenly stiffened.

The handle on the cloakroom door was turning. Mimah threw the phone into Charlie's bag.

"Hey," said Charlie, wiping her nose.

"Hey. Everything okay?"

"Yeah." Charlie bit her lip. "Mime?"

"What?"

"I'm sorry if I came across as selfish before. I didn't mean to. I know you're only trying to help. Thanks for stopping Mummy from coming to school."

"That's fine, Charl." Mimah leaned back against a rack of hanging coats. "It's just . . . I only want to make sure you're okay. If anything was up, you'd tell me, right?"

Charlie hesitated, then nodded. "Of course. But . . . I'd better go. Mrs. Gould will be taking the register soon."

"Yeah." Mimah walked her sister through the foyer and leaned against the doorjamb, watching Charlie disappear into the night.

She had the first clue. How was she going to get the next?

CHAPTER THIRTY

loody rain," George Demetrios grumbled, jerking his head at the vaulted windows in the Hasted House dining hall. Their panes were blurred by streams of water. "I am not looking forward to rugby practice this afternoon. Oi, T," he called, as Tristan slid his breakfast tray down the long wooden table. "You're team captain—can't we cancel rugby practice?"

Tristan sat down and rubbed his hands. Breakfast was the best meal of the day at school, probably because it was difficult to fuck up eggs, bacon, sausages, and baked beans, all of which he'd loaded onto his plate.

"Oh, yeah, sure," he replied, "let's cancel it. Totally. I'm sure the Brigadier will think that's an amazing idea. It's not like our biggest game of the year is coming up in two weeks or anything."

"Shut up," George snorted, stealing a piece of bacon from T's plate. "Sarcasm is the lowest form of wit."

"I guess that's why you understand it, then," T grinned.

"Ouch!" Jasper yelped from across the table.

"What's your problem?"

"I spilled bloody tea on myself." Jas dabbed at his navy and green tennis tie, then threw down his napkin. "People, this week sucks. The weather's shit, I've got a ridiculous amount of prep and there are no parties to look forward to now that the Young Leaders Ball is over."

"I've been thinking the same thing," belched George, his mouth full of bacon. "We need another one to cheer us up."

"George, come on," Seb said, glancing up from the newspaper he was reading. "We've had at least three parties in the past two weeks."

"Yeah, and now we're on a roll. Never quit while you're ahead, mate."

Seb rolled his eyes. "Um, I hate to ruin your argument, but I think the saying is *always* quit while you're ahead. Mate." Finishing off his coffee, he turned back to his paper.

Tristan shot his friend a look. For the past few days, ever since his date with Sonia on Sunday, Seb had been weirdly quiet. He hadn't been around much, and when he had, he seemed to have a brooding expression permanently stamped on his face. Maybe T shouldn't have put so much pressure on him to ask Sonia out. After all, Seb was a big boy—he could probably work out who he fancied and didn't fancy without his friends breathing down his neck. But still, it was only supposed to have been a bit of fun.

"All right, gang," said Rando, rocking up to the table with his tray. The downpour outside had plastered his dark brown hair to his head. "Let's hope the weather improves for Saturday. Who wants to be doing a Paper Bandits photo shoot looking like a drowned rat? Right, T? Seb?" He grinned. "Right, Jas, cowbell player extraordinaire?"

Jasper, who'd been drumming his fingers on the table, looked up. "Rando!" he cried suddenly. "Perfect."

"Yeah, I know I'm perfect. What's the reason this time?"

"It's your birthday!"

Rando gave him a withering look. "Not for another ten days. I'd have thought my cousin of all people would know that."

"Yeah, yeah, sure," Jasper said impatiently. "I mean, your birthday is the perfect excuse—er, the perfect *occasion*—to have a party!"

"Hmmm . . ." Rando buttered his toast. "Could be cool. Okay, why don't we invite a bunch of people out to Shock Box the Saturday after next?"

"Shock Box?" Jasper scoffed. Shock Box was the skankiest bar in Hasted, complete with a cheesy jukebox, cheap pints, and a sweaty club in the basement that seethed every weekend with a superhorny boarding-school crowd. "Yeah, that's right—aim high," he snorted, shoving a forkful of fried bread and baked beans into his mouth. "No . . ." Jasper waved his fork. "No, what we need is a real party. A big, old-fashioned house party."

"House party!" George Demetrios cried, stamping his feet and pounding the table.

"Oi, Demetrios," scolded a passing classics teacher. "Keep a lid on it."

"Sorry, Mr. Gilchrist."

Now Rando was looking excited. "Hang on," he said. "I've just had the most fucking genius idea. You know my parents' place in Wiltshire?"

"Of course."

"Well, for the next couple of weeks, Mummy and Dad are in Munich visiting the German side of the family and the house is empty. It's not far from here. Some of us can drive. And there's a train right nearby."

"Mate." George Demetrios's face was ecstatic. "That is goddamn brilliant. A country house party!"

"Make that a country house *pool* party," Jasper said, practically rocking back and forth with glee. "Your parents have that huge indoor swimming pool, don't they? We'll get all the girls in there. Naked! In fact, let's make it a naked party—check your clothes at the door."

"Genius," Rando grinned. "We could have naked tennis. Naked croquet."

"Naked Twister!" George guffawed. "Bring it on."

"Wait, wait, wait." T raised his hand. "Guys, sounds fantastic, really—except that you seem to have forgotten one thing. If it's a naked party, then *we* all have to go naked, too. And the last thing I want is to have to look at a hundred naked dudes all night—never mind play fucking Twister with them."

"Ugh." George Demetrios eyed the sausage that he'd skewered and put it down. "Gross."

"Good point," Jasper grimaced. "We're not a bunch of gays, after all."

Everyone chewed their food in silence. Then Tristan banged down his fork. "I've got it. What's the next best thing to a naked party?"

Rando shrugged. Jasper shook his head.

"A white party!"

"Huh?" George grunted.

"Just think about it," T said. "Everyone has to wear white. Girls in white bikinis. White see-through dresses. Wet white T-shirts . . ."

"Shit, yeah," Rando chimed in. "And we can have white drinks. White wine, white Russians, white rum."

"White imported cigarettes," George Demetrios bellowed, swinging his chair back on two legs.

"Done," Jasper declared.

"Done," echoed everyone else.

Well, everyone except Seb. Tristan studied his best friend. All through the discussion, Seb hadn't said a word. He'd been staring at his newspaper, his lips pursed, his knuckles white—and it was weird, but T could have sworn he was still reading the exact same page.

CHAPTER THIRTY-ONE

*D*ylan hopped off the number ninety-four bus that she'd caught from her mother's house in Holland Park and fought her way across Oxford Street. The Saturday afternoon shopping crowd was as bad as in New York: Everyone was elbowing each other, shouting abuse, charging toward so-called bargains like zoo animals at feeding time. By the time Dylan made it through, her coat had been torn open and her hair was a mess. She took a minute to catch her breath, then pulled out her phone and dialed.

"Yes?" came a voice on the other end. "Jasper speaking."

"Hey, it's me." Dylan bit her lip, feeling a pang of uncertainty. Jasper sounded so brusque and businesslike—maybe he hadn't really wanted her to come. He was just finishing off a day of work with Tristan, Seb, and Rando—they'd been shooting publicity photos according to their new agent's orders—and he was probably trying to make a good impression on the photographer. As well as on his new bandmates.

Dylan fiddled with one of her dangly earrings. "Um, I'm on Park Lane. By Marble Arch."

"Right, cool." Jasper cleared his throat, sounding a bit friendlier. Dylan relaxed a little. Of course he'd wanted her to come. He'd been chasing her for weeks. "We're in Shepherd Market," he said. "It's a little piazza down past the Curzon, that art-house cinema. You know the way, right?"

Dylan chuckled. "Uh, no. I'm not from this city, remember? You're lucky I even found this part of town. But I'll get there."

"Okay, well . . . this part of Mayfair's kind of confusing. Call me if you get lost."

"Don't worry, I won't. I have a good sense of direction."

Dylan hung up and studied the map on her iPhone, then set off down Park Lane, filling her lungs with cold autumn air. Today was one of those windy London days when clouds whipped across the sun, making the streets flash sparkling bright one second and gloomy gray the next. Across the road, Hyde Park stretched flat as far as she could see, its paths teeming with joggers and cyclists, and scattered with rusty leaves. Tossing back her head, Dylan let her hair stream out behind her. It was funny, but she was almost beginning to like London. Maybe because this was one of her last weekends here. Her dad had e-mailed this morning. He'd booked his ticket. Next weekend he was flying over to win her mother back and take the whole family home.

A tour bus thundered past. Dylan blinked out of her reverie

and turned off Park Lane into Mayfair. It was elegant here and hushed. The parking spaces were filled with Ferraris and Aston Martins, Bentleys and Lamborghinis; the pavements were dotted with men wearing shiny shoes and women carrying Mulberry bags. After a few minutes, she spotted a cinema on the right, advertising films with French- and Russian-sounding names. That must be the one Jasper had been talking about. Shepherd Market was supposed to be around here, somewhere.

Dylan checked her map again and swung into a narrow street. She wound down it, past cafés and restaurants that took up almost every square foot, finally coming to a halt at the edge of a small square. Here, the golden afternoon light shone at a deep angle, throwing shadows into the cracks and crevices in the old paving stones. The buildings' redbrick façades glowed. Dylan pulled her coat closed against a gust of wind. It was hard to believe this place was here—it felt like a tiny village, in a different world from the Oxford Street chaos.

She huddled in the alleyway, spying on Jasper. He was standing with the others by an old green pub in the corner, listening to instructions from a long-haired photographer. His arms were folded and the expression on his chiseled face was so earnest that Dylan almost cracked up.

Usually, Jasper went out of his way to make everything he did seem effortless and cool. He spoke in that offhand tone. He walked with that give-a-shit swagger. He watched things with that arrogant gleam in his eye. But right now, when he thought no one was looking, he'd dropped the attitude—and Dylan realized how much he must have longed to be part of the Paper Bandits and how adorably determined he was not to fuck up on his very first day.

Dylan felt something soften in her heart. Memories from last weekend at the ball came crowding into her head—how Jasper's fingers had caressed the small of her back. How his tongue had explored her mouth. How his body had pressed against hers as they kissed against a wall. How sweetly he'd led her to her front door and kissed her good night. . . . The blood rushed to Dylan's cheeks. If this was going to be her last weekend in London, then she wanted to make the most of it. And she knew how to do that—she was going to go all the way.

"Hey!" Jasper called. He'd seen her and was waving her over, his mouth curved into a smile. "You found us! Come meet Yusuf. He's the photographer."

"Hello," Dylan said. She held out her hand.

"All right, sweetheart," Yusuf grinned, shaking it. "Sorry to keep you, we're just doing this last shot and then your boy's free to go."

"Cool. Mind if I watch?"

"Knock yourself out."

Dylan stood back and the boys grouped themselves into a tableau. Seb and Jasper leaned against the wall of the pub. Tristan and Rando peered off in different directions. It looked ridiculous. And Yusuf obviously thought so too.

"This isn't working for me," he said. "I like the background, but we need a focus. Hmm, Tristan, why don't you tell a joke that the others can laugh at? That'll draw you together as a band."

"Okay. Yeah. Cool." Tristan struck a pose with his hands spread apart, his eyes manic, and his mouth open wide. "How's this?" he said. "Does it look like I'm telling a joke?"

"Er, no." Yusuf sighed. "It looks like you're about to eat a bus. You have to actually tell a joke. If you just pretend, it'll look fake."

"Right. Yeah." T scratched his head. "Okay . . . Joke . . . Shit, man, I can't think of any."

"Come on, mate," Jasper drawled. "Don't be lame."

"Chill, cowbell player—if you're such a comedian then you think of a joke."

"Ummm . . ." Jasper scratched his chin.

"How about, er . . ." Seb furrowed his forehead. "Uhhh . . . never mind."

Rando snapped his fingers. "I've got one! So, there were these two . . . Wait, what was the punch line again?"

On the sidelines, Dylan rolled her eyes. This was pathetic. "Why did the chicken cross the playground?" she yelled.

"Why?" Jasper called back.

"To get to the other *slide*!"

Everyone groaned.

"Boo!" Jasper heckled.

"Rubbish!" Rando joined in.

But the whole group was howling with laughter, including Dylan. Their guffaws rang across Shepherd Market.

"That's the worst joke I've ever heard," T gasped. "I'm telling it for the camera. Ready?"

"No. Hang on." Yusuf held up his hand. He was peering at the group through his lens. "I have a better idea. Sweetheart, blondie, how would you feel about being in the picture?"

"Uh . . ." Dylan glanced at Jasper. "I guess I wouldn't mind."

"Ace." Yusuf looked round, then darted over to one of the pub's window boxes and yanked out a few flowers. "Let's hope no one saw that," he winked, handing them to Dylan. "Right, can you walk past the boys carrying this bouquet? Excellent. Boys, you all stand by the pub scoping her out, trying to get her attention. A hot babe with flowers: It's competition time. Let's see what you're made of."

Dylan slicked on more lip gloss and smoothed her hair. Thank goodness she'd made an effort for her date with Jasper this evening and was looking photo ready. Coyly sniffing her flowers, she sauntered out into the square and glanced at the boys from the corner of her eye. Their whistles and catcalls got more and more ridiculous.

"Hey, beautiful, do you come here often?"

"You must be tired—you've been running through my mind all day."

"If I could rearrange the alphabet, I'd put *U* and *I* together!"

"Nice legs! What time do they open?"

Dylan burst out laughing. "Gross!" she called.

"Aw, come on baby, don't be like that."

"Your dad should be arrested—he stole the stars and put them in your eyes."

Suddenly, Dylan heard footsteps race up behind her. A pair of arms caught her round the waist. "Got her! She's mine," cried Jasper. He pinned her arms to her side and planted kisses all over her face.

"Cheat!" called the others. "Yellow card! Send him off!"

"And that's a wrap," chuckled Yusuf. "Well done, guys, I think we got some good stuff. I'll send a selection along next week."

"Bye!" Tristan waved. He grinned at Dylan and Jasper, who were play wrestling in the middle of the now twilit square. Okay, so maybe he hadn't been sure at first about Jas going out with his ex, but they looked so good together he couldn't help being happy for them.

"Wicked day, mate," Jasper said, swinging one arm round Tristan's shoulders and keeping the other round Dylan's. "My first as one of the stars of the Paper Bandits. I've gotta say, I'm a bit sad to see it end."

"Yeah," T said, "it's been fun. But I've got a date with Alice, and it looks like you two have a hot night planned, so—hey!" he exclaimed.

"What?" jumped Dylan and Jasper together.

"How about if we join forces?"

"H-huh?" Dylan stammered.

"You mean like a double date?" Jasper asked, lighting a cigarette.

"Yeah. The more the merrier. Think about it—it'll be romantic *and* sociable at the same time!"

"Hmm, not a bad idea." Jasper squeezed Dylan's hand and blew a puff of smoke into the freezing evening air. "What do you reckon, Dill? The four of us out together—drinking, dancing, partying—how fun would that be?"

Not fun in the slightest. Dylan opened her mouth to say the words, but then, catching sight of the enthusiasm on both boys' faces, she snapped it shut. After all, it was just a double date . . . with Alice Rochester . . . How bad could it be?

CHAPTER THIRTY-TWO

*A*lice drummed her fingernails on the table at Sketch bar in Mayfair. Tristan was ten minutes late and it was embarrassing. She stared down and pretended to read the latest issue of *Grazia*, which she'd bought at Hasted train station on her way into London, but it didn't work. She definitely looked like a no-friends loser. There was nothing more cringeworthy than someone sitting alone in a bar, especially if it was a ridiculously romantic bar like this one, with a posh crowd, trendy cocktails, and white leather walls that glowed with soft pink light.

Alice checked her watch again. Maybe she should order a Manhattan. T loved Manhattans. She could order one for him, as well, and then he'd have the same drink as her, waiting for him when he arrived, which would be completely adorable. It was hardly even four thirty, but who gave a shit? Everyone else in here was guzzling booze. Alice craned her neck for the waiter.

"Sorry I'm late!" came a cheerful voice.

Alice jumped. "Finally!" she pouted. "I was about to give up on you."

Letting T kiss her hello, Alice gazed into his face. He was flushed from the cold outside. His eyes were bright and his hair had that sexy tousled look she loved. Her eyelids fluttered. It was such a shame T couldn't stay over at her house tonight—she had to be up early for a formal luncheon at her grandmother's tomorrow and it would be far too awkward having him around in the morning. That was why Alice had been planning all day to make this evening as romantic as possible. She and Tally had spent ages accessorizing her strapless black tulip dress and dusting her eyelids a mysterious, smoky green.

"I've got a surprise for you," T said. He straightened up. "Look who's here!"

"Oooh, who?" Alice clapped her hands. "Is it someone famous? Where are they sitting? Is it—Oh. My. God." Her smile froze on her lips. "Jasper. D-Dylan." She grimaced. "What the hell are you doing here?"

"Surprise!" grinned Jasper, kissing her on the cheek. "You weren't expecting that one, were you, Ali babe? Happy to see me—the latest, greatest star of the Paper Bandits?"

"Hey, Alice," Dylan said, raising her hand awkwardly.

Tristan was glancing round. "Let's find some more chairs. This table's a bit small, but it'll do. Waiter! Do you think we can fit two more round here? Excellent. Thanks a lot."

Alice gaped. What the fuck was happening? Was T actually inviting Dylan and Jasper to *stay*? She glared as the waiter pulled up two more chairs and whisked away the romantic vase of flowers. One little candle now flickered forlornly in the middle of the table.

"I really hope we're not interrupting your evening," came a small voice.

Alice flicked her eyes up. Dylan fucking Taylor was talking to her, gazing at her with those sickly baby-blues. Alice shot her a death stare, too quick for the boys to see. "Oh, *don't* worry," she said sweetly.

"I know it must seem a little weird, us turning up," Dylan smiled nervously. Her nails were a dark, shiny red—she'd clearly just had a manicure. Try-hard. "I mean, Jasper and I can always go sit at a separate table or something. Or find a different room. It's just that he and T were having such a good time by the end of the photo shoot, they thought it'd be fun to have a few drinks together."

Alice stared. Was Dylan actually still babbling on? And had she actually just referred to Tristan as "T"? Who the hell did she think she was? *Get the fuck out of my space!* she wanted to scream, but that would be far too uncouth. And, anyway, there were other ways of getting rid of people.

"Oh my god, I completely understand," Alice said, her voice still saccharine. "I totally see why Jasper would want to include me and good old T in your evening. It can get really boring talking to the same person all night. Especially if they're not quite from the same social level."

"Hey, babe, glad you're having fun," T said, catching sight of Alice's honeyed expression. He punched her shoulder as he sat down. "I knew you'd be up for some company. Al's always game for a party," he informed Dylan. "Hey, Al, remember last Christmas when you and I went for a quiet drink, just the two of us, and we started chatting to the people at the next table? You ended up inviting half the pub back to my place for a lock-in!"

"Mmm," Alice said pointedly, "that was before we were going out, wasn't it? Those were the days. Manhattan!" she called to a passing waiter. "Sweet, straight up. And make it strong."

"And three mojitos," T added. "With a glass of water. I'm thirsty."

Alice pursed her lips. "Oh. Mojito? I thought you were getting a Manhattan too. I thought you liked them."

"I do!" Tristan said. "But Jas and I had such a good day, we thought we'd celebrate with something tropical."

"The photo shoot was fantastic, by the way," Jasper gushed. "The weather was perfect, and I actually found the whole posing thing incredibly easy. I think I'm a natural."

Tristan rolled his eyes. "No, really? A natural poser? You?"

"Shut it."

Tristan laughed. "But really, Yusuf says he thinks we got some good stuff."

"Um, Yusuf?" Alice blinked. "Excuse me, but am I supposed to know who that is?"

"Oh." Tristan ran a hand through his hair. "I thought I told you—he's the photographer."

"Hm. Fascinating." Alice glanced at her magazine and then back at T, as if it were taking all her effort to stay in this tedious conversation.

"So, er, anyway," Tristan said, "we were out there scouting locations for ages. By the time Dylan came to meet us, we—"

"Hang on." Alice narrowed her eyes. She could feel fury, real fury, rising in her chest. "*Dylan* came to meet you?"

"Oh. Yeah. Jas invited her."

"My, my." Alice grabbed the Manhattan that the waiter had just put down. "Wasn't that nice of Jasper. I don't remember being invited."

"Aw, poor baby," T grinned, playfully tugging a few strands of Alice's hair. "Come on, babe, you know you wouldn't have enjoyed it—you'd have been bored out of your mind. You hate standing round in the cold." He raised his mojito. "Cheers everyone! Here's to double dates!"

"Double dates!" said Jasper and Dylan.

"Double dates," Alice echoed loudly a split second later, gulping her Manhattan. She slammed her glass back down. Dylan was definitely looking at her.

"Hey, Al." Tristan touched her arm. "Are you okay?"

"Yeah, I'm fine. Totally fine. Why?"

"No reason." T smiled uncertainly. "You just seem a bit, I don't know, tired?"

"Sweet!" came Jasper's voice.

216

Alice looked up. Jasper was stroking a small bouquet of flowers pinned into Dylan's hair.

"I didn't realize you'd kept these, Dill. They're the ones Yusuf gave you for the photo shoot, right?"

Dylan smiled coyly. "Yeah. I had such a nice time earlier that I didn't want to throw them away. Do they look stupid?"

"No," T joined in, "they look pretty." He brushed the petals with his fingertips.

Alice stared at his long, delicate hands, that should have been entwined with hers right now, that should have been stroking her knee while she and T sat here, *alone*, gazing into each other's eyes.

Alice swallowed. Her rage and resentment were bubbling to such a frenzy that she could feel tears pressing at the back of her throat. Yanking her magazine from the table, she stared, without seeing, at some stupid story about animal-print shoes. This was it. The night was ruined. She hated everyone, everyone hated her, and there was no way she was going to feel better. Around her, the others' voices hummed like wasps. She longed to swat them away.

Tristan turned to Jasper. "So, what do you guys have planned for later?"

"Hmmm . . ." Jasper winked. "I'm not sure I can trust you with that information."

"Hee-hee!" Dylan half-giggled, half-hiccuped. "Want to know a secret?" She was trying to drink her mojito slowly—she had no intention of doing a repeat of last weekend's sloppiness—but still, the rum was going to her head. She grinned widely. "My mom's sleeping at her boyfriend's place tonight. So I invited Jasper back to my house."

"Oh, reeeeally?" Tristan teased. "Lucky Jasper."

Alice stiffened. Without glancing up from *Grazia*, she raised her eyebrows. "Interesting," she sneered. "Back to your house. That's brave of you."

Dylan frowned. "Brave?"

"Yeah. Brave." Alice lowered her magazine so that it covered the candle flame, plunging the table into dimness. "You know what they say: When boys get invited back to girls' houses, they're only expecting one thing. And I just think it's a big decision—you know, to lose your *virginity*."

Jasper coughed on his drink.

Alice smirked.

Dylan's eyes bulged. "Excuse me?" she gulped, her voice shaking. "Are you implying something about my personal life?"

Alice shrugged innocently. "I'm not implying anything— I'm just repeating what you told me yourself. Oh, sorry—was it a *secret*? You did announce it in front of a roomful of people."

"I did not announce it," Dylan snapped. "I admitted it in I've Never. And everything said in that room was supposed to stay in that room. That was the pact."

"Oops. Forgot."

"Hey, Al . . . ," Tristan began. He shifted uncomfortably.

He'd seen Alice like this before, many times. But somehow it didn't seem so easy to handle now that she was his girlfriend.

Dylan's hand was trembling. Rum sloshed onto her wrist. "Yeah, I guess I *am* a virgin," she said, as evenly as she could. "Well, so what? At least I don't lie about it." Dylan stared into Alice's eyes. She was daring herself to say it. . . .

Alice's heart jolted. She turned pale. Dylan couldn't possibly know . . . could she?

"Anyway." Alice flung out in desperation. She had to keep her advantage. "I don't care what you are, it's none of my business. I'm just advising you to think hard before you do anything."

She picked up *Grazia* and held it in front of her face.

T sniffed the air. "Ugh, what's that smell? Is one of the chefs having a fit?"

Jasper crinkled up his nose.

"Arrrgh!" Dylan screamed. "Smoke! Fire!" She pointed at *Grazia*. The corner of the magazine had caught alight.

"Shit!" Alice flapped it round in circles.

"Here!" T cried, chucking his mojito at her.

"No!" yelled Dylan and Jasper together. "The rum will make it worse!"

Sure enough, the flames shot even higher as the alcohol burned.

"Let me," Dylan panted. Reaching across Tristan, she grabbed his glass of water and threw it over Alice. The fire fizzled out. But there was liquid everywhere. It was puddling on the table. It was streaming onto the floor. It was dripping from Alice's face.

"Fuck me!" Jasper guffawed, pointing. "You look ridiculous. Ha-ha! You have got to see that sprig of mint leaves on your head."

Tristan doubled over in convulsions. "Awww, it's a flower decoration just like Dylan's! Al, you're so cute; you look like a drowned hamster."

Alice crushed her fingers into fists. Why were boys so fucking mean? *Plop.* An ice cube rolled off her shoulder and into her lap. The tears were coming. She could feel it.

"I'm going to the bathroom," she choked. Her voice sounded unsteady, saturated. Wrenching herself from the table, she bolted through the doorway, dashed up Sketch's curving white staircase, and threw herself into one of the bar's famous podlike bathrooms. Finally alone, she covered her face, but she couldn't stop the flow. Tears of rage and disappointment leaked through her fingers, down her cheeks, into her mouth. She felt so alone.

"Alice?"

Someone was tapping on the door.

Alice didn't answer. She stuffed her knuckles into her mouth to muffle the sobs.

After another second, the door opened a crack. Shit. She'd forgotten to lock it. She sank down onto the toilet, trying to hide her face against the wall.

"Hey, are you okay?" Dylan asked, squeezing into the

bathroom. "Oh, no." She tore off a piece of toilet paper and handed it over. "Here, take a tissue. What's wrong?"

"I-I-I'm just so up-upset," Alice gasped. She dabbed at her eyes and immediately soaked the tissue through. "Th-this was supposed to be a sp-sp-special d-date. . . . And he just invited y-you two and ruined it and doesn't even c-care. And now everyone h-hates me!" Alice hunched over, her elbows on her knees, her hair straggling over her hands.

"Calm down," Dylan said soothingly. "That's not true; no one hates you. Boys are just stupid and insensitive. You should have seen Tristan's face when you ran off just now. He cares about you so much."

Alice sniffled. "I don't know. The way he acts sometimes— it's like we're still just friends. Like, he didn't even tell me I looked p-p-pretty tonight." She stifled a huge sob. "Doesn't he get it? Doesn't he know things are different now?"

"I'm sure he knows," Dylan reasoned. "But being in a relationship—it takes getting used to. Especially since you two are such old friends. I'm sure he was *thinking* you looked pretty, he's just not used to saying it. Here." She handed Alice another tissue.

The tears had slowed now, but Alice's face felt swollen and hot.

"Thanks," she sniffled, looking up at Dylan. "W-why are you being so nice to me?"

Dylan pursed her lips. "Hmmm," she mused. "Good question. Maybe I'm just a really good person." Leaning back against the white wall of the pod, she scratched her chin. "Yeah, I guess I must be, since you've always been such a total *bitch* to me."

Alice's bloodshot eyes widened. "Oh, right. I thought we were bonding here," she sniffed. "Obviously not." Then she caught Dylan's eye. Dylan was smirking. "Wh-what's so funny?"

"You!" Dylan giggled. "You crack me up, Alice Rochester. For fuck's sake, I've never seen anyone take themselves as seriously as you!"

"Piss off," Alice protested. "I don't take myself seriously. I laugh at myself all the time. I'm permanently laughing at myself. I . . . I . . ."

"Oh, yeah," Dylan guffawed. "You're like a fucking circus clown!"

Alice rolled her eyes. But Dylan's chuckling was infectious, and she could feel the laughter bubbling up inside herself as well, replacing the fury she'd felt at Tristan and the exhaustion she felt after her tears. She slumped forward on the toilet seat, shaking with giggles, feeling the tension drain from her, letting her body go limp.

"Oh, god," Dylan panted. "For a second there I wasn't sure if you were gonna laugh or punch me."

"It was a toss-up," Alice gasped, wiping her eyes. "Anyway, I'm glad you and Jasper are having a good time at least." She blew her nose. "By the way, I heard you might be leaving London."

"Oh? Where'd you hear that?"

Alice tossed her hair. "Hm, can't remember. Jasper probably told me. Is it true?"

"I'm pretty sure it is. My dad's coming next weekend."

"But do you want to go? I mean, how about Jasper? How about school?"

Dylan grimaced. "School," she snorted. "I think you guys have made that place pretty hard to miss. Especially Sonia—she's not exactly an ideal roommate, you know? But then again . . ." She squinted at a spot above the mirror. "When I first got here, I totally hated everything about this place."

"And now?"

Dylan smiled wryly. "Well, it would be kind of lame to change my mind just because I've been dating a boy for two weeks, wouldn't it?"

Alice grinned. "Um, no. That's exactly what I'd do."

Dylan laughed again. "Yeah, well, Jasper's pretty hot. And I like him a lot. I just hope he doesn't get scared off now that he knows I'm a virgin."

There was a silence. Alice fiddled with the hem of her dress, not wanting to meet Dylan's eye. Maybe outing Dylan as inexperienced wasn't the coolest thing she'd ever done.

"Hey," she cleared her throat. "I have a question."

"Yeah?"

"I was just wondering . . . when you said that thing before about lying . . . lying about being a virgin . . . who were you—"

"You," Dylan cut in. "I was talking about you."

Alice's cheeks burned red. "But I'm not—"

"Don't even try. I know you lied in I've Never—you lied your ass off. And don't ask me how I know—I found out by mistake." Straightening up, Dylan checked her makeup in the mirror and sniffed. "But don't worry—since you seem to think that being a virgin is, like, the crime of the millennium or something—your secret's safe with me. See you downstairs."

Alice chewed her lip as Dylan disappeared through the door, her curvy hips swaying, her straw-blond hair flowing out behind her.

"Yeah," she said pensively. "See you downstairs."

CHAPTER THIRTY-THREE

*A*re you sure your mum's not home?" Jasper whispered.

"Of course I'm sure." Dylan unlocked the front door of the huge house her mother had bought a few months ago in swanky Holland Park and led Jasper into the black-and-white-marble-tiled foyer. It was past five in the morning. The place was dark and silent. It smelled of new paint mixed with freshly cut flowers.

"Only my sister, Lauren, and the au pair are home," Dylan went on. "The last time my mom stayed here on a Saturday night, it was because she had the fucking flu. She doesn't even bother to make an exception when I'm home. She and her stupid boyfriend—"

"Victor Dalgleish," Jasper grinned.

"You mean *Vic*. That's what he likes me and my sister to call him." Dylan snorted. "They always stay at his place on the weekends. He's got some kind of bachelor shag-pad near

Portobello Road, full of leather couches and plasma TVs. He probably has black bed sheets. Gross. Thank god my dad's coming next weekend."

Jasper smirked. "Well, I'm disappointed. The only reason I let you drag me back here was that I wanted to meet him. My nanny used to make me and my brothers watch *MindQuest* with her when we were in elementary school. I had no idea how the game worked but I used to be captivated by his sideburns. They were like furry little rats stuck to the side of his face."

"Ew!" Dylan squealed, swatting him. "Can you please stop talking about my mother's boyfriend? It's grossing me out."

"Mmmm . . . ," Jasper murmured seductively. "Sideburns . . . Greasy hair . . . Polka-dot ties . . . Horsy white teeth . . ."

"Stop!" Dylan shrieked.

Laughing, Jasper caught hold of her, scooped her into his arms, and started up the stairs. "Which way to your room?"

"Sorry, but it's all the way at the top. I seriously doubt you can carry me for five floors."

"Don't be ridiculous!" Jasper said gallantly. "You're light as a feather. You're . . . Oh, argh . . ." He pretended to stagger. "Excuse me while I have a heart attack."

Dylan giggled. Maybe Jasper was only being silly like this because it was 5 a.m. and he was tired, but still—it was good to know he could drop his supercool veneer. It was reassuring. Because the truth was, Dylan was nervous. She hadn't changed her mind since the afternoon: She wanted to go to bed with Jasper. She wanted to do everything. But she knew Jasper's reputation. He must have slept with tons of girls. He must have seen them all naked, he must have memorized what each of them was like in bed. He'd probably compare her to them as soon as they got started. Isn't that what people did?

"In here," Dylan whispered. They'd reached the top floor. "We have to be quiet—my sister's sleeping down the hall."

"Quiet's fine with me," Jasper murmured. He drew Dylan close and kissed her, softly, lingeringly. His palm pressed into the small of her back. Sweeping up her hair, he nuzzled her ear and kissed her neck. Dylan shivered. It felt so good. Jasper clearly knew exactly what he was doing. He was slick.

"Come to the bed," she said, tugging his arm with one hand, untying her floaty halter top with the other. Its strings slithered down over her shoulders

"Hang on," Jasper said. "We don't have to go so fast. We can take our time."

"I know," Dylan smiled shyly. "But I want to do this. I've known all day that I want to. Don't you?"

"Of course. But . . ." Jasper took a step back. "What Alice said . . . Is this your first time?"

"Yes. So?"

"Well . . ." Jasper's habitual superior look flickered over his face. "It's quite a big responsibility, taking someone's virginity. It'll probably mean loads more to you than it does to me and I just don't want anything to get awkward. I'm not sure I want the responsibility."

"Responsibility?" Dylan put her hands on her hips. "Oh,

please. Get off your high horse. Everyone has to have a first time, don't they? And you don't need to worry—I won't hold you responsible for 'deflowering' me or anything like that." She rolled her eyes, putting finger quotes round "deflowering." "This is the twenty-first century; I've made a decision; it's my business and it has nothing to do with you."

"Whoa . . ." Jasper raised his eyebrows. "You certainly know how to make a guy feel wanted. It's like I could be any dude who just happened to come along."

"Oh, no." Dylan draped her arms round his shoulders. "Don't get all sensitive, for god's sake. I didn't mean it like that. I really like you—I want to have sex because it's you. I just meant— Oh shit." Suddenly grinning, she let her head fall back. "You did that on purpose! You just wanted me to say how into you I am. How could I let you trick me like that?"

"Trick you?" Jasper chuckled. "What do you think I am, a conman? I like you, too—that's why I'm here. I had a great time with you tonight. You're . . . you're the first girl I've really liked in ages." Reddening, he brushed his dark brown hair off his forehead. "There. Was that embarrassing enough for you?"

"Yes," Dylan whispered.

She pulled him onto the bed. They kissed, rolling on the new blue check duvet that her mother had bought at Ralph Lauren, or one of her other favorite stores. Dylan felt a rebellious triumph in hooking up with a guy like this, on the new sheets, in the new bed, in the new house her mother had forced on her when she'd dragged Dylan to London.

Jasper slid down her halter top. He unbuttoned her jeans, pulled off her pants. His kissing was getting more urgent, more passionate. He pressed her into the mattress. He ground his hips against hers.

"Let me get a condom," Dylan breathed. Sliding out of bed, she streaked over to her dresser and found the box of Durex that she kept buried in her underwear.

"Here," she whispered, ripping one off and holding it out to Jasper. Her hand was sort of shaking, but she tried not to let him see.

"Thanks." He got up on his knees. It was dark, but Dylan could see him silhouetted against the wall, fiddling with the condom, trying to slide it on. She didn't try to help. Jasper was the expert at this—she'd probably just mess things up.

"Fuck," he muttered.

"What?"

"I've totally wasted that one. I couldn't get it on. Let me try another."

Dylan watched. Jasper's hands looked weirdly jerky as he worked with condom number two. But he knew what he was doing. She took deep breaths. They were going to do it. Relax.

"Goddammit!" Jasper cried. He flung down the bit of rubber and flopped onto the bed.

"Are you okay? What's up?"

"Nothing." Jasper laughed sourly into the pillow. "Nothing's up. That's the problem. Great. I bet you think I'm really stupid now."

"Of course I don't. Talk to me. Why would I think that?"

Jasper covered his face. "Because. After all that crap about me taking your virginity and you getting too attached—now I'm the one who's fucking the whole thing up. I'm the one who's too nervous to do anything."

"Nervous?" Dylan's eyes widened. "But I thought you'd slept with loads of girls."

"I have! Well, maybe not *loads*, but, yeah, quite a few." Jasper sniffed. "It's different though, when . . . when it's someone I like. Fuck." He closed his eyes.

"Hey." Dylan took his hand. "Please. Don't be embarrassed. I'm not expecting you to put on some kind of amazing show. I mean, it's my first time. Whatever you do, I'll probably think it's right. I don't have anything to compare it to."

Jasper blew out through his nose and Dylan thought she detected the ghost of a smile through the darkness.

"Okay," he whispered. "Maybe if . . . Maybe if I went to the bathroom, tried to put it on there, that might help. I might not feel so pressured."

"Okay, it's down the hallway. First on the left." Dylan waited, hearing her own heart beat in the darkness. Somehow it made her feel more comfortable, knowing that Jasper was nervous too.

After a minute, a figure slipped through the door and the bed dipped as he climbed back in.

"Did it work?" she whispered.

"Yeah." Jasper kissed her. "Ready?"

"Ready."

And then they were doing it.

"Are you okay?" Jasper kept murmuring. "Are you okay? Does it feel good?"

"Yes," Dylan whispered. And it did. It hurt, too, but not in such a bad way, not in the way she'd worried it might. It was amazing being so close to Jasper. It was unlike anything else: Every breath they took was shared, every part of his body was touching hers, sliding against her. His lips grazed her ear, whispering how good it felt, how glad he was to be with her.

Afterward, they lay next to each other. Jasper's arm was draped across Dylan's body. He kissed her drowsily, and his breathing became deep and regular.

A glimmer of dawn broke through the curtains. The little neon clock on the bedside table flashed 7:08.

I'm not a virgin anymore. Dylan tried out the words. *I'm not a virgin. I just had sex.*

She must have drifted to sleep, because the next thing she heard was the front door slam and raucous laughter from downstairs.

"Hellooo! Dylan, Dill Pickle! Lauren! Hurry downstairs girls, we have news. If you don't come down, then I'm coming up."

Dylan sat bolt upright in bed. The clock said 10:03. And that was her mother's voice.

CHAPTER THIRTY-FOUR

*J*asper rubbed his eyes groggily. He didn't have a clue where he was. Then he remembered.

"Dill?" he croaked, peering over to the other side of the bed. It was empty. "Dylan?"

But Dylan was nowhere to be seen. She must have gone to the toilet. Or maybe she'd gone to make him breakfast in bed. That would be excellent. He could do with some hangover-friendly food. His family's Filipina maid was probably serving up their Sunday eggs-and-bacon feast right this second.

Yawning, Jasper folded his arms behind his head and inspected Dylan's bedroom. It had been so dark earlier this morning that he hadn't been able to see a thing, but now the pale winter sunlight floated through the curtains, sweeping the shadows into the corners. He blinked in surprise. Dylan's room was desolate. It was completely bare. Okay, maybe that wasn't entirely accurate. There was the bed. The bedside table. The dresser. There were a few cardboard boxes shoved against one wall and a half-unpacked suitcase against another, but they only made the place seem starker. Girls' rooms were usually full of jewelry and handbags and photos and perfume bottles and silky ribbons and things. Jasper knew that. He'd spent plenty of time nosing round the bedrooms of potential conquests; you could learn a lot of helpful stuff that way. But all the colorful clutter he'd seen in the past—there was nothing like it here.

Jasper bit his lip, feeling weirdly down. He'd realized before that Dylan wasn't exactly ecstatic to be in London. That was why she was so looking forward to her dad arriving and taking her family back to New York. That was why she made such a point of insisting that she didn't belong here: "I'm not from this city, remember?" To tell the truth, Jasper hadn't really cared all that much before, apart from the fact that he fancied Dylan and would prefer not to have the object of his lust disappear before he'd sealed the deal. But last night had changed things. He felt closer to Dylan now. And it was clear that this place wasn't a home to her. It was just a house. A house where she was doing her best to remain a guest.

"No!" came a shriek from downstairs.

Jasper jumped so violently that he hit his head on the wall. "Stop!"

There came a crash, followed by the tinkling of glass. Jasper jumped out of bed. What the fuck was going on? It sounded like an intruder. Holland Park was a respectable area, but you never knew what riffraff might be lurking on a Sunday morning, trying to take advantage of the unsuspecting upper class. One thought flashed through Jasper's head—*help Dylan*. He bolted for the door, then suddenly caught a glimpse of himself in the mirror above the dresser. He was stark naked. Shit—if the police turned up, they'd probably arrest him instead of the real criminal.

Almost falling over his feet, Jasper pulled on his jeans, not bothering with his pink check shirt, and shoved his feet into his Vans. He hurled himself out the door and down the stairs.

"Just stop!" A woman's voice echoed through the landings. It had to be Dylan's. What was the intruder doing to her? Jasper clenched his fists. If only he'd had time to grab a weapon. . . .

He tiptoed into the front hall—surprise was key—and crept through the living room, the TV room, the library. There was no one here. The noise must have come from the kitchen. Jasper bolted, on tiptoes, downstairs to the lower-ground floor, skidded into the kitchen—and froze.

"Oh my god!" screamed a tall, thin, blond woman. She clapped her hand over her heart.

"Identify yourself!" demanded a man wearing bright red trousers and a 1970s biker jacket. It was Victor Dalgleish. There was no mistaking his sideburns. Or his ludicrous dress sense. He seized the first thing within reach—a cheese grater—and shook it, advancing on Jasper. "Hands in the air!"

"Wait, I'm sorry, sir, Victor, I . . . I'm—"

"He's my friend," called an infuriated voice.

Jasper darted his eyes to the table and noticed Dylan glowering behind it, next to the double doors that opened on to the garden. She looked stunning. But that was partly because her face was livid. Her cheeks were flushed and her eyes were wild.

"Oooooh, a new 'friend'?" said someone else. Jasper turned to the other end of the table. A pretty girl was standing there. She was an inch or two taller than Dylan and was grinning widely at him. This must be Lauren.

"Nice of you to mention your 'friend' before. What happened to his shirt?" Lauren took a bite of the almond croissant in her hand. Jasper peeked at the table and realized it was piled with croissants and Danish pastries and *pains au chocolat*, all fresh from the bakery. Inappropriately, he felt his stomach grumble.

Dylan's mum slapped the countertop. "Young lady," she snapped, "you are in serious trouble. It's completely unacceptable, not to mention irresponsible, to bring strange boys back to the family home."

"Oh, yeah? Why don't you practice what you preach?" Dylan shot back. "You're the biggest hypocrite I've ever met. What? It's okay for you to bring *him* here, but it's not okay for me to bring my own guys back?"

"You're sixteen years old!" Dylan's mum cried. "Of course it's not okay. How dare you talk back to me like that?"

"Piper kitten, calm down," Victor purred, stroking Dylan's mother's hand. "This boy looks like a decent fellow. Attractive, too. Got to let the younger generation discover their sexuality. Personally, I hope they had a wild night up there. Grrrr." He licked Piper's ear.

"Barf," Dylan spat. "Am I the only person in this family who thinks that's disgusting?" She turned to Jasper, her voice rising. "Do you know what these two just did? They just burst in here, first thing in the morning, and announced that they're getting *married*!"

Jasper raised his eyebrows. "Oh. Wow. Congratulations," he said, mustering the most charming smile he could under the circumstances.

It was then that he registered the bottle of Krug on the kitchen table. And the fact that Lauren, Victor, and Dylan's mum were holding champagne flutes. Glancing down, he glimpsed shards of broken glass glittering around Dylan's feet. That must have been the crash he'd heard upstairs.

"Congratulations? What do you mean, congratulations?" Dylan fumed. She wheeled on her mother. "How could you do it?"

"Dylan, please," Piper said. "It's not appropriate to involve strangers in our family discussions."

"He's not a stranger," Dylan insisted loudly. "I've already told you, he's my friend."

"That's enough!"

Jasper pursed his lips. Dylan's mother seemed as cold as a glacier. The hot temper clearly came from her father's side of the family.

"But how can you be getting married?" Dylan ranted. "You've known each other for less than six months. And, anyway," she was practically screaming now, "you're still married to Dad."

Piper cleared her throat. "Well, sweetie, your father and I are getting divorced. I thought you knew. I'm having my lawyer notify him this week."

"But he's coming next weekend! He's coming to London."

Piper's cheeks paled. "What?"

"He's coming to London. He's got his tickets and everything. I invited him. I wanted him to bring us home. He has presents for you: He's bringing jewelry and flowers and everything." Dylan was almost crying. "It was supposed to be a surprise."

"Oh, Dylan . . ." Piper's face softened. For the first time since Jasper had entered the room, she actually appeared to have feelings. "Darling, you shouldn't have done that. And he should never have agreed to come."

"But he did." Dylan wiped away a tear. "And I thought it would be okay. I thought we'd be a family again."

Jasper cleared his throat apologetically. Every household had dirty laundry and that was fine—as long as you kept it hidden instead of flapping it in people's faces, exposing every stain and unpleasant whiff.

"Er, Dylan," he said, "I'm terribly sorry to interrupt, but I think I'd better be off."

"Yeah," Dylan said, not meeting his eye. "Okay. Bye. Sorry you had to see this."

"Don't worry at all. It was nice to meet everyone."

"Nice to meet you!" Lauren called, as Jasper left the room.

Two minutes later, hurrying out the door with his pink check shirt neatly tucked into his jeans, Jasper sighed with relief—and with trepidation. Until this morning, his thoughts about his future with Dylan had got about as far as them sleeping together and then stopped. He liked her, of course, but Jasper had never been into commitments. He was into his freedom. He was into joking around with the guys. He savored the thrill of the chase. While he'd thought Dylan was leaving London, the whole situation had seemed complication free. Now that she seemed to be staying, however, things were bound to get sticky.

CHAPTER THIRTY-FIVE

Mimah slapped her physics test onto Mr. Vicks's desk on Monday afternoon and bolted out of the classroom twenty-five minutes before the bell. That was the rule in physics: If there was a quiz, you were allowed to leave as soon as you'd completed the paper—meaning that, today, Mimah was in luck. She'd spent the past week trying to work out how the hell she was going to sneak into Charlie's room to investigate her sister's suspicious behavior and here was her chance. Right now, the entire freshman class would be gathered in the small theater, yawning their way through their weekly PSHE talk. Which put them safely out of the way.

Mimah smirked as she hurried through the foyer of Locke House. Poor little freshmen, having to sit through all that boring PSHE crap. PSHE stood for Personal, Social, Health, and Economic education, and it was where you blabbed about things like tampons and birth control and why it was hurtful to be cliquey and bad to do drugs. In other words, it was one long opportunity to pass notes and whisper bitchy comments about people's acne, as long as you sat in the back.

Her heart pounding, Mimah cracked open the door to Charlie's attic dorm. *Yes.* It was empty. But she'd better get her ass in gear; the science block was halfway across the school from Locke House and she'd already used up five valuable minutes just getting here.

Charlie shared a desk along one wall with one of her other roommates. Mimah located her sister's glossy white MacBook, which she'd decorated with shiny star stickers, and pressed the keyboard to wake it up.

Please let Charlie be signed into her e-mail account. Please let Charlie be signed into her e-mail account. . . . It would make things impossible if Mimah had to mess around trying to guess her password. Especially since she only had eighteen minutes left.

She was in luck! Charlie's school e-mail program was minimized at the side of the screen. Mimah opened the inbox. Where to start? Georgie was the most likely source—she was Charlie's BFF, and if Charlie was going to write to anyone about whatever shit she was up to, it would be her.

F-o-r-t-e-s-c-u-e, Mimah typed, and hit search.

Five hundred and twenty-three results popped up.

Fuck. Did Charlie never delete anything? Randomly, she clicked on a message from two weeks ago.

Yehhhhh baby, it read.

Great. That was going to be a really big help in getting

to the bottom of the mystery. She chose another message: `booored. send me hugz.`

And another one: `Charleeee how long is our history essay meant to be, not crazy long right?`

Mimah skimmed several more before throwing back her head in frustration.

She thought for a second. What were those initials the texter had used again? Shit. She was such an idiot not to have written them down. They'd started with an F. FGH? No. Duh. That was just the alphabet. Grabbing a scrap of paper, Mimah started scribbling random letter combinations. FTH. FTB. FHT. No. She'd know it when she saw it. *Come on, come on!* FHD . . . FHB. That was it! She keyed it in.

Nothing. She checked again. Nothing at all.

Okay . . . How about that other thing—the nickname the texter had used? "Xx awesome," whoever it was had signed off. She typed *a-w-e-s-o-m-e*, hit search and pounded her fist on the desk in frustration. Three hundred and fifty-seven hits. Of course. How could she have been so fucking dumb? Charlie and her friends used that word all the time.

Mimah glanced at the clock at the top of the computer screen: 3:59 p.m. Six minutes to go. Six minutes before the bell rang for tea and Locke filled up with freshmen hurrying to dump their bags at the end of the day. Mimah felt a film of sweat on her forehead. She had to find something. She had to. This could be her only chance before Charlie got herself kicked out.

She opened her sister's hard drive. There was nothing in DOCUMENTS—it was just a list of essays and assignments arranged by subject. Surprisingly meticulous for someone who seemed so scatty.

She clicked on PICTURES. Maybe there'd be a random photo of this FHB "awesome" person. Then at least Mimah would know who she was dealing with.

Suddenly, an icon caught her eye. It was a PDF file, weirdly out of place among all the holiday photos and party pics. It was called "maps." Maps to where? Since when had Charlie given a shit about cartography?

Riiing!

That was the end-of-lessons bell. On a last, desperate hunch, Mimah clicked "maps." It opened, infuriatingly slowly, in Adobe. And when it did, Mimah stared. No way. This had to be something.

She was looking at a hand-drawn trail. It was labeled and ran from Locke House to a spot in the woods about fifteen minutes' walk from the edge of the St. Cecilia's grounds. In the top right-hand corner was yesterday's date and the words, `W11/17 2:30, S11/27 1:15. C u there. FHB.`

FHB! Finally. Something.

At that moment Mimah heard voices from below. She glanced out the window. Freshmen were trickling through the gate into Locke's front garden. No sign of Charlie yet, but she'd appear any minute. *Hurry up. Hurry up.* Her hands shaking, Mimah pressed print. She held her breath, her nostrils flared, and as soon as the paper slid out, she grabbed it, quit Adobe, minimized Charlie's mail, and hurled herself through the door.

Footsteps were echoing up the stairs to the attic. Instinctively, Mimah darted across the hallway and into the bathrooms, where she locked herself in a stall and uncreased the map. "W11/17 2:30. S11/27 1:15." Those looked like dates and times. W must be Wednesday, November 17: Elective day, when every student was supposed to spend the afternoon playing sports or learning skills or doing community service. It was when Mimah had her main lacrosse practice of the week. That meant that S11/27 was a week from Saturday. Quarter past one was just after lessons would be over for the day. The whole thing made sense. So far, at least.

Mimah's lips curved into a triumphant smile. She was on the trail. And Wednesday was less than forty-eight hours away.

CHAPTER THIRTY-SIX

Try kicking it," Tally whispered.

"You kick it," Alice retorted. "I'm wearing my new Miu Mius."

"Fine. Shove over."

Hoisting her leg in the air, Tally rammed her studded ankle boot into the old attic door. A cloud of dust exploded in her face. She and Alice waved their arms frantically, trying not to cough. Once the air had cleared, they crept over the threshold (avoiding the lethal broken floorboard) and into a big, low-ceilinged storeroom stacked with paint cans and broken easels and dirty canvases and random still-life props: a stuffed parrot lying sideways on top of a heap of red velvet, a bunch of fake sunflowers, a cracked violin.

"The Grubhouse," Tally grinned. "God, I love it up here. We haven't been in ages."

"Too risky," Alice said. She stuck a cigarette in her mouth

and held one out to Tally. "If we sneaked here too often, someone would definitely notice."

Tally nodded and lit up. She and Alice had discovered the Grubhouse one evening back in their freshman year and since then it had been their favorite, most secret, smoking hideout. No one ever came up here to the eaves of the art block, which made it the perfect place to sneak a cigarette safe from prying eyes. Especially on rainy days like today.

"Ew," Tally groaned, plopping herself onto an old workbench. She leaned her forehead against a garret window and tried to see out, but the glass was so smeared with rain and dirt that the Great Lawn below looked like a giant snot. "I hate this weather. How much do you wish we could jump on a plane to Miami right now?"

"Don't tempt me." Alice settled herself next to Tally and took a drag. "It better not pour like this for the big Hasted House–Glendale's rugby match next week. Remember two years ago when it totally pissed it down and Tristan and Jasper turned into mud monsters and we all got colds?"

"That was horrific. By the way, what's up with you and T? Have you forgiven him yet for being a bastard at Sketch?"

"I suppose." Alice heaved a long-suffering sigh. "I know he didn't mean anything by it, like Dylan said. Boys just have a way lower mental age than girls. I'm giving him a chance to make it up to me this weekend at Rando's party. Speaking of Rando . . ." Alice paused and exhaled. She watched the tendrils of smoke curl round the legs of easels and old stacked chairs, and tried to suppress the tremor that had inexplicably crept into her voice. "Speaking of Rando, we have to discuss your seduction plan for the weekend. What's the strategy?"

"Eeek!" Tally gripped Alice's wrist. "I don't know. I'm so nervous! You have to help me. What should I do? What should I wear?"

"Hang on. First of all, it's going to be difficult seducing the birthday boy. He'll probably be busy trying to talk to all the guests and plus he'll be stressing about his house getting trashed."

"Uh, no," Tally laughed, elbowing Alice. "That's what *you'd* do. I reckon Rando will be too drunk to care if anyone starts using his parents' porcelain collection as target practice. At least, that's what I'm counting on."

Alice giggled. "I've got it. Here's what you should do: bring an extra bottle of champagne and hide it really well—but in, like, a sexy place."

"What, like in the hot tub?"

Alice rolled her eyes. "Yeah. Hide a bottle of champagne in a hot tub. That'll work *really* well. Not. No, I mean hide it in his parents' bedroom or something, where you can be private. Then when all the good alcohol runs out, tell Rando you've been saving some. Lure him away, make sure the two of you end up drinking all alone, and then . . . pounce!"

"Yes!" Tally clapped her hands. "Genius. This is so happening."

Alice took another drag. "Can I ask you a question?"

"Duh."

"In the beginning you were kind of only into Rando 'cause you wanted to forget about Mr. Logan, right?"

Tally blinked at the floor and shrugged. She still wasn't comfortable with people mentioning Mr. Logan's name.

"Well, is that still the same, or do you actually like Rando?"

"Why? Are you worried about his feelings or something?"

"No. I'm just curious about yours."

"Yeah, I do really like him," Tally sighed. "Especially since that night at Guy Fawkes—how sexy was it, the way he rescued you and Dylan from the townies? And, anyway, I'm starting to feel left out. I mean, you and T have each other, Sonia's got Seb, Jasper's getting it on with Dylan, Mimah's acting kind of weird so she doesn't count. I'm like, the only person left who's all alone."

She ashed into a paint-encrusted palette and pouted jokingly, but Alice watched the frown lines at the side of Tally's mouth. It was true—her best mate hadn't had a boyfriend in ages. It was time to get her one.

CHAPTER THIRTY-SEVEN

*M*imah peered anxiously into the mirror as she went through the first steps of her plan just before 2 p.m. on Wednesday. After dabbing her face with talcum powder, she rubbed circles of black eye-shadow under both eyes, blending carefully so it looked as little like makeup as possible. Next, she layered three heavy sweaters over her lacrosse uniform, wound a pashmina round her shoulders, and draped another over her head like a hood. Finally, she sucked in her cheeks, widened her eyes, and hurried out the door.

"Jemimah, where have you been?" demanded Miss Colin, the lax coach, when Mimah rocked up to the field a few minutes later. "The others have already started. As team captain, you're supposed to set a good example. And what's with that ridiculous getup?"

Miss Colin had always been a blunt, no-bullshit kind of teacher. Mimah prayed her plan would work.

"S-sorry Miss Colin," she said, shivering. "It's just so c-cold out today."

Miss Colin scoffed. "Don't be pathetic; it's warm out. You've just been sitting in lessons too long. Go on, run round a bit, and you'll soon warm up."

Mimah rolled her eyes. Not a good start. She was going to have to ham it up.

"G-good idea," Mimah stuttered, wrapping her arms round herself. "I've been l-looking forward to l-lax all day. *Aaatchoo!*" she sneezed, convulsing into a trembling fit.

Miss Colin folded her arms. "Jemimah, is something wrong?"

"What? Oh, no. I'm f-fantastic. My body's a bit achy and I have a head . . . head . . . head *aaatchoo!*—headache, but I think I'm just excited about playing lacrosse. I'm d-dying to get onto the field."

"Hmmm . . ." Miss Colin, who was short and stocky, peered suspiciously under her student's hood.

Smiling feebly, Mimah lowered the pashmina that was covering her head.

"Bloody hell!" Miss Colin jumped as soon as she saw Mimah's face. "Pardon my language, but what's happened to you? You look like a ghost."

"G-ghost?" Mimah bit her lip. Maybe she'd overdone it with the talcum powder. "Oh, dear. You mean I'm p-pale? I wonder why. I hope I'm not getting *ill* or anything. I'd hate to be *ill.* If I was *ill,* I wouldn't be able to play l-lacrosse today." She blinked at Miss Colin and started shivering again, so violently that it looked like an interpretive dance.

Miss Colin rolled her eyes. "Jemimah, if you're waiting for me to tell you not to play this afternoon, then you're wasting your time. You certainly don't look well, but only you can tell me if you're feeling fit enough for practice. You're my team captain and you're almost seventeen years old. You can make your own decision."

Mimah's eyes widened. "Oh, okay." She gave a sniffle. "Well, now that you mention it, I think it'd be better if I spent the afternoon in b-bed. After all, as captain, I don't want to catch pneumonia and be laid up for the rest of the season. And I'd feel so terribly guilty if I infected anyone else on the team."

"That's fine, Mimah," Miss Colin replied. "I hope you feel better. And next time, just ask if you want to be let off practice. I can't stand sympathy-mongers."

"O-okay, Miss Colin. Thanks."

Mimah hobbled away from the field in the direction of Tudor House, her cheeks going pink under the talcum powder. She rubbed most of it off with her sleeve. Whatever. So what if Miss Colin had been totally unsympathetic? She was still a complete fucking genius. Now that she'd got out of lax, she was free to track Charlie to her rendezvous and finally find out what the hell was going on. She'd better hurry, though. Charlie was meant to be meeting FHB in fifteen minutes and Mimah had no idea how long they'd stay in one spot. Suddenly, a thought occurred to her: How had Charlie managed to get off her own elective in order to attend this little get-together in the woods? Charlie had signed up for Community Service this term as part of her Duke of Edinburgh Award. That must have been one of the lessons she'd got in trouble for bunking off.

Mimah waited until there was no chance she could be seen from the lacrosse field. Then, abruptly, she switched direction. Cutting straight across the Great Lawn, she headed uphill toward the big school theater, a brick building with state-of-the-art equipment, partly hidden from view by a line of knobbly oaks. Suddenly, Mimah thought of the last time she'd taken this route to the woods. It had been back at the beginning of term, when she'd been pretending to be Dylan's friend. She smiled, remembering how she'd brought Dylan up here to get her stoned for the first time and how Dylan had drooled, practically passing out with her head on a rock. Mimah laughed out loud. To tell the truth, she hadn't had to pretend all that hard to like Dylan—the girl was sharp and funny and eager to please. But, at the time, Mimah had had other things on her mind.

She skirted the theater. Less than six feet ahead was the barbed-wire fence that divided the school grounds from the woods. All she had to do was dash up to it, duck through, and she'd be home free to find Charlie. She took a deep breath, and—

"You!" called a man's voice. "Why aren't you at your elective?"

Mimah froze.

It was the eccentric old Head of Physics, walking his three yappy terriers. He had a reputation for doing this—patrolling the circumference of the grounds, setting his dogs on unsuspecting runaways.

"Mr. Vicks," Mimah said, pulling down her hood. "Hi. Nice to see you."

"Jemimah! I didn't recognize you in that getup. What are you doing all the way out here?"

Mimah chewed her lip. It might be dangerous to tell two different lies to two different teachers, but then again, she couldn't exactly see Miss Colin and Mr. Vicks having a good old gossip. They weren't each other's type.

"Well, it's lacrosse practice at the moment and Miss Colin wanted us to focus on our fitness, so I came up here for a run. The hill's pretty tough," Mimah said, wiping her forehead.

"I'm not surprised you're hot with all those layers on," Mr. Vicks said. "Listen, I'm glad to bump into you. I was going to e-mail you later on, anyway. Have you got time for a chat?"

"Oh, um . . ." Mimah looked at her watch. Two thirty-three. She was already late. "Well . . . what about?"

"Cambridge. What's your decision about applying?"

"I'd definitely like to," Mimah said. "I guess I should decide what college to go for and stuff, right?"

Mr. Vicks nodded. "Though, actually, I've got a few ideas myself. My first choice for you would be Trinity College. It's big, it's eminent, and I know several of the tutors there. I went to Trinity, myself, in fact. Here." He took his wallet from his jacket pocket and pulled out an old photo. "A picture of me at my graduation."

Mimah looked. A younger version of Mr. Vicks (there was no mistaking those eyebrows) was standing in a huge court-yard, wearing a black cape with a furry hood and a proud smile on his face. Behind him were the most stunning build-ings she'd ever seen—golden sandstone, with turrets and flourishes and archways. "Wow," Mimah gasped, "amazing."

"Isn't it? Now," Mr. Vicks went on, tucking the photo care-fully back into his wallet, "you know, of course, that you won't be applying until the beginning of your senior year. But you should start building up your CV now. How about you come back with me to my office and we can map out a strategy?"

"Oh . . . right now?"

"Of course, right now. When else?"

"But I don't think I have time. I'm kind of . . . busy."

Mr. Vicks's expression changed. "That's disappointing, Jemimah. If I'm going to groom you for Trinity, then I need to know you're one hundred percent committed—otherwise it's a waste of both our time."

Mimah hesitated. She thought of that picture of Trinity. She thought of all the things that going to Cambridge could mean.

Mr. Vicks tapped his foot.

She looked toward the barbed-wire fence and beyond it into the woods, where somewhere in that labyrinth of trees Charlie was getting up to god knew what. . . .

Finally, Mimah took a deep breath. "Okay," she said, turning back to Mr. Vicks. "Okay, I'm committed. Let's make a plan."

The mystery of Charlie could wait. Who said she had to put her own future in jeopardy for the sake of her stubborn sister? And, anyway, there was always a week from this coming Saturday—the second date on the map.

CHAPTER THIRTY-EIGHT

*W*ait, wait, don't open the door yet!" Tally pleaded as she buckled her strappy, white ankle boots.

"Hurry up, then. I'm dying for a drink," Alice ordered, adjusting her sequinned boyfriend-blazer over her tight white dress. It was nine thirty on Saturday night and she, Tally, Mimah, and Sonia had just arrived at Rando's country manor from the train station. The Randall-Stubbses lands were so extensive that it had taken their taxi at least five minutes to drive from the property's front gate to the house itself—but apparently that still hadn't been enough time for Tally to sort out her shoes. Typical.

"Looks like loads of people are here already," Alice said, peering through a window into the entrance hall where grime music was bursting from giant speakers. "The place is packed." She jumped back as the door burst open.

"Girls," Rando beamed, "welcome!"

"Happy birthday, darling," Alice cried, planting a kiss on his cheek.

Tally swooped in behind her. "Gorgeous place, sweetie," she exclaimed. "How come you've been keeping it a secret from us all term?"

Rando grinned. He'd only started at Hasted House in September and none of the gang had ever been to his house. "I suppose I don't think about it that much. It's been in my family for generations, and it's not often that my parents go away and I get it all to myself."

"I guess this is our lucky weekend then," Tally chirped. She inspected Rando's outfit. He was wearing a black tuxedo with a black shirt and black bowtie. "Hang on a minute; I thought this was a white party. What are you trying to do?"

"Stick out like a sore thumb?" Rando gave an adorably sheepish grin. "It was Jasper's idea: He insisted that I couldn't just blend into the crowd at my own party. I would have been perfectly happy that way, but Jas can be very insistent."

Tally beamed at Rando, her sea-gray eyes glowing. Of course Rando would have been happy blending in. He wasn't out to be a hero or a stud. That was why he sat at the back of the Paper Bandits and played the drums. That was why he'd been so modest about rescuing Alice and Dylan. "Why don't you give us the grand tour?" she said, linking her arm through his.

"Right this way." Rando led them into the lofty front hall, which was decorated with candles, lanterns, and balloons. Streamers ran up and down the grand staircase. Throngs of people dressed in white were dashing round, laughing and drinking and smoking and dancing to grime. Alice recognized students from boarding schools like Malbury Hall, St. Swithin's, Glendale's, and Rando's former school, Stoke, as well as St. Cecilia's and Hasted House.

"Not a bad turnout so far, is it?" Rando yelled above the noise. "My friends from Stoke decided to hire a coach to drive them here, and they all got wasted on the way. I reckon it's gonna be a wild night. Cheers!" He knocked back a huge gulp of booze.

"Cheers!" Tally responded, and caught Alice's eye. Excellent. Rando was on his way to being exactly where she wanted him.

"So, birthday boy," she said, sauntering closer with a naughty gleam in her eye. "I hear you have a pool. Why don't you show us where we can strip off?"

Dylan tiptoed out of the changing room and into the Randall-Stubbses magnificent pool suite, trying not to look as self-conscious as she felt. Judging from the mirror she'd just checked, her new white one-piece swimsuit made her boobs seem even more enormous than usual. She looked like a sack of soccer balls, for fuck's sake, even though the saleswoman had assured her this suit was "body sculpting." What was it supposed to sculpt you into? A half-melted snowman? Whose stupid idea had it been to have a white party, anyway? Definitely some perverted boy's.

Dylan screwed her eyes shut and sat at the edge of the

pool. Speaking of boys, she'd been here almost forty-five minutes and still hadn't laid eyes on Jasper. In fact, she'd hardly heard from him all week, apart from a couple of lame texts, and she was worried. That family shitshow last Sunday had been enough to put anyone off—who'd want to go out with a girl who had a stepdad like Victor Dalgleish? But, no, Jasper had probably just been busy. After all, he was a popular guy. And he had rugby to practice. And it took a lot of energy to organize a big party like this.

For the hundredth time, Dylan put her fingers to her newly wavy hair. She'd made a special effort to look gorgeous tonight, with Farah and Emilia's help. She'd worn a white halter-neck dress that her friends back home always said made her look like Marilyn Monroe. The hair and the red lipstick she'd put on were supposed to dramatize the effect.

Lighting a cigarette from the pack at her side, Dylan gazed around. Without a doubt, she was in one of the most beautiful rooms she'd ever seen. Three of its sides were glass and looked out into a stunning walled garden that shone with landscaped spotlights. The ceiling was arched and supported by old, marble columns. Giant stone urns were scattered around the pool, their leafy plants trailing over the marble floor. On the fourth side of the room, set back from the water, was a fireplace flanked by a bar and clusters of couches and chairs. Hidden speakers blared out music. Melissa and Olivia Wyndham-Rhodes gyrated to it as they sipped from champagne flutes and Dylan snickered.

Those two sisters were ridiculous; Jasper had told her all about them at YLB.

Suddenly, Dylan's smile froze. There he was. Jasper.

He was sitting near the fire, scrunched up very close to a pretty blonde on a chair that was clearly meant for one. He was definitely flirting. Dylan watched him give that bitch the same playful smiles that he'd used to seduce her. She watched him reach out and touch the necklace dangling between the girl's boobs. Dylan's blood boiled with rage. Then, the next second, her rage melted into desolation. Maybe Jas had lost interest now that they'd slept together. Maybe he was onto his next target. Wasn't that, like, the nightmare story every girl got warned about before she gave it up? Dylan shook her head. No—Jasper really liked her, he'd said so. He'd said it *after* she'd told him she wanted to sleep with him. So why would he lie?

"Woo-hoo! Hot bikini," someone called out, whistling.

Miserably, Dylan looked round. George Demetrios was leering at Alice Rochester, who'd just skipped out of the changing room.

"In your dreams, George," Alice called, swinging her hips like a catwalk model.

"I was talking about Sonia."

"Ew!" Sonia squawked. "Keep your hairy paws off me."

Behind her, Mimah and Tally tittered.

"Watch out!" cried a voice. Freddie Frye whizzed past like a skinny, bucktoothed horse, hurled himself off the edge of the pool, curled into a cannonball, and landed in the water with an almighty splash.

"Seven out of ten!" roared Tom Huntleigh.

"Oh, for fuck's sake." Sonia stamped her foot and glared at Tom, even though he looked fit in his white swim trunks—probably from all the rugby he'd been playing. "Don't you dare have a splash competition. I won't stand for it!"

"Sit down, then," Tom smirked.

"Oh, shut up," Sonia said. But she settled down by the side of the pool and coiled her hair round one shoulder, just like a graceful, lovelorn mermaid. Now all she needed was her prince.

"Looking for Seb?"

"Wha—?" Sonia jumped. Mimah was crouching next to her. "Oh. It's you. Maybe you should stick your nose in your *own* business, little Miss *Cambridge*."

"Whatever," Mimah snorted. She'd told the gang about her meeting with Mr. Vicks the other day and was beginning to wish she hadn't. "You're so transparent. Oh, but . . . hang on, I thought Seb ran away from you when you kissed before. Don't you think that was, I don't know, a hint or something?"

Sonia tossed her head. "For your information, I've already told you my theory about that: Seb was psychologically disturbed in his father's wine cellar. Tonight we're at Rando's house, and he's never been here before, so it won't have any mental associations. It's neutral territory. Now, if you'll excuse me. . . ."

Sonia scanned the room for her darling. At last her eyes

found him. He was sitting by the fire, drinking beer, and talking to Marcus Hungerford, that leechy boy from the Young Leaders Ball. Sonia splashed her foot in the water. Hopefully that would make Seb notice her. Hopefully he'd spot her in a second and come rushing over.

"I don't think so!" bellowed a voice at the other end of the pool. Sonia jumped, then noticed that Tristan and George Demetrios were play wrestling, struggling to dunk each other's heads under the water.

"Alice, Sone, help!" Tristan bellowed, straining toward the girls.

Sonia giggled.

"Children," Alice muttered, rolling her eyes.

"Gotcha!" George howled, grabbing T's hair. "Oh my god, can you imagine if Brigadier Jones saw us now? Next weekend is the biggest rugby match of the year and here we are drinking our asses off and trying to drown each other. He'd have a fit."

"Oh, shit," T said, yanking himself free of George's grip. "Don't talk about the match."

"Why? Are your parents coming, by the way?"

"No, they're in Paris, thank fuck. But I'm still totally shitting it. We've got to win or we'll be letting everyone down—especially Alice and the girls. We can't let all their cheering go to waste."

Alice folded her arms. "Interesting. You seem pretty confident that we'll be there and that we'll be on your side. I guess you'd better make sure you're a good boyfriend till then."

"I'm always a good boyfriend." T grinned.

"Yeah. Whatever."

Tristan studied her, his smile fading. He'd thought they were just joking around, but Alice looked dead serious. Girls— he'd never understand them. What on earth was wrong now? PMS? He hoped not—if Alice had her period, it would make his plans for later a whole lot more complicated. He thought of the key he'd hidden in his pocket, in his pile of clothes in the changing room. . . .

"Come on, you wimp," George boomed, interrupting T's thoughts. "Since you lost our wrestling so badly, maybe you can redeem yourself in a diving competition. Al, will you judge?"

"Fine," Alice shrugged, stretching out a long, tanned leg. "But make it good, or I might fall asleep."

Her eyes stayed glued to Tristan as he hoisted himself out of the pool, his expression as excited as a little boy's. His body was dripping wet. His torso gleamed. But Alice folded her arms. She wasn't going to let T's hotness distract her from her goal: to make him repent for his behavior last Saturday.

"Ready?" George bellowed. His voice was so loud that several of the other swimmers jumped to attention.

"Yippee! Go, George," cried the Wyndham-Rhodes twins, who were wearing matching crochet bikinis. They linked arms and danced a cancan of encouragement.

"Thank you, ladies." George made an elaborate bow and took a running start from the back of the diving board. He leapt into the air, turned two somersaults, and landed in a dive.

"Hoorah!" cheered the spectators.

"My turn," called T, flexing his chest. "Ali, are you ready? Watch me! This is for you."

"Oi, no fair!" George waved his fist. "No influencing the judge."

Tristan flipped him the finger. Then he positioned himself backward at the edge of the diving board. He bent his knees. Alice watched his muscles strain. She ran her eyes over his tight butt and his beautiful, strong back.

With a graceful movement, T sprang off the board. He turned a backflip in the air, then jackknifed into a front dive, his legs perfectly together. The audience burst into even louder applause than before.

"Tristan wins!" Alice howled, beaming despite herself. Her boyfriend was so skilled.

He cut toward her through the water. "Why don't you come in for a swim?"

"Maybe in a minute," Alice smiled coyly.

"Hm . . . Or maybe now!" Tristan cried, grabbing her.

"Eee!" Alice squealed. Her drink spilled into the pool, but she didn't care. Tristan's arms felt so good around her, so hard and strong. Her bikini hardly covered anything and neither did his swim trunks. They were about as undressed as they could get in public and it was hot. Alice kissed him. She felt his tongue in her mouth.

"Oi," protested George Demetrios. "You two, get a room!"

He splashed them. Alice splashed him back. Suddenly, they

were at war. Shrieks and yells filled the cavernous room and arms and legs flailed in the water.

"Ow!" cried someone as Alice rammed into the side of the pool.

"Oh." Alice tossed her soaking-wet hair. "Dylan." *Why don't you and your boobs stay out of the bloody way?* Force of habit pushed the bitchy words to the tip of her tongue. Then Dylan glanced back to where she'd been gazing before and Alice followed her eyes.

She frowned. There was Jasper, lounging by the fire, practically drooling over another girl. One guess what that meant: Dylan had gone all the way with him last weekend and now he'd lost interest—as always—and left another heartbroken conquest in his wake.

Alice sighed, remembering last Saturday in the bathroom at Sketch.

"Hey, babe," she said suddenly, digging her elbow into Dylan's ribs. "What are you standing on the sidelines for? Get in the fight! Help me beat the boys!"

Dylan stared at her. Then, all of a sudden, light broke over her face. "Let's get 'em!" she cried, slapping Alice five.

The once-serene pool now looked like a stormy sea. Water flew everywhere. Arms and legs flailed. The tiles were soaked.

"Oh, shit!" Tally cried, skidding as she returned from the bar with a fresh rum and Coke. "My drink—it's spilled all down my front. Oh well, only one thing to do."

Deftly, she untied the strings at the back of her bikini top and whipped it off, flinging it across the room.

"Bravo!" bawled George Demetrios, together with a crew of Glendale's boys.

Tally gave them a topless twirl.

Looking up a second later, she saw Rando. He was standing on the other side of the pool, staring right at her. Then, as he noticed her watching him, his cheeks flamed red and he blinked away.

Cheers! Tally toasted herself with what was left of her drink. So far so good. And the night had just begun.

CHAPTER THIRTY-NINE

George Demetrios drained the dregs of his beer and waved the bottle in the air. "Number thirteen!" he burped. "I am the champion."

"Oh. My. God," Sonia sneered from the opposite side of the circle, crossing her fingers in front of her to ward him off. "The champion of freaks, you mean. How can you drink thirteen bottles of beer? I'd die if I drank that much."

"Yeah, you probably would," George slurred. "But I'm a big powerful man and you're a dainty little lady. Tiny as a bird. *Cheep cheep.*"

"How rude," Sonia retorted, struggling to keep the self-satisfied smile off her face. She couldn't let George realize, but she really did adore it when people called her tiny. After all, she spent every waking moment resisting delicious chocolates and cakes and pastries and pastas and potatoes so she could look like this. It was gratifying when people noticed.

George reached for another bottle of beer. It was four in the morning and the whole crew was lounging on cushions around the fire in one of the Randall-Stubbses dens. The party was still rocking. A few people had passed out on sleeping bags, a few more were snoring on random pieces of furniture, and several couples had disappeared to hidden nooks and crannies—but most of the guests were still going strong.

"Wait just one minute," Jasper said. He caught hold of George's bottle before George could chuck it into a corner. "Did you say this was your thirteenth bottle? That makes it lucky, mate. We should put it to good use."

George grinned. "Hmmm, interesting. I wonder how we should do that? Maybe if I spin it, it'll land on the person I want to snog."

"Oh my god, Spin the Bottle!" Tally clapped her hands. "I haven't played that in ages. Do it, do it, do it!"

Seb chuckled drunkenly into a mostly empty bottle of Jameson. Alice giggled. She loved this part of the night, when everyone lost their inhibitions and anything could happen.

"Go. Go. Go. Go. Go," the group chanted and George placed his bottle on the rug. Ten pairs of eyes stared as he flicked his wrist and the beer bottle whirled and whirled, slower, slower, until it finally stopped.

"Sonia," Alice screeched. "That's definitely you."

"Snog, snog, snog," Tally and Mimah chanted.

"Nooo!" Sonia shrieked. She folded her arms over her white jumpsuit. "Oh my god, this is so unfair. George Demetrios,

KATE KINGSLEY

you totally rigged that. You've been wanting to kiss me all evening."

"Didn't look like he rigged it to me," Tristan grinned, taking a gulp of gin and tonic. "Did it look like he rigged it to anyone else?"

"Nope." Jasper shook his head.

"Nope."

"Nope."

"You've got to do it," Mimah added. "Or there's a penalty."

"Yeah," Tally jumped in. "If you refuse to kiss someone, you have to run naked round our entire circle."

"Hear, hear!" Rando drummed his fists on the floor and Tristan clapped his hands.

"Go on, Sone, get your clothes off, then."

"Why are we waiiitiiing? We are suffocaaatiiing. . . ."

"Ugh. *Fine.*" Sonia stood up. "Come on, you stupid caveman, let's get this over with." She grimaced as George Demetrios lumbered into the middle of the circle and slid his arm round her waist. Tilting her chin up, she closed her eyes, bracing for a horrible, slobbering tongue.

But the next thing she felt was George's lips press gently on hers. Without thinking, Sonia parted her mouth and breathed in. George smelled kind of sexy. His stubble brushed her skin. It felt rough and prickly, but manly, too—so different from Seb's boyish, hairless face.

After a few seconds he pulled away and Sonia opened her eyes. She swayed on the spot.

268

"Wooo!" Insinuating catcalls rose from the rest of the gang. Flashes from pocket cameras went off in all directions.

"That was hot, guys," Alice heckled, waving the picture on her iPhone. "Want to do it again? You could always go into the broom cupboard."

Sonia sneaked a glance at George. He was grinning widely and sticking out his tongue like a demented baby. Rolling her eyes, she shoved him in the gut.

"Idiot," she huffed, lowering herself to her cushion as gracefully as possible. But George's taste still lingered in her mouth.

"My turn," said Jasper, grabbing hold of the bottle.

Next to her, Alice felt Dylan stiffen and knock back most of her drink.

Jasper spun.

"Tally!" everyone cried. "It's Tally. Snog, snog, snog, snog."

In the middle of the circle, Jasper took hold of Tally's belt and tugged her toward him, grinning.

"Ready, babe?"

Tally cracked up. "Ready."

They kissed for at least ten seconds, with the cheering growing louder every moment. Jasper swooped Tally backward and slid his hands down her body. Cameras flashed. Finally, Rando leaned forward and pushed them apart.

"All right, you two, break it up. That's enough."

"Oi," Jasper protested. "I was enjoying myself."

Dylan gripped her plastic cup so hard that it crunched in the middle. Why were boys so fucking insensitive?

"Yeah, no shit you were enjoying it," Rando replied. "That's exactly why I had to put a stop to it—there's only so much I can take of watching my cousin stick his tongue down someone's throat."

Tally's eyes sparkled as she plopped back onto her cushion. Rando had yanked her and Jas apart! That must mean he was jealous. Which meant he liked her. His excuse about Jasper being his cousin was completely lame. She hugged herself, thinking of the special bottle of champagne she'd brought with her and hidden in the depths of the house . . .

"I'll take that," Alice declared. She grabbed the bottle from Jasper and blew on it for luck. "Give me someone good. Give me someone good," she chanted, placing it on the rug.

Tristan chuckled. "Someone good? I guess that's me, then. Who else here would you want to kiss?" He sparked up the joint he'd just rolled. "Don't answer that."

Alice grinned, watching the bottle spin, then get slower, slower, slower . . .

"Mimah!" everyone roared.

"Oh, shit!"

"You blowing on the bottle must have made it lucky for me!" George Demetrios rhapsodized. "I've been wanting to see two babes get it on all night."

"And every night," Seb said, elbowing him.

Alice blushed. "Well, don't count on too much of a kiss," she said, giving Mimah an eye roll as they entered the circle. Mimah grinned. A silence fell over the group as she and Alice stepped right up close to each other, their bodies almost grazing, but not quite. Alice closed her eyes and felt Mimah's mouth brush hers. It was soft—incredibly soft—much softer than a boy's. She had the urge to reach up and touch Mimah's short black bob, but then she remembered where she was, and who she was kissing, and stepped back.

The biggest cheer so far rose up from the group.

"Niiicely done," George Demetrios called.

"Damn nice!" added Jasper. The next second, he narrowed his eyes as Dylan picked up the bottle and, without looking at anyone, gave it a spin. The next minute, she and Tristan were standing opposite each other in the middle of the circle.

"The exes face off!" George bellowed.

"For fuck's sake," Alice snapped, "why do you always have to be so loud?" Okay, so she'd changed her stance on Dylan, but that didn't mean she wanted the girl to go round snogging *her* boyfriend. She poured herself another G and T.

Tristan and Dylan stepped toward each other. Their lips met. Jasper's jaw tightened. No—he couldn't watch—even though it was a game and even though he'd been doing his best all week to get Dylan out of his head. He fumbled for his cigarettes. Tonight had been difficult enough already: the moment when Dylan had ambled over to the pool in that hot white bathing suit that showed off all her curves. . . . It hadn't even been a bikini, but it was still one of the hottest things he'd ever seen.

"Whose go is it now?" Jasper snapped, fiercely striking a match.

"Give it here, I'll take a spin," Rando grinned. "I'm beginning to feel left out that I haven't snogged."

"Awww, poor randy Rando," Mimah cackled. "Hasn't had a snog. Don't worry, we'll fix that."

Taking a last toke of the joint he was holding, Rando passed it on to Seb and claimed the bottle. It whirled round, round, round, then slowed and was still.

"Who's that on?" Mimah squinted.

Everyone leaned closer. The bottle was pointing to a space between Jasper and Alice.

"Definitely Jasper," Tally blurted.

"No way," Sonia argued, "it's Alice. It's *so* Alice."

"Jasper!"

"Yeah, Jasper."

"Alice. No question about it."

Alice chuckled amid the debate. She turned to wink at Rando across the circle—but, as soon as their eyes met, something sparked. He immediately flicked his gaze away. Alice's face flushed hot. She covered her cheeks with her palms. What the hell was going on?

At that moment: "It's Jasper," Seb declared. He'd borrowed Tally's belt and used it to measure who was closest to the bottle.

"Bloody hell," Rando groaned. "You mean I'm supposed to kiss my cousin? That is *wrong*. I refuse."

"You can't refuse!" Mimah tittered. "Unless you want the penalty, that is. . . . Anyway, in some places it's legal to marry your cousin. So it's fine."

"Rank." Rando stood up. "I think I'll take the penalty, thanks."

"Penalty! Penalty!"

"It's the full monty. No excuses."

"Strip! Strip! Strip! Strip!"

Everyone started hooting as Rando pulled off his T-shirt, followed by his jeans. Tally stared at his bare chest. His body was pale and smooth, lean and muscular. Her heart beat faster as the rest of his clothes came off.

"Don't watch, you perverts!" Rando guffawed, taking off round the circle, totally nude, amid screams of hysterical laughter. Just as he finished and grabbed his boxer shorts, Tom Huntleigh showed up.

"High five, Rando," T called, reaching across the group. "That was brave. Respect."

"Respect for what?" Tom asked. "Mates, I can hear your racket from three rooms away. What the fuck's going on?" Peering into the middle of the circle, he whistled. "Spin the Bottle? Bring it on. Can I play?"

"Of course," declared T, still shaking with giggles at Rando's display.

Tom crouched next to Tally and sent the beer bottle wheeling.

"Come on!" he urged it. "Come on, bottle, give me someone

good. Oh, shit!" The bottle had stopped and was pointing directly at Seb.

"Yes!" George Demetrios guffawed. "I guess it serves you right for elbowing into our game. Ha."

Seb chewed his lip as he and Tom stumbled into the circle. Tom was his friend—they had economics together and had always gotten along. But, more than that, Tom was hot. He was tall and sturdy, with sandy-colored hair like Prince Harry's and a bright white smile.

"You've got to kiss properly, now," Jasper said. "Like Mimah and Alice. None of this pecking on the mouth and running away."

"Exactly," Mimah agreed. "At least five seconds. That's what Al and I did."

"Oh, Christ," Tom groaned, slapping his forehead and looking at Seb. "Mate, what have I got us into? I'm sorry about this."

"It's all part of the game," Seb murmured, stepping closer, looking up at Tom's lips. He closed his eyes and, after a moment, felt Tom's mouth meet his. He felt the rasp as their chins grazed.

He felt how right it was.

Flash. Someone snapped a picture.

"Tongues!" someone heckled from the circle. "We want tongues."

Both boys opened their mouths. Seb reached up and touched Tom's hard, strong arm, just for the briefest of seconds. Then Tom broke away.

KISS & BREAK UP

"Phew," he said, shooting Seb a relieved grin. "Thank fuck that's over."

"Yeah," echoed Seb. "Thank fuck."

Tristan yawned. "I don't know about anyone else, but I reckon I'm just about done watching other people slobber down each other's throats. Hey, gorgeous," he whispered, leaning against Alice and nuzzling her ear, "guess what I saw earlier on, when the boys and I got here this afternoon to set up?"

Alice giggled. "What?"

"A summerhouse out in the grounds. It's beautiful, all glassed in. And it has a sofa. I checked."

"Hmmm, maybe you should show me," Alice purred. As she kissed T and got to her feet, she heard Tally's voice from a few feet away:

"Oh look, Rando darling, your glass is empty."

"Yeah, I s'pose it is."

"Hey! I have an idea," Tally said. "I've just remembered, I left a bottle of lovely champagne up in one of the bedrooms. It's in my overnight bag. Why don't we go and find it?"

She took Rando by the hand. "Night T. Night Al," she said, giving Alice a wink as the four of them strolled, in two couples, out of the den.

CHAPTER FORTY

*I*t's locked," Alice groaned, shivering as she rattled the door to the summerhouse. "Great. It's, like, five a.m. All the beds in the house will be taken. Now what are we supposed to do?"

"Hmmm . . . I guess there's only one thing we *can* do," Tristan winked, his eyes sparkling as he slipped his hand into his jeans pocket. "Unlock it." He pulled out an old iron key.

"T!" Alice bounced on the balls of her feet. "Have you been hiding that all night?"

"If keeping it in my pocket constitutes hiding, then, yeah, I guess I have." Chuckling with delight, Tristan kissed her. "I knew we'd want somewhere private to, ahem, *sleep*, and when I found this place, I just had to . . . well . . . you'll see. Go in."

His smiled confidently as Alice pushed the glass door and stepped onto the summerhouse's wooden floorboards.

"Oh, T," she gasped. "It's lovely."

Tristan had turned the place into the world's most romantic

hideaway: He'd piled the couch with pillows, duvets, and quilts so it looked like a bed. He'd picked flowers from the garden and arranged them in vases on every table and shelf. Their perfume filled the room. He'd laid out a bottle of red wine, together with two crystal glasses. And there were candles everywhere.

"Babe," Alice breathed, as T began to light them, "where did you get all these? You must have scavenged them from all over Rando's house."

T looked bashful. "Actually, these were Seb's idea. He remembered how much you like candles and all that stuff. So, what do you think?"

"I love it." Alice draped herself over the sofa, her hair tumbling over her shoulders, her white dress unbuttoned as far as was decent. Not that it would stay decent for long.

"And I love *you*," T whispered, kicking off his shoes and lowering himself on top of her.

The candles flickered and reflected in the dark glass windows, making the summerhouse glitter like a jewel box. It was hidden in the dip of a hill five minutes' walk from the manor, so Alice knew that she and T could make love for hours without anyone finding them.

Tristan unbuttoned her dress all the way to her navel and slipped his hands inside. He bent down and kissed the soft flesh of her stomach.

"Wait," Alice whispered, looking into his soft, hazel eyes. "I want us to be naked." She tugged at T's clothes.

He yanked her dress over her head.

"Careful! You'll tear it," Alice hissed. "It's new."

"Sorry," T murmured, drawing his hands away.

He watched as Alice stripped off her silky pink bra and silky pink panties. In a few seconds there wasn't a shred of fabric between them. T's body glowed in the candlelight: his skin a light caramel, his eyes dancing with the flames. Alice kissed him deeply, pressing into him, savoring the warmth of his skin in the coolness of the room.

"Let's do it now," she whispered. "Right now." *Before anything can go wrong*, she added in her head.

"Yeah," T breathed. He slid a condom from his jeans pocket, put it on, and rolled back on top of her.

"Ow, ouch," Alice croaked. "You're too heavy. You're crushing me."

"Shit, sorry." T propped his weight on his elbows. "Better?" he breathed into Alice's neck. Heat rippled down her skin.

"Yeah."

The next second, he was inside her. Alice gasped as pain and pleasure both shot down her body at once. She gripped T's strong arms. "Does it feel good?" she winced, closing her eyes.

"Better than good," T whispered. "I love you." He kissed her eyelids, her nose, her lips—kissing away the hurt, kissing away the fear. Alice sank her head into the pillows, starting to relax. The feeling of Tristan was unlike anything she'd ever known. He was on top of her, underneath her, inside her.

She grabbed his back and thrust upward, deeper, deeper. It was like her body knew exactly what to do, exactly what it wanted.

But then T groaned—and, almost as soon as it had begun, it was over. Shuddering, Tristan pressed his face into Alice's hair where it lay spread on the pillow. His body slackened.

"Hey." Alice stroked his shoulder blade. "Um, are you okay?"

T nodded.

"What happened?"

"I, uh . . ." Tristan's voice was muffled. "Sorry, I couldn't help it—I guess I got overexcited and, er . . ."

"Oh," Alice whispered. She listened to T's breathing, trying not to feel disappointed as he lay tangled in her arms. First times were hardly ever good; everyone knew that. Mimah had told her she'd slept with three different boys before she'd got it right. But still, Alice had wanted everything to be amazing. What was the point in waiting so long to lose your virginity if it wasn't going to be incredible?

"Don't feel bad," she whispered, as much to herself as to T, smoothing back a lock of his chestnut hair. "Practice makes perfect. We can practice again in the morning. I love you," she added.

But T's eyelids fluttered. He was already fast asleep.

Somewhere outside, a pheasant squawked. Wings flapped. Alice cracked open her eyes and immediately blinked them shut. Cold, piercing light was shining through the glass walls on every side. The summerhouse smelled of burnt-out candles. Her nose was cold. In fact, her whole body was cold.

"T," she whispered, snuggling over. But where T's body should have been, there was nothing but a piece of plastic, rustling under her fingers. Huh? Alice's eyes popped open. A condom wrapper. Frowning, she reached for her phone—it was quarter past nine and she had a text.

YAY!!! Tally had written.

Alice rubbed her temples. It didn't take a genius to work out what that meant: Something had happened with Rando last night. Something big. Something good.

Suddenly, a figure strode through the door.

"Who's there?" Alice screamed, snatching the duvet.

"It's only me," Tristan laughed, flinging himself down beside her. He was already wearing his jeans. "Sorry, I left the door open. Brrr, it's freezing." Snuggling under the blankets, he kissed Alice's cheek. "We haven't even had breakfast and today is already a great day. I'm so happy!"

"Mmm. Me too." Alice kissed him and stretched luxuriantly.

"Really?" T propped up on one elbow and gave her a perplexed smile. "How come? What happened? I thought you were asleep."

"Huh?" Alice's forehead creased. "I was. I was talking about last night. I mean, this morning. You know . . ."

"Oh, yeah." T chuckled. "Duh. Silly me."

"Excuse me?" Alice inquired, narrowing her eyes.

"My mind was totally on something else," Tristan said, taking Alice's hand, playing with her fingers. "I meant I was happy about the phone call I just got. It was Dick Crawley, the agent? He's got *Stella* magazine on board to do an interview with us. He pitched us as a hot young group and they bought it!" T leapt to his feet. "Hey, what are we doing in here? Let's run to the house and tell the others. Or, no, maybe I'll just text them; it's kind of cold out. Hey, Al, could you— Al? What's wrong?"

Alice was staring at the ceiling, her arms flat against her sides, her jaw clenched. "Wrong?" she repeated. "Oh, nothing. Nothing's wrong. Why should anything be wrong?" Abruptly, she turned on her side.

"Al," T sighed. "Ali, don't be all girly like that. What did I do?"

"Nothing!" Alice almost shrieked, shoving him away. "It's what you didn't do."

"Huh?"

"Like just now—you didn't even remember that we had sex last night."

"Of course I remembered!"

"It took you ten seconds to get what I was happy about. You didn't bother to be here when I woke up this morning, and—"

"I got a phone call," T objected, looking baffled and indignant. "I ran outside so it wouldn't wake you up."

281

"A phone call about your band," Alice yelled. "Why can't you turn your fucking phone *off*, once in a while? That band is ruining my fucking life." She couldn't stop herself. She was tired, hungover, irritable—it was all coming out now. "Last weekend at Sketch it was supposed to be our special date and you were late and you brought the others and went on about your photo shoot the whole time—how do you think that made me feel? And the weekend before, when we were about to . . . you know . . . and your stupid agent interrupted. And the Young Leaders Ball—do you know how I felt when you played that song? About your backyard?"

"But—but I wrote that song for you." T threw his hands in the air. "I don't get it—I thought it was romantic."

"Oh. Yeah. It's really romantic that you think I've just been 'waiting' for you in your bushes for the past ten years. What do you think I am? Your pet goat?"

Tristan burst out laughing.

Alice's jaw dropped. "Oh my god, that is *it*!" she cried, grabbing her clothes and pulling them on under the covers. "I can't believe you're laughing at me. I'm pouring my heart out, trying to tell you how hurt I feel, and all you can do is *laugh*."

"Ali, Alice, wait. I thought you were trying to be funny . . . I . . . I . . ." Tristan clutched his hair in dismay as Alice threw back the duvet, grabbed her shoes, and left, slamming the glass door behind her.

CHAPTER FORTY-ONE

The quarter past seven bell for Prep echoed through the stone courtyards of Hasted House. Footsteps pounded in the corridors as streams of boys rushed back to their rooms, racing to reach their desks before they got bollocked by housemasters on patrol.

A knock came at Seb and Tristan's door.

"C'min," Seb called.

"All right, guys, it's me," Rando said, sticking his head inside. "Oh, Seb, hey. Is T around?"

"Yeah. Here," Tristan grunted, straightening up at his desk, over which he'd been hunched for the past half hour.

Rando laughed. "Sorry, mate, didn't see you! What are you hiding for? George and I are gonna do our Italian prep together and we were wondering if you wanted to join?"

"Oh. No." Tristan dragged a hand through his hair, which was looking even messier than usual. "I mean, thanks for asking, but I'm in the middle of something."

Rando shrugged. "Cool. Well, good luck with that. I'll try not to be offended. See ya later, boys."

"What'd I tell you?" Seb asked, grinning as the door clicked shut behind Rando. "He's been looking well pleased with himself since the weekend. He and Tally must have shagged, even though he's refusing to tell anyone. Don't you think? T?"

"Yeah, whatever," Tristan snapped, letting his pen fall. "Whatever you say, I really couldn't care less." He grabbed his iPhone, checked it, and slammed it back on the desk. Why couldn't Alice just call him back? It was two days since their spat on Sunday and he hadn't managed to get a word out of her in all that time. Why was she being such a fucking drama queen? Tristan snorted to himself. Stupid question. Alice was always a drama queen. He'd known her for sixteen years and she'd never been anything else.

"Mate." Seb shook his head. "Look, I'm sorry you're upset about this whole thing with Alice, but—"

"Upset?" Tristan interrupted. "I'm not upset, I'm fucking furious. I should have known this would happen—no matter how much effort I make, Alice always goes crazy if things doesn't go exactly her way." He rubbed his eyes and massaged his temples.

Seb sighed. Yeah, right: T wasn't upset at all. . . .

"And this is the annoying thing," Tristan ranted on, "I used to be able to laugh at this shit when Alice and I were just friends. Her over-the-top outbursts were a challenge, but

I could talk her out of them. But now—fuck." Slumping his head, he pounded his fists on the desk.

Seb swung his chair back onto two legs. T usually needed to calm down a bit before he'd talk about his feelings—Seb knew that much from experience.

"T," he said, "I'm sorry you're feeling so miserab— I mean, angry. Let me know if there's anything I can do."

"Yeah. Thanks."

As T stared toward his bed, wishing he could climb into it, pull the covers over his head, and turn off the lights, he caught sight of something sticking out from under the bed frame. He squinted. Oh, great—it was Alice's banner. The one she'd made him for the Glendale's match that year. He kicked it out of sight. What if Alice didn't come on Saturday? She had to. She'd always brought him luck. Glaring, T turned back to his notepad and set about scribbling again.

After a few minutes he leapt up, looking self-satisfied.

"Oi, Seb."

"Mm-hmm?"

"Listen. I just wrote a song. Want to hear it?"

Seb blinked up from his computer. "Uh-oh. Is this about what I think it's about?"

Tristan shrugged innocently. "I don't know. What do you think it's about?"

"Come on, T—I told you not to keep writing songs about Alice. Didn't I warn you she might get upset?"

Tristan shrugged. "Yeah, well, here's one she can't get upset about, cause she's never gonna hear it." He rubbed his nose aggressively. "Ready? It's called 'Kiss & Break Up.'"

He seized his guitar, but as soon as he started singing, it became obvious that the strumming was just background noise to his shouting lyrics:

> *"Whatever I do,*
> *It's never enough.*
> *When I make things smooth,*
> *You complain they're rough.*
> *When I'm having a laugh,*
> *You throw a tantrum and cry.*
> *When I say hello,*
> *You shout good-bye.*
> *Have you ever been wrong?*
> *No, you're always right!*
> *'Cause you'll never back down,*
> *You won't lose a fight.*
> *Well, it's time to shape up,*
> *It's time to get wise.*
> *You can't be my lover*
> *If you won't compromise."*

Suddenly, the music became even more frenzied.

> *"You should want to kiss and make up—*
> *You're my lover and my friend.*

But you'd rather kiss and break up,
And stay smug till the end!
Most people kiss and make up
To make a fight end.
But you'd rather kiss and break up—
You'd rather break than bend!"

"So," T panted. He was winded with the effort of practically screaming the last words. "What do you think?"

Seb didn't answer.

"Seb!" Tristan barked. Then he saw that Seb's ears were blocked by his noise-canceling headphones. Bastard! The boy must have sneaked them on just to wind him up. Well, he was in for a shock. Stealthily, T crept up behind Seb's desk. He reached out to snatch the headphones and yell in Seb's ear. Then he halted, confused. Seb was looking at Facebook—at pictures of Rando's party, to be precise. But he wasn't looking at normal pictures—not ones of people swimming or dancing or pouting. He was staring at a shot of himself during Spin the Bottle—a shot of him and Tom Huntleigh, kissing. Tristan furrowed his forehead. He wavered behind Seb for a good ten seconds. Then:

"Hey!" he called, chucking his guitar-pick at his best friend's head. "What are you doing? What's so fascinating about you having to snog Tom? Trying to relive the romance, are we?"

"Oh!" Seb pulled off his earphones and fumbled to close the page. "No way, dude. Kissing a guy was gross. I was just reminding myself of what happened at Rando's party—I was so pissed, I forgot half the shit that went down." He chuckled. "Crazy night."

Tristan studied him thoughtfully. "Yeah," he said at last, "it was a crazy night."

CHAPTER FORTY-TWO

"*M*ime, you can't disappear *now*," Tally complained, frowning as Mimah ran past the common room door, throwing on a plaid duffel jacket. It was one o'clock on Saturday and lessons had just ended for the week. "You've got to help us finish the poster."

"Sorry, can't." Mimah slipped a hand into her pocket, apparently checking for something. "I have an appointment. But, don't worry," she added, seeing that Tally was about to protest, "I'll be back in time to get to the match."

"You'd better be!" Sonia called. "You've only got half an hour. And we're not making ourselves late just so we can wait for you!"

But Mimah was already gone.

"Fantastic," Sonia grumbled. "Now it's just the two of us." She glared at the jumble of paints and poster paper and color markers that she and Tally had dumped on the coffee table.

"How are we supposed to make a fabulous banner for the boys with such limited resources? Maybe we should hire some sixth graders to do it for us. Or at least to do the menial work."

Tally rolled her eyes and sat for a minute, looking thoughtful. "What kind of appointment could Mimah have now?" she mused. "It's lunchtime. All the teachers will be taking a break."

"Hmph," Sonia pouted, hacking at a bit of paper with a gigantic pair of scissors. "Who cares! She's probably gone to the library to study up for Mr. Vicks and *Cambridge*. Who'd have thought Mimah would be such a goody-goody? I can think of plenty of people more talented than her who aren't being given the same attention. *Ahem*." She cleared her throat. "Maybe I should file a complaint."

Tally ignored her. "I swear," she mused, "that girl's been acting so weird recently. I've been trying to get her to open up about it ever since fall break, but you know what she's like. I can't work out what her problem is."

"Maybe she's a lesbo," Sonia smirked. "I saw the way she kissed Alice during Spin the Bottle. Maybe she's gone off to some secret lesbian society. Let's go ask Alice what she thinks."

"OMG, grow up," Tally declared, tittering despite herself. "Anyway, you're just jealous that *you* weren't the one who got to snog Alice. You kiss her ass so much, you're practically gagging for it."

"I am not!" Sonia shrieked. "I'm gagging for *Seb*. I tried to snog him again at Rando's, but he disappeared."

"Whatever," Tally said. "Just leave Alice alone right now,

okay? She said she didn't want anything to do with the rugby match today, and, knowing you, you'll make her fly off the handle."

Mimah jogged across the stone patio that surrounded the theater, checking her pocket yet again. Yes, she'd remembered the map. She'd remembered the compass. It was five past one—she had ten minutes to get to Charlie's rendezvous point with FHB. That might be a push. It wasn't that the walk was so far, but she had to be furtive or she might bump into Charlie on the way. Plus, once she was in the woods, the map called for a bit of orientation. It was hand drawn, after all, and it didn't look like this meeting place was on any kind of path. Only morons met to do illicit things in obvious places like paths, after all. And Charlie was a lot of things, but she wasn't a moron. For a start, she'd learned rule breaking from a master.

Suddenly, as Mimah reached the corner of the theater at a run, she ran smack into a small, wiry figure.

"Ouch!" seethed a reedy voice. "Be careful where you're going."

Shit. Mimah stopped short. The Ho.

"Mrs. Hoare," she cried, breathing hard. "I'm so sorry. Are you okay?"

The Ho sucked in her cheeks. "I'm fine. I wish I could say the same for my coffee." She patted her frizzy, triangular haircut and glared down at a puddle of steaming brown liquid.

"Oh, dear," Mimah cried, "I am sorry. Please let me buy you another."

"No," Mrs. Hoare snapped, but she looked slightly appeased. "It only cost 30p from the vending machine in the theater." After a second, her eyes narrowed again. "Well, I can see you're feeling better this week."

"Better?"

"Why, yes. Miss Colin told me that last week you were convinced you were coming down with the flu. I said I hadn't noticed anything, but, then again, teenagers seem to recover from certain maladies very quickly indeed." She stared at Mimah, hard.

Mimah took a step back, forcing a smile. "Yeah, it's true, isn't it? My friend's older brother once broke his leg. They said it would take two months to heal, but four weeks later, he was back to playing rugby!"

Mrs. Hoare pursed her thin, overlipsticked lips. "What an inspiring tale. Speaking of rugby, I thought you'd be preparing for the match at Hasted House. What are you doing up here?"

"I'm, uh, just running an errand," Mimah said. "I think I left something in the auditorium."

The Ho frowned. "What did you leave? I was just in there teaching a Shakespeare class and I didn't see anything out of the ordinary."

"Oh, no, you wouldn't have, because it's very small. A very small necklace. Well, I'd best be off to look for it. Sorry again for bumping into you."

"Yes, well, make sure you're signed out before you leave the school grounds for the rugby. Or there'll be trouble."

"Will do. Bye," Mimah said, and strode round the corner. Thank fuck she'd shaken the Ho off. For a second there, she'd thought this was going to be a repeat of last Wednesday—a full-on teacher sabotage.

Up ahead were the barbed wire and the woods. Mimah skidded under the fence, dodging its vicious spikes, and threaded her way into the trees. She knew the woods well from years of sneaking out of school, but she moved slowly, cautiously, on the lookout for Charlie. Every so often a branch cracked behind her. Something rustled in the undergrowth. She stopped. Listened. These woods were full of animals, though: birds, rabbits, deer. There wasn't a human soul in sight.

Finally, Mimah checked her compass, took one last look at the map, and dropped them both in her pocket. FHB's drawing indicated a circle of tall, thin trees, exactly like the one in front of her. Stealthily she began to creep round it, toward the west. After a minute or so, she heard a giggle. Charlie's. Then she saw the end of a gigantic fallen treetrunk, its roots at least six feet tall. This was it. The spot.

Mimah inched closer over the dried leaves and ducked. She drew in her breath. There was Charlie. She was straddling the tree-trunk—and she was snogging someone. A boy. He had bright blond hair that contrasted with the dark blue of his Hasted House hoodie.

Suddenly, guilt hit Mimah like a punch. Shit. What an idiot. She was interrupting a date! She was spying on her own sister's love life. Slowly, she began to back away, but—what was that? Mimah squinted. The boy had pulled away from the kiss and was taking a small, orange cylinder from Charlie's hand. He opened it. He popped out a tablet. It looked like . . . It looked like—

"Charlie!" Mimah yelled, before she could stop herself. She stood up and crashed through the weeds to her sister. "Stop this right now."

The boy leapt up like someone had lit a fire under his ass.

"Jemimah?" Charlie's face was shocked. Horrified. "What are you doing here?"

"What are *you* doing here? And what the hell are these?" Mimah snatched the pill bottle from the boy and examined its prescription label. "Mrs. Theresa Calthorpe de Vyle-Hanswicke," she read, her voice shaking. And then the name of the drug. "Xanax. You *stole* these from Mummy? What the fuck? Do you know what they do to you?"

"Excuse me," said a posh male voice. "I know what they do to you and I'll tell you. They make you euphoric. Dreamy. Floating-on-a-cloud happy. Got a problem with that?"

"Yeah," Mimah spat, "because they also make you suicidal and aggressive and completely out of it. And they can kill you if you OD. No wonder you've been acting so weird recently, Charlie. Idiots!"

"But we've been using them responsibly," the boy insisted. His face was so roguish that Mimah might have thought it was cute if she hadn't been so enraged. "Charlie had me to take care of her. Why don't you try one? It's fun and you might chill out."

"Felix," Charlie warned. "Don't."

"Felix . . . ," Mimah whispered to herself. "Felix . . . Hey, what's your full name?" she demanded.

"Felix Hedley-Bunk," the boy announced, taking Charlie's hand. "Why?"

Mimah closed her eyes. Felix Hedley-Bunk. FHB. She looked at the pill bottle again. Xanax. *Xanax* . . . That text on Charlie's phone . . . "Can't w8. Xx awesome."

Oh my god. Of course. It all made sense: Awesome hadn't been a code name at all—Xx was the code name. It stood for Xanax. *Xanax is awesome.*

Mimah turned on Charlie. "Who is this? Is he your boyfriend?" she hissed. "And what the fuck are you doing with Mummy's prescription drugs? How long have you been stealing them? How long have you been taking them? How did—"

But before she could blurt another question, there came an unmistakeable sound. *Crunch. Crunch. Crunch.* Someone stomping over dead leaves.

"Jemimah!" called a sharp, reedy voice.

Mimah paled. "*Hide.*" She pointed to the tree root. "Behind there."

"Jemimah," shouted the voice again. "I know you're out here."

"Shit," Charlie whimpered.

"*Go*," Mimah ordered, shoving her.

Charlie grabbed Felix and dived to the forest floor. Mimah pushed the pills into the pocket of her duffel coat.

The next second, Mrs. Hoare appeared.

"*Jemimah*." The housemistress's eyes were glinting. "You're going to have a hard time explaining what you're doing out here, in the middle of the woods, off school grounds."

Mimah gulped. No, it was okay. The Ho had nothing on her.

"I-I'm sorry," she squeaked. "I just came out for a stroll. It was stupid but . . . but sometimes being at boarding school gets a bit much. I wanted some time alone."

The Ho folded her arms. "Do you really expect me to believe that sorry excuse for a lie? After you lied to me about losing something in the theater? After you lied to Miss Colin about being ill?"

"But it's true!"

"Don't even try. You came out here for some other reason. What was it?"

"Nothing." Mimah widened her eyes. "I swear."

"Were you smoking? Were you meeting someone?" Mrs. Hoare's expression narrowed. "You were meeting someone. That's it. Where is she? Or *he*." She took a step toward the fallen trunk.

"Wait," Mimah said.

The Ho stopped. "Yesss?"

"I . . . I . . ." Mimah couldn't think of anything to say. How dare her wits fail her at a time like this?

The Ho turned and advanced again toward the trunk. In about three seconds, she'd see Charlie. Mimah couldn't let that happen. She couldn't let her little sister be kicked out of school. That was what they did if you got caught taking drugs. Charlie's life would be ruined.

"No!" she cried. "Wait. Don't waste your time."

The Ho paused.

Her mouth dry, Mimah slid the bottle of Xanax from her pocket. "Here. This is why I came out here. To take these." She handed the bottle to Mrs. Hoare and hung her head. "I took them from my mother. She hasn't been very well and . . ." Mimah bit her lip. "I like the way they make me feel."

"I see." Mrs. Hoare's voice was very quiet as she stared at the bottle in her hand. "Very well, Jemimah. Come with me. This is a serious offense. We'll see what the headmistress has to say."

Mimah swallowed. Mrs. Traphorn: This was worse than she'd thought. She knew the headmistress's policy on drugs, especially drugs that weren't marijuana, and it wasn't soft.

As she followed Mrs. Hoare out of the woods, Mimah clenched her fists, thinking of all the good things in her life. Physics. Lacrosse. Alice. Tally. Yes, even Sonia. And how about Cambridge? A lump rose in her throat. Cambridge had been part of her future. Maybe all she had now was a past.

CHAPTER FORTY-THREE

*W*here the hell's Mimah?" Sonia yelped, wringing her hands as she and Tally ran upstairs to get their coats. "She said she'd be here. I knew she wouldn't. I knew this was going to happen. Disaster!"

"Will you please fucking chill?" Tally snapped. "Mimah's a big girl. She can take care of herself. She'll probably meet us there."

"Well, she'll have to," Sonia announced, "because I'm not waiting a second longer. No way am I missing the opening ceremony—the boys look so hot when they run onto the field. Ta-da!" she cried, bursting through Alice and Tally's bedroom door. "Ali baby! What do you think?"

Alice glanced up from *Gone with the Wind*, which she was reading in the entertaining nook (a weepy, swashbuckling romance was exactly what she needed right now), and grimaced. "Ugh. What do you want me to say?"

Sonia's face fell. She and Tally lowered the masterpiece they were holding, a big poster declaring, WE LOVE YOU HASTED HOUSE!!! MWAH MWAH! in blue and maroon letters, the colors of the boys' rugby team. They'd been slaving away at it for the past half hour.

"Oh, but, I thought you'd like it," Sonia sulked. "It doesn't say T's name, or anything. I thought you might change your mind and come with us and help us wave it during the match."

Alice positioned her bookmark meticulously in *Gone with the Wind*, placed it on the coffee table, and gave Sonia a cold stare. "How many times do I have to tell you? I am so furious at Tristan Murray-Middleton that I'd rather die than have him think I'm supporting him at his stupid rugby game. And if I turn up and start flapping that sign, that's exactly what he *will* think."

Tally pushed past Sonia and plopped onto a cushion next to Alice. "Babe," she said, "I totally understand. T was completely insensitive the other day. But this is a major social event; you'll be so pissed off if you miss it. Come on, it's not like T owns Hasted House. You can totally ignore him and have a bit of fun."

"Fun?" Alice echoed dramatically. "That's easy for you to say. You're going to be all over Rando, making gooey eyes at him, whispering how amazing the sex was on Saturday night, and I'll be out on the sidelines, watching T get the hero treatment." She clenched her fists. "I can't believe you and I had sex on the same night and now I'm completely desolate and you're all starry eyed."

Without thinking, Tally smiled dreamily. "Yeah. Rando was amazing. I wasn't expecting him to be so skilled, or so gentle and strong, but he totally swept me off my—"

Oops. Tally shut her mouth. Tact had never been her strong point, especially not where romance was concerned. Tally had had sex with one other boy before Rando: an experienced Frenchman who she'd met on the beach in Barbados last spring. It had been wonderfully romantic, but in a reckless, one-enchanted-evening kind of way. This thing with Rando, on the other hand, felt real. Tally had never been tempted to date anyone in their social group before and now, all of a sudden, she was dying to give it a try.

Sonia bounded over to the entertaining nook and flung her arms round Alice's neck. "Ali babe, please come. It won't be the same without you. Go on, change your mind."

"Four words—" Alice replied, "No. Way. In. Hell." She stuck her nose back in her book and refused to speak another syllable.

Finally, Tally and Sonia exchanged glances and disappeared out the door.

Tristan lined up at the head of the Hasted House rugby team, trying not to let on how shit-scared he was.

"Yeah, team!" he shouted, wheeling round and pumping his fist at the rest of the squad.

"Yeah!" they roared back. Tom Huntleigh jumped up and down on the spot. Jasper shook George Demetrios by the shoulders.

"Be afraid. Be very afraid," George threatened, glaring at the line of Glendale's boys standing parallel to theirs. He was looking particularly fierce in his protective black helmet.

"You be afraid, you fucking pussies!" the Glendale's captain growled back.

T punched his fist into his palm and bared his teeth. A bit of friendly heckling was all part of the buildup to each match. Plus, it helped take his mind off his nerves.

In front of him, the heavy wooden doors of the Hasted House school hall were shut tight, and on the other side of them, out by the rugby field, he could hear the swell of glasses clinking in the refreshments marquee, of parents chatting, of pupils laughing, of girls practicing cheers. No one had talked about anything but the rugby all day. During chapel, the headmaster had fired everyone up with battle cries. During breakfast, boys in every year had crowded Tristan's table, wishing him luck. During warm-ups, Brigadier Jones had piled on the pressure. And now, the hour of truth.

The hall doors swung open. The Glendale's team darted outside to hoots and whistles and applause. Then it was Hasted's turn. Amid ferocious cheering, Tristan burst through the archway, raced down the stone steps at the back of the hall, and ran onto the field. The racket crescendoed. Hundreds of people had turned out—the whole of Hasted House, most of St. Cecilia's, parents, siblings, teachers. Spectators crushed round all sides of the field.

T couldn't help himself—as he took his position for the coin toss, he scanned the crowd, his eyes full of hope. If Alice was here, she'd be at the front. She had to be here. She'd never missed a big match. He looked down one side. Nothing. He looked down another. Nothing. Then, halfway down the third side of the field, T saw it—the big blue and maroon sign waving against the cloudy sky. There were Tally and Sonia, each holding a corner. There were Seb and Rando, yelling through cupped hands. Alice must be there too. T darted his eyes back and forth—and finally, the hope in them died. He saw no tall, sleek figure; no head of flowing brown hair; no familiar face, beaming with excitement and encouragement, that he'd known and loved his whole life.

Suddenly, T wished his mum and dad were here. At first he'd been relieved that they were in Paris and couldn't get back in time, but now he felt an empty space in his chest.

Tweet!

"Ready?" the referee called, barging between Tristan and the Glendale's captain with his coin.

"Ready!"

"Ready," T echoed, the word barely more than a rush of air.

The coin twirled up toward the sky, hurtled down, and landed with a smack on the referee's palm.

"Hasted to kick off!"

"Hoorah!" the crowd roared.

Tristan blinked, trying to push Alice out of his mind. He swallowed, focused, and curved toward the ball.

"Move. Excuse me. Move."

Dylan heard the bossy voice before she felt the fingernails dig into her back. She twisted round, which was difficult in this dense part of the crowd, and, "Alice!" she exclaimed.

"Quiet," Alice ordered, even though there was no chance of T hearing anything from all the way back here. "Keep it down. I found you because I thought you'd be *subtle*."

"Uh, okay," Dylan snorted. "What, are you undercover? Because, if so, maybe you should have worn a disguise. Like that weirdo over there." She pointed to a woman wearing the most gigantic sunglasses ever, even though it wasn't sunny, and at least three silk scarves wrapped round her head like a fortune-teller.

"Shhh! That's Tom Huntleigh's mum!" Alice almost giggled, then remembered what a bad mood she was in and frowned. "Of course I'm not undercover," she said, "I'm just furious at Tristan and I don't want him to realize I came. He doesn't deserve my presence."

Dylan studied her. "So why did you come?"

"Look around you." Alice rolled her eyes. "This is a major social event. Why shouldn't I come and have a bit of fun? I can totally ignore Tristan. It's not like he owns the school."

"Gooo, Tristan!" shouted someone a few rows ahead.

"Tristan! Tristan!"

"He's such an *amazing* team captain," gushed a tall eighth-grade girl, a few feet away.

"And so brave. Those Glendale's bastards keep trying to take him out."

"That's 'cause he's our best."

"As I was saying," Alice glowered, "Tristan does not own the school. Both my brothers went to Hasted House. In fact, my little brother, Hugo, is still here. He's only fourteen."

"Huh. I guess he'll be meeting my sister, then." Dylan was looking straight ahead.

"Your sister? Why? What do you mean?"

Dylan sighed. "I just talked to my mom before the match. She called to tell me that Lauren's coming to St. Cecilia's in a few weeks. She managed to get them to squeeze Lauren in at the last minute. 'Special circumstances.'" Dylan put air-quotes around the last words.

"Special circumstances?" Alice stared at her.

"Yeah. My mom's getting married to Victor Dirtbag Dalgleish. I guess she wants both her kids out of the way." Dylan shook her head in disgust.

"Shit, you're getting Victor Dalgleish as a stepdad? I'm sorry. So you're not leaving after all?"

"Guess not. Now all I have to do is figure out what I did wrong with Jasper, and—"

"Hurraaahhh!"

A wall of sound sprang up from the crowd. Cheers, screams,

yells. Alice and Dylan strained on tiptoe to see the field. Tristan was streaking faster than light over the grass, clutching the ball in both hands, gaining on the goal. The number eight on his back was almost a blur.

"He's gonna score!" Alice squealed, forgetting her fury. "He's gonna score!"

"I have no clue what the rules are, but this is fucking awesome!" Dylan grabbed her arm.

"Eee!" the eighth-grade girl squealed. "He looks so adorable covered in mud."

"Tristan, Tristan!"

Then, out of nowhere, a Glendale's player bolted in on the diagonal. The boy was enormous—as wide as a refrigerator, and taller—and he was heading straight for T.

"Watch ooouuut!" Alice screamed.

A split second of silence enveloped the crowd.

Crack!

Tristan flew a foot in the air, crumpled, and crashed to the ground.

The spectators gasped. The whistle shrieked.

T's body lay twisted on the earth. He didn't move.

CHAPTER FORTY-FOUR

*A*lice wiped her tear-streaked face. Then she pushed through the glass doors into Hasted Hospital, hugging a single yellow rose to her chest. The smell of disinfectant burned in her throat as she surveyed the sterile space. It seemed like a century since Alice had last been to this place—but in fact, it was only three years since that afternoon in eighth grade when she'd sliced her finger open during art. The doctor had stitched her up, given her a lollipop, and sent her back to school, where she'd milked everyone's sympathy for at least two weeks.

If only life were still that simple.

"I'm here to see Tristan Murray-Middleton," Alice told the receptionist, trying her best to control the tremor in her voice.

The young man at the desk gave her a sympathetic look. He had acne all over his cheeks and his nametag read, NEIL. Funny the things you noticed when your world felt like it was falling apart.

"Tristan Murray-Middleton is just down the hall," he said. "There's a boy in with him right now. Oh, hold on, here he comes."

"Seb!" Alice cried. She rushed at the skinny blond figure striding down the corridor and flung her arms round his neck. "I'm so happy to see you. How-how is he?"

Seb bit his lip. "Unconscious. I just sat there for a bit, watching him breathe. Apparently he's got a concussion and a dislocated shoulder. But he should be okay." Furtively, Seb slipped his whisky flask from his pocket and took a sip. "Want some?"

"Thanks." Alice poured a few drops down her throat, letting the liquid warm her chest. It was the first comforting thing she'd felt since T had collapsed. After that terrible moment, she'd clung, shivering, to Dylan, hardly seeing as the ambulance screamed into the school grounds and the paramedics huddled over Tristan, shifting him onto a stretcher, shutting him from sight, shuttling him away. She suppressed a sob.

"Darling, don't worry," Seb said, rubbing her shoulders. "His parents are flying back from Paris. They'll be here this evening to take care of him. Go on, go in."

"Thanks, Sebbie. I'll-I'll call you later." Dabbing her eyes, Alice slipped through the door to Tristan's room and, as soon as she saw him, heaved a shuddering breath. T was lying on the bed, his shoulder bound up in a sling, his face swollen and bruised, his eyes closed. In all the years Alice had known him, she'd never seen him look this battered, this bruised. A wave of tenderness welled from her heart.

"T," she whispered. "Oh, T."

His eyelids flickered.

Alice gasped. She flitted toward the bed. "Wake up, T. Wake up, *please.*"

Tristan's eyelids fluttered again and, slowly, opened. His pupils were huge, bleary, dazed. Then they focused on her.

"A-Al?" His voice was croaky.

"Yes, babe, it's me." Alice dropped her rose and grabbed Tristan's hand, weaving her fingers through his. "Thank god you're awake. Thank god. I was so worried. I saw you get hit and I . . . I . . ." She stifled another sob.

T's eyes widened as much as they could with all the swelling. "You were there?" he asked, his words barely a whisper.

"Of course I was there."

"But I thought you were furious at me. I thought you were never going to speak to me again."

"Oh, T." Alice squeezed his hand. "How could I never speak to you again?"

"Easy." T tried to smile, but winced with the pain. "You're Alice Rochester. You can do whatever the hell you want."

Alice smiled. "And you're my best friend. You know that. What would my life be like if you weren't in it?"

T shut his eyes and lifted her hand to his lips. "I love you."

Alice swallowed, feeling her throat constrict as if it might not let out the words. But she did love T. In a confusing, controlling, infuriating way. But she did. She'd love him as long as she lived.

"Oh, I'm sorry." A voice spoke from the doorway. "I didn't mean to interrupt."

Alice flicked up her gaze. A tall figure was silhouetted against the corridor's fluorescent lights. Rando. For some inexplicable reason, her heart lurched.

"That's okay," she said. "Come in."

"Oh . . . no, maybe I should come back later."

"Rando, mate," T rasped, "is that you? How was the end of the match? Did we win?"

Rando chuckled. "Glad to know you've got your priorities straight. No one won, mate. We stopped the game. We were all too worried about you."

"So the gold cup is still ours to win."

"Indeed it is." Rando's dimples deepened as he caught Alice's eye across the bed. Again, something sparked inside her. Something intense, frightening, irresistible.

What was happening to her?

At that moment a nurse bustled into the room.

"Hello, dears," she smiled, straightening T's sheets. "I'm sorry, but I'm going to have to ask you two to leave. Doctor's orders. Our patient's tired; he needs all the rest he can get."

Alice looked down at the pillow. It was true—T's eyes were already half closed.

"Bye, sweetie," she murmured, kissing his pale, bruised cheek. "I'll come back soon."

"Bye, mate," Rando echoed.

The two of them walked side by side down the corridor, past reception, and through the hospital doors. As they reached the cold, gray parking lot, Alice plunged her face into her hands.

"Hey, sweetheart," Rando uttered, pulling her toward him, "don't cry. Don't worry. He's going to be fine."

"I know he is. I know," Alice sobbed. She wasn't sure what she was even crying about anymore. She hugged Rando close, letting the tears stream down her cheeks. He smelled of delicious, warm, comforting boy.

"Come with me," he murmured in her ear. "Let's get you a drink. I know just the place to go."

Rando draped his arm around Alice's shoulders and led her toward the center of town. She leaned against his chest. He'd come to the rescue again.

KATE KINGSLEY has lived on both sides of the Atlantic, spending time in New York, London, Paris, and Rome— so she's more than qualified to chronicle the jet-set lives of the YOUNG, LOADED, AND FABULOUS girls.

Kate also writes for magazines such as *GQ* in New York, where she's had the enviable task of interviewing fashion designers like Paul Smith and celebrities like James McAvoy. She's currently hard at work on her next book about the YL&F crew. Visit her at www.katekingsley.com.

Jammed full of surprises!

LiP SMACKER.
LOUNGE